M000208829

none of this is serious

none of this

catherine prasifka

is serious

CANONGATE

none of this is serious

catherine prasifka

CANONGATE

First published in Great Britain in 2022
by Canongate Books Ltd, 14 High Street, Edinburgh EH1 1TE

canongate.co.uk

1

Copyright © Catherine Prasifka, 2022

The right of Catherine Prasifka to be identified as the
author of this work has been asserted by her in accordance
with the Copyright, Designs and Patents Act 1988

British Library Cataloguing-in-Publication Data
A catalogue record for this book is available on
request from the British Library

ISBN 978 1 83885 552 9

Typeset in Bembo MT Pro by Palimpsest Book Production Ltd,
Falkirk, Stirlingshire

Printed and bound in Great Britain by Clays Ltd, Elcograf S.p.A.

MIX
Paper from
responsible sources
FSC® C018072

To everyone who understands why some of this might be serious.

1

The taxi splashes water over the pavement as it pulls up
to the house. I pay the driver and get out, pulling my
coat against my skin, and duck for cover under a tree by
the gate. I check the time on my phone and scroll through
the group chat. No one has said anything since Grace
messaged:

Can someone pick up some extra paper cups?

The house looks warm. Its bay windows flood light onto
the grass. There are deep grooves in the gravel driveway,
channelling water to a puddle at the gate, which I jump
over. The house is one of the older ones on the street;
Grace's parents bought it during the boom. I can't imagine
the fortune they spent. A fortune they're still paying off,
Grace tells me sometimes, after a few glasses of wine.

As I approach the door I shake these thoughts out of
my head as if they are cobwebs clinging to my hair. I
take a deep breath, smile, and knock. A beat thumps
through the walls of the house, and I wonder if anyone
will hear me outside. I open the group chat again.

hey
can someone let me in

Dan replies:

Hangg on
Grace's om theway
*on the way

I refresh Twitter as I wait and check my lipstick in the camera of my phone.

After a minute, Grace opens the door, a drink in her hand. Noise from the party pours out. I don't recognise the song. Multicoloured balloons roam free-range on the floor. People are dancing in the kitchen beyond the hall, some of them well. It all washes over me.

'Soph! I'm glad you're finally here!' Grace spills a few drops of Prosecco as she hugs me, and they splash down my leg. She looks effortlessly glamorous, something I know she puts an incredible amount of effort into. She's simultaneously chic and casual, and it makes me feel both overdone and underdressed. I smile at her and hug her back.

'God, you look like a drowned rat, come in come in come in, I didn't even notice this rain starting.' She pushes me through the door. 'Need a drink?'

I wave my bag. I've picked up the second cheapest bottle of wine from the off-licence before heading over.

'Well, that's all right then, but there are G&Ts in the kitchen if you want any. I cut up some limes as well. In the big bowl – better get to them fast, Dan's already dared several people to eat the entire thing, and some of us are drunk enough to start trying.'

2

I nod and someone calls her name from the kitchen. She tells me I can dump my stuff wherever and that she'll see me in there. She skips down the hallway. Instead of shoes, she's wearing fuzzy slippers.

Other people are chatting in the hall. They don't notice me coming in or taking off my jacket, even though I give them ample opportunity to. I watch myself in the mirror as I slide it off, feeling as though I'm slipping off my skin and revealing myself to be entirely formless beneath.

I open the door to the study and leave my bag in the corner, after taking my bottle of wine out. It's quiet inside, and I take a moment to look at myself in the darkened mirror. When I try out a smile, I see that lipstick is smudged onto my teeth. I straighten out my damp hair, contemplate my shoes before kicking them off, and return to the hall.

I squeeze past the crowd, nodding to the people that I know or recognise. Some of them nod back. Finn is amongst them, but he's deeply engaged in conversation with a girl I don't know and he doesn't see me. He keeps laughing and touching her shoulder. I can see the bubble of personal space around her pop every time he does it. I bite the side of my cheek.

I find the others sitting at the dining-room table, and I join them. Dan says, 'Nice hair,' and I shake off rain droplets at him in response. A stray balloon brushes against my leg, and I pick it up and hold it in my lap.

They're playing a drinking game of quick-fire questions, where the only way to avoid answering is to respond with a question directed at someone else. The game appeals to me in the same way that a cliff edge does.

I take a gulp of wine straight from the bottle and

angle my face so I'm visible from the hallway. I picture the scene from the outside and imagine I look like a regular girl having a good time, and it fills me with delight.

Steph clinks her glass against my bottle and takes a big swig. I feel small, like a puzzle piece clicking into place. I don't want them to leave me behind for their shiny new adult lives. Nearly everyone is emigrating somewhere: London, New York, Sydney. Part of me wants to go with them; it would be nice to abandon my past life for a state of constant present. I watch the game and encourage the feeling with my tepid wine.

'Lucy, who do you like better: Mike or Ross?'

'Dan, who do you like better: Mike or Ross?'

'Ouch. Steph, who was your first kiss?'

'Sophie, what's really going on with you and Finn?' The question startles me. I wasn't expecting them to direct anything my way.

Steph wiggles her eyebrows at me. 'Too slow, drink.'

My mind is blank as I answer. Absolutely nothing. I hold the wine in my mouth for a moment before I swallow it. It's bitter. The image of the regular girl departs, but I don't look away from the game. It feels like everyone's looking at me, and no one is.

'If you say so, but I think you should drink again,' Dan teases me. He always teases me; it's part of how he shows affection.

I raise my bottle in cheers. I suppose to them it seems like nothing's happened. I'm not conscious of the words I say to get them to move on, but eventually they work.

The game continues buzzing, but I've lost interest. I take my wine through to the kitchen table and look at all the snacks that are laid out. I watch one of Grace's friends pick up a handful of popcorn and eat without thinking about it. She's so skinny, too. I sip my wine and walk away from the table, my thighs brushing against each other as I go. I feel as if I'm made of butter, just congealed lumps stuffed into an outfit that's too small for me. I look at myself in the mirror across the room. Maybe all anyone can see when they look at me is butter.

I flit between social bubbles, each one with a slightly different rhythm. The girls I know from school are the same as always, each personality moving against the others in a well-practised dance. They welcome me into their group, but I have nothing to say to them. Niamh asks me, 'What are you up to now?' as though we've not spoken in months, and I remember that we haven't. I wonder at what point I became an outsider and if it's their fault or mine. They don't try to convince me to stay when I stand up and mumble an excuse; they are too engrossed in each other's lives.

The debaters Grace knows from college are exchanging proper nouns at a speed that makes me dizzy. Sentences lose their meaning. There's someone arguing for free speech, and someone else explaining the difference between that and actively platforming someone. I hear the phrase 'the marketplace of ideas'. One of them tries to engage me in conversation, I think to help bolster his point, but I haven't been paying attention.

I'm watching the party as if behind glass, each person totally estranged from me. I'm repeating ordinary party questions in my head over and over again. *Hi, what are you up to now? Hiya, oh yeah, I'm fine. How were finals?* It's giving me a headache. Every time I try to force words out of my mouth, the timing feels off and I choke. No one notices except for me.

As I'm making my way to the bathroom, Grace appears, grabs my hand and pulls me inside. I feel as though I'm being pulled through syrup. 'I'm glad I found you.' The bathroom is a huge white marble and faux-concrete thing. There's a claw-footed bath against one wall, and the opposite wall is lined entirely in mirrors. I'm not sure Grace understands that I actually have to pee.

'That's fine, I won't look.' She sits herself down by the sink, resting her head against the porcelain. 'Fuck, I'm drunk. Not in a fucked-up way, in a good way, I think.'

I'm not sure there is a good way, but that's never stopped us before.

'Look,' she says, 'I need to tell you something. I just heard it, and I don't want you to be upset or anything, and I didn't invite her, by the way, it just happened, but I thought I definitely had to be the one to tell you. But finish peeing first, please.'

My insides go cold and squirm inside me. I already know what she's going to say. I can only be confronted with so many Instagram stories and rescheduled hangouts before it slaps me in the face. I flush the toilet, wash my hands and sit down next to her. I run my fingertips over the grooves between the floor tiles.

'Okay, so, I only heard this third-hand, so maybe it's not true but, you know, it might be. Anyway, that girl here with Finn? Apparently, they're dating.'

I nod slowly and look her in the eyes to prove I'm unmoved by this information. The girl's face is familiar;

I've seen her pop up as a suggested friend more than once.

'You're not upset? Because you know he's a prick, right? He's a stupid prick, and I wouldn't have invited him if I thought I could get away with it, but you know how these things are – it's more trouble not to.'

I see my reflection in the mirror stare back at me as I say the appropriate words aloud, and I watch my face make the appropriate emotions. It's hardly ever worth being honest with Grace; she'll just twist my words until she finds the meaning she's looking for. It's never important what I say.

Grace says, 'Yeah, but he messages you all the time, he's not fair. You actually just can't trust men.'

Last night, Finn messaged me asking what time I was thinking of arriving, so he wouldn't be the first one here. We stayed up late chatting about poetry and his parents. He didn't mention anything about bringing this girl. I look at the messages on my phone now as Grace talks, and they take on new meanings. I was foolish to think they meant he wanted to spend time with me.

'Okay, if you say so, but you shouldn't put up with it. I wouldn't put up with it if I were you. You need to say something to him, honestly.'

Grace is always telling me to say what's on my mind because she can as good as read it anyway. I'm a science experiment to her, something to be figured out and dissected. She reads thoughts I'm not even sure I'm having.

Someone knocks on the door and yells at us to get out.

'Shut up, it's my house!' Grace yells back through the

door, but we stand up anyway and she gives me a hug. 'Well, let me know if you need anything, and I mean anything.'

I leave the bathroom and go to the kitchen. I drink two full glasses of water, standing at the sink by myself. Through the window, Finn smiles as someone takes a photo of him. I refresh my feed until he posts it, scrolling past photos of people's dissertations and images of some war crime taking place somewhere in the world. When I see Finn's face, I stop for just a moment and use my thumbs to zoom in. He's captioned it boys' night out, even though that's obviously not what this is. I put my phone away without liking the photo and grab the bowl of crisps Grace left out on the counter. They're not my favourite flavour, but I eat them anyway. The bowl shakes in my hand. I wipe the dust from my fingers on my jeans.

I pour myself another glass of wine, drink half of it, then bring the bowl outside with me and start chatting to the smokers. The second-hand smoke makes me dizzy. Steph offers me part of her cigarette, and I take it. I breathe in the smoke, and I want so badly to die. I hold the thought for a moment, letting it fill me, and then I exhale. It evaporates into the night.

Finn grabs a few crisps from the bowl and smiles at me graciously, then goes back to talking to the others. He holds his cigarette in his hand as he gesticulates, and I think I'm the only one who notices that he barely touches it. I watch it burn down to his fingers, the smoke emphasising whatever point he's making. I asked him about it once, when I was too drunk, and he told me that sometimes he just forgets. I remember breathing in that moment and tasting the smoke.

Grace is beside me, and I hear her whisper, *'Prick.'* I take another crisp and let it go soggy in my mouth before chewing it.

'You can't just lean into normative feminism, you have to subvert it first,' Steph is adamant. 'You can't just go along with the whims of the hegemonic capitalist patriarchy and call it empowerment.'

'But the only way we get empowerment is through the system, we'll never actually break it down otherwise.'

'What system? How are you going to break it down? There's no self-destruct button.'

'All I'm saying is get empowerment where you can, right? Life's hard enough otherwise.'

'All right then, so wearing make-up is empowering, is it?'

'Could be.'

'Some people *do* find it empowering.'

'Yeah, right. And by the way, what does empowerment mean? I don't feel fucking empowered every time I use a fucking tampon.' Grace's voice is loud beside me.

'You know full well what it means.'

'Yeah, but it's just a concept, it's not like voting rights or the ability to afford food. Who cares?'

'Fine, well, maybe you'd rather we were all disempowered? That's socialism, right?'

The discussion is making my head hurt. I've lost track of who's saying what. I want to contribute, but the words are clunky on my tongue. I sip my wine and eat a crisp every time someone looks at me. The boys know to be silent, and it's like I can hear them performatively listening. I want Steph to give me another cigarette.

Someone says, 'Why do you girls always have to make

these things so political? You can feel however you want about your tampons, right?'

'Oh, sorry.' Grace is cold. 'I'd forgotten that politics only exists when it's about women, otherwise it's all just "normal", is it? It's only political when you disagree?'

I hear the smoker back down. Grace continues on a monologue I've heard so many times before that I barely register it.

Finn pulls at my sleeve and asks if we can go and chat somewhere. I nod mechanically. My mouth is dry, so I stop along the way to refill my wine glass.

We sit on the love seat in the corner of Grace's sitting room. It's cold inside, so I pull the blanket on the armrest over me. Without words, Finn grabs it too and gets under it with me. He pulls my legs over his lap.

I drink some of my wine, and he tells me that his parents are arguing again, and he doesn't know who he can talk to about it. I hear myself say things like 'oh' and 'ah' and 'I'm so sorry'. He doesn't seem to be listening to me as he speaks. I wonder if he's told anyone else this, and if I should feel guilty that it pleases me he probably hasn't.

He rests his head between my breasts and I stroke his hair. I think about leaning down and kissing him, and I drink more wine. He can probably feel my heart beating under his head, if it isn't obscured by a layer of fat. I hum gently as I listen to him talk. I could easily drift off to sleep. My hand is resting just below his chin, and he bends his head to kiss it.

Grace enters the room and asks me to help her clear up. It takes a moment for me to understand what's happening. Finn moves and releases me. I follow Grace into the kitchen, and she shakes her head at me. When I look over my shoulder, Finn is looking at his phone as though nothing's happened, and perhaps it hasn't.

'What, and I mean *what*, was that about?' I don't know what Grace means, but she pours me a glass of water and makes me sit and drink it. To make me feel better, she has one too. 'Thank God that girl already left. I'll kill him,' she says, to herself more than me. We sit together in silence, nursing our water. Grace holds my hand when she notices a tear rolling down my face. 'Things are going to change now, and change for the better, don't worry,' Grace says to me, but I find it hard to believe her. Things are ending, and yet I still feel the same. I'll always feel this way.

'Look, Soph, a shooting star. Make a wish!' She points through the window, up to the night sky.

I look up and see a streak of light. *I wish I wasn't alone.* The thought comes to me unbidden; it's a secret between just me and the star.

As if I've anchored it, the star refuses to leave me. It traces a long purple scar that disappears over the horizon. Someone yells, *'Holy shit!'* from outside, and the deck is lit up by everyone's phones.

We go outside and look up at the sky. Where before there was only light pollution, now there's a hairline fracture spanning as far as I can see in either direction. It's lit from within by a violet glow that seeps across the night sky.

I keep blinking, as though it will vanish as quickly as it arrived, but the light only grows stronger, outcompeting whatever stars have the audacity to still shine. My mind spirals through various explanations – fireworks, coordinated LEDs on drones, an overzealous night club – but the eerie purple light feels too alien to be man-made.

I'm struck by the fear that this thing will consume us. It's like the jaws of a great beast, threatening to open and swallow the world whole. For as long as I can remember, I've been told the Earth is dying, that we had to reduce, reuse, recycle. But I never expected it to happen so suddenly. There's too much to take in all at once. I over-balance and fall backwards onto the deck, catching myself with the heels of my palms. I look at everyone around me, and in the purple light they're all strangers.

Someone pulls me to my feet. My phone looks cracked, but when I click it on I realise it's just the reflection of the sky in the screen. I can't tell if it's my imagination, or if the light is really pulsing. A phone goes off, and then another. No one is speaking, all I can hear are message tones and countless people typing.

I feel seasick; the only thing keeping me centred is my phone in my hand, which is alive with notifications. Someone vomits into one of the bushes.

My feed is full of photos, so many that they don't all load at once. One by one, my phone presents me with different areas of the world lit up purple, blurred from how hastily the users took the photos. Most of them are too grainy to make out, but I find a gif someone's posted of the star shooting across the sky. I watch it on repeat, each time feeling like something inside me is tearing apart.

Politicians and celebrities are beginning to tweet about it. They're urging calm, but they don't know what's happening. A few of the posts look a little bit too prepared, and people are already speculating about why. I show the gif to Grace and she looks at me with wide eyes. Neither of us can say anything. She goes upstairs to wake her parents, and the party evaporates like so much smoke on the wind.

2

The next morning I wake early, with a dryness in my mouth and a cold purple light filtering through the blinds. When I look out the window, I see the long scar the star has cut across the sky, somehow more eerie in the morning light. Purple tendrils flicker and dance around it, stretching out until they merge with the blue of the sky. It's impossible to tell how far away it is, only that the rules of reality have shifted in the night. I look down at my hands and stretch out my fingers to test the fabric of my new life, and confirm it feels just the same.

My phone is a living creature in my hand, my notifications its heartbeat. Every piece of content on the internet is about the star, or the crack, or whatever whoever's decided to call it. There's no escape. People are calling it a climate catastrophe; a hoax; the worst disaster in a hundred years; nothing compared to World War II. There are threads explaining how to preserve food in case of power failure and how millennials don't know anything about real survival. The more I scroll and read, the more my anxiety grows, but I can't stop. I flick through the profiles of journalists on Twitter, trying to confirm things my friends have put up on their Instagram stories.

Separating fact from fiction seems impossible, although I don't believe what my uncle's posted on Facebook.

It isn't dopamine hitting my brain, but it's addictive all the same. Scrolling helps me to shut out my gnawing thoughts. It keeps alive the possibility that there might be an answer on the next thread.

I take a photo of the crack, with the intention of adding it to the countless others, but on my screen it looks small and insignificant. I look between my phone and the sky, and try to reconcile the two; the photo is so at odds with the sheer terror I feel. Thinking about the star is like imagining time running straight into a brick wall; I can't see past it, and I'm not sure anything exists on the other side. So, instead, I drink in the internet.

I can't decide if the haziness of the data makes me more or less uncomfortable. No one knows what it is; there isn't even a leading theory. A tech billionaire has started a campaign to send a car through it. The campaign's getting ratioed on Twitter, but the Kickstarter is doing well.

I absorb it all like a sponge, trying to give my own thoughts substance. I hope for clarity, but instead my head is regurgitating content I've read on loop. Maybe Aldi will start selling home canning kits in the middle aisle. I don't have anything to add to the discourse. It just looks like a crack in the world to me.

I try to come up with a relevant tweet to articulate this feeling, but erase it halfway through. It's not clever or succinct enough.

I can't focus on the crack any more, so instead I think about the party. I replay the events of the night in my head as I shower, picking through every detail as the water runs over my skin. I fight through the alcohol to pinpoint each interaction. I remember the game, but comfort myself in knowing that no one else would have found it significant. I dreamt about Finn last night. I can still feel his phantom presence against my body. I decide I'm not jealous.

I feel the parts of my body that bulge and watch soap bubbles form on them. I've gained weight in the last few months. Maybe I won't eat all day, just to see what that feels like, if it gives me some sense of purpose or control.

When I dress and go downstairs, the house is empty. My parents have left some food for me in the fridge. My stomach churns with anxiety as my phone screen flickers with notifications from messaging apps and news alerts. Steph keeps sending memes into our group chat that I ignore because the kind of content she shares serves only to increase everyone's anxiety levels. She finds her memes on an Instagram account that steals content from Twitter, which in turn steals from reddit, and somehow none of these acts of filtration make them funny. They normally feature pictures of wine glasses, the minions from *Despicable Me* and troubling social values. The latest one features a white lady holding an enormous bottle of wine with the caption: The only supplies I need for the end of the world.

I turn on the TV and flick through different news channels to quell my rising panic. It's wall-to-wall coverage of the crack, but I find it hard to understand what any of the reporters are saying. The broadcasts have the feeling of improvisation, as though the networks expertly placed their anchors against backdrops of the crack, and then told them to just riff. I look at the crack in the sky, and I have nothing coherent to say either.

Mum sends a picture of some ducks on a lake into the family group chat. I don't recognise the location. She doesn't comment on the sky, even though the crack is visible in the photo. I want to ask her about it, but I normally avoid the family group chat, and sure enough Hannah replies with her own photo after a minute. Hannah says she's looking forward to coming home soon, especially if there's an apocalypse. I turn my phone face down on the coffee table and eat the leftover pasta to fill the abyss that opens within me.

It's been peaceful with her away in Glasgow at college. It evens out our relationship, being apart. Sometimes I think that I'm the product of an unhappy place, or I myself am just filled with some kind of melancholy, but the majority of these feelings dissipate the moment she drags her suitcase out the door.

When I hear her voice in my head telling me to just be better, to not eat, to grow up, it's like she's still here. But life's better when I don't always have her face to reflect mine. She didn't want to stay in the UK with Brexit, so she's coming home. It's just one more thing to blame the Tories for.

I sit down on the sofa and read through my notifications, wondering if everyone's feeling as panicked as I am. I have thirty notifications in a group chat of school friends that I never usually read, but which I'm too awkward to leave. There's no reason to be in it; Grace tells me everything relevant that's happening in their lives. She sees them far more than I do. They're talking about the party last night. I open the messages, scroll up to see if they've said anything about me, and when I see that they haven't, I immediately exit the app.

Grace sends me a photo of her house post-party, saying her dad's counted the empty bottles left behind and is shocked that there are thirty-seven. She sends me the eye emoji, which in this case means that she hasn't told him that she's hidden thirty more bottles in a bag in her wardrobe and asked people to take some rubbish with them. She also says that he's not the least bit interested in looking at the sky, which is just typical.

Grace asks me what I think it all means, and I link her a few of the articles I've read and summarise them as best as I can. The concepts I'm describing are just out of reach, and it makes me feel stupid. I'm frustrated at the things I can't explain.

Those are really interesting, but I meant what do you think it all means. Like in general, for us.

I think about it for a minute. It feels as though I'm losing a game I haven't agreed to play.

i don't know
everything's so uncertain

But that's exactly it, it's uncertain. I've had enough of uncertainty. I think our whole generation has.

what do you mean?

Then:

is it even possible for the future to be certain?

18

She sends me a voice message.

'Okay, so I've been thinking about this a lot,' it begins. Grace is always thinking about things a lot, although she says she never overthinks, it's always just the right amount. Overthinking is a criticism she reserves for me. 'I don't remember a time when I had a clear idea of what the future was going to be like. Everyone kept telling me it would be one way, I kept seeing what the media wanted me to see – happily-ever-after and all that – but I never believed it. I remember being in school and the recession happening, and my mum saying that it would be fine because the economy would recover by the time I was looking for a job. And now that we've just finished college, a big crack opens in the sky? No one can tell us what to expect any more. It's like . . . We're in totally unknown ontological territory.'

> you're very fatalistic
> but you have a point
> i remember being content when i was about 6
> but my grasp on the future then was pretty loose
> maybe we're trapped in a constant present?

Yes!!

I always like it when Grace agrees with what I say; it makes these conversations feel worth it.

> Our idea of what's normal is based on the past, a past that never existed, and now with this crack it's like . . . We're mourning the loss of a past that was never ours, that was always a fantasy. And now we have no lens to view the future. What even is normal any more?

yes
when i woke up i was glad it was still there
like, I'm glad it's still real
what do you think is behind it
anything?

Would it be worse if there's nothing?

if nothing's behind it then we'll be consumed
by the void and I won't have to worry about
getting a mortgage

You're obsessed with houses.

it's because I'll never own one
none of us will

We talk back and forth about the housing crisis. Grace sends me a link to a property she's found in Rathfarnham that's just a converted shed with a bed and a microwave in it. It's going for over two hundred thousand.

Searching for the average property value in Dublin leads me to article after article about the unliveable rooms for rent, where you can watch your dinner cook and your clothes wash from the comfort of your bed. 'Studio' as a word has slowly shed its artistic and independent connotations and now conjures up images of the tenements.

I tweet out that thought and replies start to roll in. The British people who follow me are confused; the word 'tenement' signifies something else to them. I try out different replies in my head, wondering if it would be funny to bring up the Famine, or 1916, but by the time I've settled on a clear explanation, someone in the replies has already worded it better than me.

I watch debates start to branch out, stemming from the least charitable interpretations of everyone's thoughts. Arguments start to morph and abstract themselves, and it's clear I'm no longer in control of the meanings people take from my words. I delete the tweet to avoid becoming today's protagonist, and move on. I bounce between social networks, reading comments and threads, buoyed along by my phone's currents.

I refresh the feed every minute and continue to consume, growing fat. I'm like a vampire, leeching off the content of other people's lives. I'm not even really interested in anything I'm reading. I read a thread about possible theories of what's causing the crack, before real-ising that the poster is some American alt-right conspiracy theorist. His avatar is a fox wearing a suit, which should have tipped me off.

Finn's posted some photos of the crack in the sky above his house from several angles. Some of them are good, but most of them are weirdly filtered and overexposed, draining all colour from the landscape. He recently bought a camera that sends the photos directly to his phone, and he's become an amateur photographer, or at least that's what his Instagram bio says. I like them and message him to ask how his parents are. He doesn't respond. Those conversations are reserved for the comfort of night and one too many glasses of wine. It's a familiarity that hums between us.

Mum calls me and I consider letting it go to voicemail, but after the fourth ring I answer.

'Hi Sophie, it's Mum, did you eat the food I left for you? I hope you have, because it's going to go to waste otherwise . . . Great, that's great. I'll be out for the afternoon, so if you could put the chicken into the oven . . . Oh and yes, I've just been on the phone with Hannah, and she'll be coming home this time next week.'

I haven't forgotten.

'Anyway, I'm just calling because I'm wondering if you've had a think about what you might like to do for your birthday?'

I know that Hannah's already decided that she wants us to have a birthday party, so there's no point in having this conversation. I pace around the kitchen as I listen to Mum talk.

'No, that won't do,' she says. 'You have to do something. Why don't I send Grace a text and see if she has any ideas? What about going out for dinner at that Indian place you like in town, the one we went to last year?'

It's actually a Chinese restaurant, and she knows the difference.

'Yes, that's the one. Or we could have people over? Hannah said she might like to do that.'

We've reached the point in the conversation where I don't need to keep pretending. Once, when I was fifteen, I asked my parents if we could have two separate parties, but Hannah invited her friends to mine anyway. All of my gifts were rummaged through, the envelopes torn open and the money stolen.

Mum chats to me some more about the plans. I feel myself slipping into a sullen mood, so I catch myself. I take a deep breath and hitch a smile onto my face. I can almost feel the endorphins. It's easier to play the role of the obliging daughter. I forage in the cupboards until I find a packet of crisps and open them quietly away from my phone's microphone.

She asks me about my day, and I have no plans, but I try to sound upbeat about it.

'And what about this whole sky business as well, what are they calling it? Anyway, it's frightful. I didn't know what it was when I woke up, we heard about it on the radio, and of course I hadn't a clue what he was talking about until I opened up the curtains. Anyway, I'm sure it's nothing.'

I've been waiting for her to comment on the crack, and I try to persuade her it's probably something, but she goes on speaking as though I haven't said anything at all. I sit down at the kitchen counter and open my laptop, thinking about my mother's worldview. Her aspiration for a normal life has always been strong enough to generate one out of chaos.

'Did you see the Taoiseach was on the news and said that there's nothing to worry about, business as usual?

I search for the video and read the captions as Mum speaks. I find it hard to be surprised. Doing anything like advising people to stay home while a giant hole opens in the sky isn't worth it: it might disrupt the economy.

Mum scoffs at me. 'Oh, stop moaning, the economy is important if you ever want to get a job!'

The economy is something some men made up one day, and if it functions for anyone, it certainly doesn't function for me. As I talk, I refresh job sites, and the lack of anything appealing underscores my point. Mum ignores me and keeps talking, as though we aren't watching the slow decline of human civilisation. She's interrupted by

Dad, who wants to say hello to me, but then accidentally hangs up the phone.

I send Grace a message about my birthday party, and she replies saying she's already on it. I send her a gif of someone rolling their eyes.

Look I'll make it actually fun. Promise!

> *you're welcome to try*
> *you know how Hannah is though*
> *especially about these things*

Just leave it with me, okay?

Grace is the only one who understands how I feel about Hannah. Hannah's impossibly nice to everyone she meets, she's incredibly competent, and things just seem to happen for her. The problem is she has a way of making sure things never happen for me, of undermining me and my confidence at every turn. Grace is the only one I've ever shown the bruises to.

Fuck that bitch anyway.

> *anyway.*
> *drinks later?*

Sure.

I send a message to the group chat asking the others if they want to join. I watch their replies scroll across the banner on the top of my screen as I read Twitter.

A notification pops up. It's a new follower, and when I look at the profile picture I don't immediately recognise who it is. He's following a few other people I know, including Steph and Grace. I search his name on Instagram, and he has a public account, which I find significant. It's not that the photos themselves are risqué, but rather the act of having an open account.

I recognise him then: he was at Grace's party. I have a dim memory of chatting to him about something and feeling bored, although he's handsome, in a bookish kind of way. I can't decide if he uses product in his hair or if it does that naturally. I stop looking at him, because it feels like an invasion of privacy. I delete my search history in case the app judges me, or the algorithm starts getting ideas.

I put the chicken into the oven, and my parents return just as it's ready, so we sit in silence watching the news. I don't feel like eating and confronting the complicated feelings that it leads to, but I eat anyway.

There's another announcement from the Taoiseach. My body is tensed up with anticipation about what he's going to say; it feels like it's going to be important, like it has to be important. I'm disappointed. He dodges tough questions with answers so well practised they're sharp in their vagueness. The news ends and I still haven't been given a name for the dread that's pooling inside me.

Dad says, 'Well, that's that then, isn't it? Nothing to worry about after all.'

'I suppose so,' says Mum. 'I wonder how Hannah's dealing with all of this? I'll be glad to have my two girls back home.'

She slaps me on the leg then, just hard enough to hurt.

I can't make myself return her smile. For our parents, we are interchangeable, forever two halves of a whole. We haven't been close since we were children; it's hard, when people think you're incomplete without someone else. Especially when Hannah's life has always been so much fuller than mine.

'Hannah's fine,' says Dad. 'She's got that job lined up, so I'm sure she won't want to be back here for too long.' He doesn't look at me when he says it, and I leave the sitting room to go and get ready.

I decide to walk into town to clear my head, but it doesn't help. There are too many houses. I'm astonished by their solidity, the lives that their walls contain. I play a little game with myself where I try to guess how many rooms they're hiding. It's a game I can't win.

Every time I see a house for sale I understand that my whole presence on the physical plane is contingent upon the acquisition of capital. I'll never be able to afford a house in this area. Maybe Hannah will. The thought makes me hate her more.

I meander through the streets of Dublin, window-shopping and grimacing as I pass building sites for new hotels, and doughnut shops that haven't been trendy in five years. Someone's painted over a mural on a building that I liked, under the guise of keeping the city clean, but really because the mural was too progressive. The sun is just setting, and the sky is a crystal blue sliced with an almost imperceptible line of violet.

When I arrive at the pub, I'm exhausted in a hollow sort of way. Steph, Lucy and Dan are already sitting at a table in the corner with drinks. They fit in perfectly with the scene, as though they're the cast of an indie movie. For a moment, I consider leaving. Then they see me and call my name. Too late. I wave at them and go to the bar to order for myself, and I message Grace asking where she is. I'm about to order a pint of cider, but then I remember an article that compared the calories in pints versus spirits, and order a gin and tonic instead.

When I sit down at the table, Lucy's bringing up a memory from when she was in school with Steph, when apparently Steph had taken something from the teacher's cupboard and got the whole class in trouble. Steph's reminding Lucy of the two separate times she's had chlamydia. Dan's doing his best to avoid the exchange, quietly nursing his drink.

'Here, Soph,' Lucy appeals to me. 'Steph's being a bitch, yeah?'

Steph makes a gesture at Lucy and then laughs, the escalating mood disintegrating around them. They love to put on play fights with each other; it's a moderately unhealthy way to air any real grievances they have before they can build up. Neither of them could say anything at this point that would end their friendship, although they like to test that every so often.

The conversation resolves itself into more civilised jokes and I'm grateful; I don't know what I could contribute otherwise. After a moment, Dan brings up what's on all of our minds.

'I was so plastered last night, I didn't remember what happened until I opened my blinds this morning.'

'Not surprising, given I had to hide the lime bowl from you,' says Lucy.

27

'They were free limes.'

'No one wanted you to eat the limes,' says Steph. 'I don't think I'm worried, actually. Climate change will take us out first.'

'It could be because of climate change, though.'

'I mean, it could be anything from aliens to some bizarre effect from nuclear testing that the US government's hushed up. Are there any actual theories from actual scientists?'

'Ask Sophie,' says Dan. 'No doubt she's read everything that's been published on it already.'

He's exaggerating, but they goad me until I put up my hands and relent, relinquishing all of the information I've gathered. The alien theory has no proof, which disappoints Dan. Steph is surprised I've had a chance to read so much about it already, but she has a job and I don't.

Steph says, 'Well, speaking of jobs, I hate mine,' as she flicks a coaster across the table.

'At least you don't have to move to London for it,' says Dan, who tosses the coaster back at her.

'At least you have jobs,' says Lucy. 'I'm stuck at home with my parents, full of existential dread. I'm thinking of taking up yoga.'

'For your flexibility?' Dan asks.

'Yeah, for riding, thanks for making me clarify.'

'Would you ever stop being so vulgar?'

'Would you ever stop being a prude?'

'Speaking of getting fucked,' says Steph, 'who are we voting for in the election?'

I shrug; I don't really care. It isn't that I'm not politically engaged, it's that nothing about Irish politics is engaging.

'Neither of the two big boys, anyway. Greens? I mean, climate really should be a hot button issue this election.'

'Should be, but won't be. And do you really think they could handle the crisis that's definitely coming?'

'Can anyone? Did you see that video of the Taoiseach going round?'

'I can't wait for the campaign slogans.'

'If you give me the money I'll run on a "no crack yes craic" platform,' says Dan.

'Only if it'll make you stay.'

'I think I could stay for a TD's salary.'

'I just wish there was someone competent we could vote for who isn't evil.'

Lucy says, 'We're stuck with the same civil war politics. What if we do another Rising and start the whole state again, with more of an emphasis on the original rebels' radical socialism?'

Steph rolls her eyes, and the conversation breaks down into an argument that no one really wants to have, where everyone's arguing the same side, as is our custom.

The evening feels like slipping on an old coat, it's so familiar. There's a joy in watching these people, in observing, and I wonder if I'll ever be as perfectly happy as they seem in this moment. I'm not sure how I can be so insecure and secure at the same time; it's like holding my breath, knowing that I can breathe when I want to. Or I could not. I hold my breath a few times just to test out how it feels and listen to the conversation go on around me.

When Grace arrives, she yells, and we echo her. She buys a round of Jägerbombs for the table and we take

29

them reluctantly, Steph holding her nose as she knocks it back in one. Someone, maybe me, says that we are too old for this kind of thing.

It feels as though nothing will ever change. But when I look out the window and up to the purple-tinged sky, I'm less sure.

3

I flick through Instagram stories until I come to Dan's. I watch it several times compulsively. It begins with photos of the night: Steph and Lucy holding their drinks, a boomerang of Grace doing a shot, and then a video I don't remember. Dan and I are pointing up at the crack, and laughing as though it's funny. I look good, at least, but it makes me fear other things I can't remember. I don't know everything I said, or how I got home. I'm transfixed by the video, enthralled by my own face, which looks as though it belongs to someone else.

I check Twitter and see I have a notification. The boy has liked one of my tweets. It's a fairly bland tweet about the crack, so his liking it could mean any number of things. I chew my lip and read through his last few tweets. Nothing immediately screams *predator*, but he rarely tweets so there isn't much data to go on. I scroll through his liked tweets for a while, feeling as though I'm reading his diary, and decide to follow him back.

I think about it for a minute, and then I send Grace a screenshot of the notification and ask her how she knows him. Part of me doesn't want to have this conversation with her. I want to hold onto it like a secret.

Oh, that's Rory. He was in Steph's course and he was
at my party.
He was outside most of the night?

I wish I could remember him. I can't find the right
phrasing to ask her what she thinks the like means, so I
keep typing and erasing my message. I know Grace can
see me doing this, which persuades me to send it. She'll
read whatever meaning she wants into it anyway; I've
never been able to control her perception of me.

Have you fallen in love with him yet?

haha
as if

Determined to die alone then? That still the plan?

I stare at the message for a while without replying,
composing my thoughts. Then:

Don't worry, we can adopt 10 cats together.

i'd rather die alone

If the crack gets any bigger, you just might.

thanks

Maybe the crack will end the world before I find a
husband, and Grace will finally be happy. She makes fun
of me both for being an eternal spinster and for falling

32

in love with every guy who makes eye contact with me. I can't even argue with her; it feels like it's true, like the joke is something I can't escape from. Engaging with it makes it determinate, prescriptive, unavoidable. Pretending it doesn't get to me is a way to take control over the situation, to let it wash over me. Inside, it makes me spit and boil like water on hot oil.

Have you seen this article yet?

She links me an article about the crack and I'm grateful for the change in subject.

yes
have you seen these?

I send her screenshots of a few tweets, along with some long exposure shots of the sky in different parts of the world. Someone's created a thread of map graphics that accidentally leave out New Zealand.

God you're so online, all of this is just gibberish to me. It's like you're part of a cult.

I stare at the message for a second, wondering if she's making fun of me. I decide it's not worth picking a fight over, even if she is.

well it's nice to be part of something

Freak.

I can't explain my need to be plugged into the internet. Sometimes it feels like my body will scream if it doesn't have three separate screens in front of it, not even to watch and enjoy any of them, but to use each one as a distraction from the others, and to drown out any independent thoughts I could have about anything.

I reply with a shrug gif and we chat about summer plans and Grace's take on all our friends and how weird they are. It makes me wonder if Grace talks about me to other people the way she talks about other people to me.

She tells me things about Lucy's sex life that I'm sure Lucy wouldn't have told me herself and peppers her comments with things like, *I don't want to slut shame her, but . . .* And I don't think she does mean to slut shame her, or to talk badly about anyone, but Grace loves talking about people to the point where it's dehumanising by accident.

I'm worried about Dan moving.

me too
he might turn full brit

No, I just think he won't like it. I'm not sure he's thought it through.

i'm not sure he has any other options

We should definitely go and visit him once he's settled in.

do you think planes will still fly with the crack?

Pretty sure Ryanair will fly through anything. Maybe they'll add an extra fee for UFO insurance.

we could sail and rail

I don't love Dan that much.

After a while I forget to reply to her.

I scroll through Rory's Twitter feed again. He retweets things without adding a comment, so it's impossible to tell if he supports the content or if he's making fun of it. He could be the kind of person who believes in freedom of speech at all costs, and I remember the debaters I overheard at the party.

There's nothing explicitly political about anything on his page, which I find frustrating. He isn't following anyone who throws up immediate red flags, at least. His bio says he 'loves food and travel', to set him apart from the guys who never eat or move.

He's retweeted someone making fun of a government account advising us to stay calm. The original post tried to create a hashtag, which is now being abused by people with nothing better to do. The feed is flooded with memes, some of which are actually funny. The one advantage of the shift in political discourse to the online sphere is that no one over the age of forty understands what they've unleashed upon the world.

I like the tweet. It's a fairly innocuous thing to do, but it will give him a notification and maybe then he'll think of me. I wonder if other people think about social interactions like this, and decide that at some level they must. I'm not sure if I want Rory to understand my motives or if I want to understand his.

I read the internet for a while, which makes me think about how it really is a coping mechanism, and maybe Grace isn't as online as I am because she doesn't have as much to cope with.

Finn and I are supposed to meet for coffee in town, and I send him a message asking if he's still up for it. He's just put up a photo in a kitchen that I don't think is his.

He replies immediately and says *of course*. He follows up with a screenshot of a meme, which I laugh at not because it's funny, but because it's deconstructing several things I know to have been funny, once.

I pick a place and get the bus into town. Someone sitting behind me is listening to the radio out loud. I cringe at it but listen anyway. It's a talk show, and the host is running through a list of callers who want to talk about the crack. It isn't a productive conversation, but the host is maintaining interest by pitting callers against each other.

One woman calls in to make the point that the crack is a punishment from God in retribution for the legalisation of same-sex marriage and abortion.

'They said all they wanted was equality, but I never believed that for a second, it's always one thing and then another if you ask me.'

The host says, 'Now, now,' in a way that means, *please continue.*

'We used to have morals, but now churches are empty and isn't Jesus weeping, and there's a crack opened in the world.'

36

I wonder what kind of crack would open in the world if God found out about the Church's sex abuse and the Magdalene laundries. I put in earphones to drown out the radio. I know how the rest of the conversation will go: the big difference between my generation and that woman's is that we are no longer okay with state-sanctioned suffering. That's why we march in the streets, and how I found myself holding Grace's hand on the plane back from England a few summers ago. We'd spent our savings on that trip, and it was the only holiday we got. And the next summer we repealed the Eighth Amendment. The woman is right about something: it is always one thing and then another. I'm relieved when the bus approaches my stop.

I thank the bus driver as I get off, and immediately step into a puddle. I feel off balance, like I've walked onto an escalator that's not moving. The day is clear and crisp, and it looks as though the crack has got bigger in the sky, although I can't be sure. Every report I've read has struggled with how to measure the crack, and how to represent the data they've managed to record. Some part of my brain is screaming that it must be expanding, the threat must be growing, but I've learnt to not trust my brain.

The purple light is affecting the daylight and the shadows in an almost imperceptible way, which makes everything feel over-rendered, like a video game. Nothing looks quite as it should, and it makes me doubt the authenticity of the landscape.

I order a coffee in the café as soon as I sit down and dump three packets of sugar into it. I'm not early, but I know Finn's going to be late. I contemplate getting a brownie, but then feel I'll regret it later. Finn might judge me for it.

I order it to spite myself, to silence Hannah's voice in my head, and then I make myself eat each bite. It isn't worth it: the brownie is dry and I can feel it stick in my throat and on my thighs. The cake counter is dressed up to look homemade and twee, but they probably order everything in frozen and wholesale.

Finn arrives ten minutes after he says he will, his hair tousled as though he's been in high winds. I've been busying myself with googling whether they've decided the crack is bigger yet; there's still no consensus.

He's wearing a coat that I know he inherited from his grandfather, because he told me. It's frayed in places and patched up with tweed. He can afford a new coat, but he prefers the aesthetic of looking like he can't.

'Sorry I'm late, you wouldn't believe the day I've had – no, really, it was hectic and terrible and awful.' He sits down opposite me and fumbles with my empty sugar packets. 'Anyway, how have you been?' he adds, as though he has to.

I look him up and down, and it's like he can't see me. I could be anyone sitting here, listening to him. I hate him for it; his latte arrives.

Finn leans back in his chair and says, 'I couldn't sleep because of the crack, I kept waking up and seeing the light and feeling weird. As though it was draining something from the air? Probably my imagination, but it was weird, anyway.'

Regardless of whether or not it's growing, there's no scientific evidence that the crack's having any effect on the atmosphere, let alone sucking anything from it. It's just something I've seen a few scaremongering sites posting about. I punctuate my comments with a sip of my coffee and throw in a few *or whatevers* so I don't appear standoffish.

'Yeah, I know I know, it's definitely psychological. I've seen too many bad movies. But the point is it set me up to be in a very bad place for today and everything earlier.'

I wait for him to tell me what happened earlier.

'Oh, it's just Cassie, you know? Cassie, the girl I've been seeing. I introduced her to you at Grace's thing?'

He didn't, but I nod anyway. Perfect hair, red lipstick, and a distinct impression of thinness flash across my vision, but I ignore it. The only people who profit off that kind of thinking are men.

'Well, her dad's just had a fall, nothing too serious, but she has to head back down to Galway – she's from Galway – anyway, she has to head back down. She's pretty freaked out, with, you know' – he gestures in the air – 'everything.'

I grimace in sympathy but can't quite tell where Finn fits into the picture exactly. I also know from her Instagram that she's from Mayo, but I don't mention it.

'Please don't think me awful, and I'm trying to be as above board as possible here, but I think I need to break up with her. I don't want to be a dick about it, and now this has happened with her dad, I don't know, but I just have to be honest with her, you know? Not dick her around . . .' He trails off and looks at me imploringly.

I sip my coffee for a moment, holding the liquid in my mouth before I swallow it. I try to understand the motivation he could have in telling me this. He knows my love life's a mess, he frequently makes fun of me for it, so I'm not sure what kind of advice he's looking for.

I refuse to allow myself to think this could be about me in any way, not even for a second.

'I know, but you understand me. You get it, and I don't know who else I can talk to. I've been in a bad place for a bit now, and I feel like I can trust you. I need you to tell me what to do.'

I swallow my pride, and what feels like an ulterior motive, and try to be objective. On paper, I know it's not that difficult to break up with someone, even if I've never done it. He nods along as I speak, his thumbs moving across his phone screen. I can feel the gap of silence between each sentence like a physical thing. I can't tell if he's listening or if he's a million miles away. My words echo through my ears like a bell in a cave.

'This is all great.' He's still looking at his phone, and I can't stop myself from picturing what's on his screen. 'Yeah, God, I'm going to have to think about this. She's great and I really like her, but I'm just not in a place for this to happen. I think the crack made me realise that.'

I nod. Finn hasn't been in a place for a relationship for as long as I've known him, but that's never stopped him. The crack certainly hasn't sucked his fear of commitment out of him. I make a mental note to look up whether or not the crack *is* affecting the atmosphere later, just to make sure I'm right.

'Anyway, how've you been? I've heard there's some kind of birthday party happening?'

I don't want to think about how many people Grace has told. The party already feels too real; I'd thought entrusting it to Grace would banish it from my mind, but instead I'm afraid of what I can no longer control.

'Am I finally going to meet your twin? What's she like?'

His words have the effect of freezing time for a moment, and I'm suddenly acutely aware of everything that's going on around me. He doesn't know anything about my relationship with Hannah, and I want to keep it that way. For the last four years I've managed to keep her away from my friends, for good reason. I picture Finn brushing her hair off her shoulders, as I've seen him do to so many other girls.

'Well, I've got a great present for you, anyway. You'll never guess what it is, but I know you'll love it. I got it in this vintage shop in town, actually, have I told you about it?'

I'm grateful for the speed at which Finn spins conversation; it stops me fixating on anything for too long. My mind keeps jumping forward to the birthday party, and all of the potential hazards it entails. I can't remember the last birthday I had with Hannah that was pleasant; perhaps there's never been one. Her resentment of me started as a childish rivalry that she never grew out of, and I could never compete with.

I listen to Finn talk for a while. It's soothing to get swept up in him. Every few days Finn tags different people in pictures of pint glasses and coffee cups. He took a photo when his coffee arrived at the table, but I haven't received a notification yet. I feel a little bit smaller because of it. I concentrate on the fact that he chose to have this conversation with me; he wanted my advice.

I let none of this show on my face. I play with the fragments of my sugar packets. He looks at me with eyes like the ocean, and I can't concentrate on the thread of the conversation any more. I'm swallowing excessively loudly.

I look at my phone out of habit, to avoid having to look at Finn and say any of the things that are racing through my mind. I have a direct message from Rory. He's shared a meme similar to the one I'd liked before. He hasn't added any comment, and I stare at it for a moment.

'What are you smiling at? Let me see.'

I hesitate and then show it to him. Passing over the phone feels like passing over some unnameable part of myself. He asks me where I saw it, and my voice hitches on the word 'friend'.

'Oh, so it's a boy, is it? A boy friend? Tell me everything.' His eyebrows are arched, and in a flash he's back to his usual self. 'This is so exciting! Maybe I can give you boy advice? We could have a weekly coffee date about relationship issues?'

Finn asks me a lot of questions I don't want to answer, until suddenly his expression clears and he sits back in his chair. He knows Rory too.

'I could set you two up if you want.' He winks and seems genuinely excited. 'He's a really cool guy, no, really, I've met him out before, and he's the kind of guy I wish I could be friends with. I think he knows Pearse? We were all chatting at Grace's. Anyway, the offer's there.'

I shake my head at him, confused. In a few seconds he's managed to upturn my entire thought process. I can't understand his angle. Grace might know, or at least it's something we could dissect for a few hours. I start to type a message to her, but I don't know what to say. I'm not sure how to frame it properly, so that I come off as detached and uninterested.

'Pearse is friends with the coolest people. Sometimes, I think we're just friends because he likes to collect people.' Finn laughs at himself then, on cue. The way he talks about his male friends is like he idolises them. They are the most important things in his life, and at the same time he's hopelessly insecure in those relationships. I wonder if anyone else understands this about him. I don't want him to become uncomfortable confiding in me, so I don't push him on it, and the conversation moves on.

An older woman is loitering near our table, close enough that she's distracting. She's dressed in an old overcoat and staring right at me. I can't keep the conversation going.

'Do you live in number seven?' she asks me.

I blink at her. Finn looks from me to her in confusion and tries to keep going with his sentence about some arthouse film or other. I widen my eyes at him to show alarm, but he doesn't know what to do. He moves as if he's going to stand up to go to the bathroom, but I grab his sleeve and pull him back down, all the while trying to keep him talking. The woman interrupts us again.

'I live opposite you in number nine.' It isn't a question, but she's waiting for some kind of answer, so I nod, and pick up my coffee cup as an addendum to the interaction. Finn is looking around, clueless.

'Been lots of deaths on the road lately, haven't there?' She isn't looking at me any more, but at the space between Finn and me. She's waiting for a reaction while also paying no heed to the reactions we give. I look at Finn for help, but he just gives a breathless, nervous laugh.

I haven't noticed any excess deaths. My relationships with the adults on the road ended when they stopped giving me selection boxes at Christmas. I barely recognise this woman, who's now touching my shoulder.

The woman continues, the pauses in her monologue not reflecting the end of her sentences but rather some other rhythm: 'Didn't the woman in number thirty drop dead, last Saturday night, and I was only talking to her on the Friday before, and of course there were police and ambulances but, they wouldn't let me in the house. And Mr Malloy in number two, died of a heart attack, when he was abroad in Budapest, left his two kids behind, a fine job he had as well.'

With each death she lists, Finn grows more and more hysterical, struggling to contain his laughter. He coughs and takes out his phone so he can pretend to be laughing at something else. I kick him under the table, and he grabs my arm in response. I clasp his hand, desperate for something to ground me. The woman is looking at me again with all the intensity of a banshee. At her every pause I force out *oh yes*s, *oh no*s, *no really*s, struggling to contain my own laughter. Finn is making it worse.

'Of course, everyone's dying these days, can't be helped, I'll be next, have you seen the work they're getting done, in number three, beautiful house, not a touch wrong with it. Of course they're tearing it down, because poor Mary's husband, drowned last September. Lots of people I haven't seen on the road lately, maybe because of this sky business. If you ask me it's something biblical.'

Finn whispers, *Jesus Christ* under his breath. I breathe in deeply and keep my face straight.

'Your sister's away, isn't she? Beautiful girl, thin too.'

The sentence hangs between us like a physical thing. I can't come up with anything to say and neither can

Finn. He sits there quietly, no longer laughing. I stare at the flaking plastic of the table. The silence extends and the woman goes away. I pick at the skin around my fingers and pretend not to notice it. Eventually, Finn breaks it and asks me if I've ever seen that woman before in my life. He starts running over the things she said, and it has me laughing again.

'And she just comes up to you and tells you someone drowned? Jesus Christ, how many people does that woman know who've died? Do you think she's murdered them, like?' The faux earnestness in Finn's voice has me in fits of giggles, so much so that I'm crying. It helps to ease the conversation onto a new topic. He can be good like that, when he wants to be, when he knows that he has the power to elevate the mood.

When we laugh together, it feels like we have some shared connection, like I can predict what he's going to say and already know it's hilarious. Reaching across the table to him is like brushing a hair out of my face: thoughtless and essential. He reminds me of all the things I like about myself, and I love him.

Finn takes out his phone again and posts to Instagram. I relax a little bit when I get a notification. He's captioned the post: Old woman warns us about the apocalypse . . . and she's right? with a lot of tenuously related hashtags. Finn's always looking for more followers.

When he hugs me goodbye, I can smell his cologne. I breathe it in and hope it stays on my jacket for a little while. He needs someone to be there for him, not another girl to want him, so I decide to not want him any more. My motives aren't always pure, but I can't shake the feeling that I'm the only real friend he has. We both need each other.

Finn tells me he's meeting other people in town and has to run, and I start to walk home alone.

The evening feels lighter. The days are getting longer, and this one stretches out in front of me. The sky's full of candy-floss clouds, backed in purple. It looks like the sky from a fairy tale, and it emboldens me. I breathe air into my lungs like I've never breathed before and wind my way through the streets of Dublin. I look at them with fresh eyes, and they suddenly feel very romantic.

I've always liked Dublin in the summer. On the rare days when it's justifiable to get an ice cream that drips down your hand, and men walk around inexplicably topless, it feels like it's full of possibilities. This summer feels different though; there's an underlying pressure. Everyone on the streets seems anxious, like something is about to burst.

At the top of Grafton Street some people dressed in matching purple T-shirts are handing out flyers. I take one out of learned politeness. The text on it warns that the crack is God's punishment. I'm surprised that the word 'nigh' doesn't feature at all. A young blonde man tries to engage me in conversation about it, but I sidestep him and pretend I'm late for something. I wonder if they paid for express delivery on their outfits, or if they already had them from something else.

When I check my phone, I have another message from Rory. This time he's sent me a link to a video essay about online authenticity. I untangle my headphones and listen to it while I walk. I write and rewrite my reply over and over again until it ceases to have any meaning. I don't know why I feel awkward and uneasy, but I do. Online you can be anyone you want to be, which is the point of the video, and yet I can't be charming or intelligent.

Possible replies continue to run through my mind and it's only after I get home that I settle on one. My thumbs fumble over the words and I accidentally send two typos.

Rory, to his credit, replies like a regular human. As we chat, it gets easier. I ask him random questions, almost as challenges, and he meets them. We like the same books, follow the same Twitter accounts, and he recommends some games he thinks I'd like to play. The feeling of judgement melts away. I tell him about the people I saw handing out flyers.

I find it hard to share their concern.
Nothing's happened?

                              it still could though

True.
Especially because we live in a dystopia.

               the crack or the decline of late capitalism?

Both?

                          a true ontological nightmare

You know I've never really understood what that word means, ontological.
I feel like I'm supposed to know all these words that no one's ever explained to me.

I hadn't realised that was something you were allowed to do, to just brazenly admit you don't know something. I'd spent a few minutes reading the Wikipedia page before sending the message to him, and the word is only on my mind because Grace said it to me. I tell him this, because I want to know how it will feel.

Sorry I refuse to believe that.
You're like one of the smartest people I've spoken to.

well you've obviously not spoken to many smart people
then

He keeps finding little ways to compliment me, saying my reactions to things are cute, or interesting. Eventually, I run out of ways to shrug them off. After a while, I don't mind, I even get used to it. It's as if, for the time that I'm talking to him, I'm allowed to believe that I'm special.

I screenshot a few messages and send them to Grace to ask her what she thinks they mean. I screenshot a few just for me.

Stop being a weirdo, just talk to the boy.

I take her advice and stop thinking about it. It's almost easy.

4

When I check my email, my inbox is full of job rejections. I open and close each one manually, cementing in my mind the reality that I'll be living with my parents until I'm thirty. Every property in Dublin that even hints at being in my price range is an hour outside the city and has bunk beds you have to jump over to get to the oven.

I didn't want any of these jobs, not really; they're all graduate jobs with ambiguous titles that I saw in Facebook groups or my friends linked to me. But I don't understand how I didn't meet their minimum skill level.

I open my social media apps out of habit, and they all load on Rory's profiles. I'd stayed up late stalking him, and I feel guilty about that now in a way I didn't at two this morning. I close them one by one, checking my activity logs and liked posts to make sure I haven't accidentally embarrassed myself.

I send Grace a screenshot of my inbox, and she replies immediately.

Are you all right?

i feel worthless

You're worth more than the value of your labour.

                              sure but not monetarily

Yes we all love cold hard cash.

                    i'm 22 and i'm already burnt out

It's not your fault, blame our boom and bust economy.
Can't wait for the inevitable recession caused by oil
markets spooking over this crack.

                         maybe it'll spark a tech boom?

Sophie, we have arts degrees.

                                   transferrable skills?

I'm not sure there's a way to articulate this kind of
dread.

          it's just the sound of every young person screaming

Clever, maybe you'll become a poet?

                                        no money in it

Maybe it'll get better?

           things haven't been getting better since 2016

I consider getting out of bed, but see no point in it. Instead, I look over my CV and then trawl through job sites looking for anything and everything I can apply for. Somewhere around the third page of results, I begin to lose hope and change tactic.

Grace is going into a Masters next year, which means she can delay the job search, at least for a little while. I thought about doing that too, but there's nothing I want to study. UCD offers a diploma in digital marketing, but it's hard to justify spending the money to confirm that I can use Twitter.

Dad's sitting watching the news when I come downstairs, and Mum is reading the paper. Dad doesn't look up as I make some food, but he quizzes me on everything I'm doing. I stare into the back of his head as I put together a sandwich on the counter.

'Are you going to eat the leftovers from last night?'

'Did you see the fresh loaf of bread on the counter?'

'Will you put your dishes in the dishwasher?'

'How's the job search going?'

We never talk about any temporal place other than the immediate present. It's best for our relationship if we don't talk about the past, or the future, and that doesn't leave room for much else. I don't know him as a person, and he doesn't know me.

When I open the cutlery drawer, the handle comes off in my hand. I've been telling them to fix it for years, but they've never listened. I stand for a moment at the counter, looking across it to the living room beyond, and brandish the handle at my parents before placing it back on as firmly as I can. Some of the yellow paint comes off under my fingernails. Hannah will tell them to fix it, and they'll do it.

Mum folds the paper and asks me about my plans for the day. I don't look at her, which I know will annoy her, but the truth is that I've nothing planned for today, and that will annoy her even more.

'Well, that's grand then, you can help me with planning your birthday.' She pats the empty sofa cushion beside her. 'I know that's more Hannah's thing, but you're the next best thing!'

She means it as a joke, and that makes it worse. It's like my parents weren't there for my childhood. They've no idea how Hannah makes me feel, or how their treatment of her makes it worse. It's impossible to even have a conversation with them about it.

The last time Hannah was home, she threw a pan full of stir-fry at the wall and called me a bitch, all because I'd called her out on stealing my expensive hair dryer. Hannah's a difficult person, and she acts without consequence. My parents are just grateful every time she doesn't blow up; they always have been. I'm the one responsible for keeping peace in the house, if only by not reacting to Hannah. I've been marking off the days until she comes home on my phone's calendar, and they've run out.

'I know you know more than three words. It would be nice to hear them sometimes! I thought you'd grown out of your mumbling phase. And please put your phone down while I'm talking to you!'

I grew out of that phase more or less around the time Hannah left. The pressure of someone always speaking over me had taught me to not speak up for myself. It's something I'm still conscious of every time I trip over

52

my words because I haven't had enough practice saying them out loud. Hannah used to playfully slag me when I couldn't pronounce a word on the first go, and at some point, it stopped being playful. It was just another way she could prove she was better than me.

The reporters on the news are discussing the crack, and my dad turns it up high, which cuts off the conversation. For the first time, I don't mind.

They're saying that the crack has widened. It's something I'd expected, anticipated even, but having it confirmed is so much more awful than I could have predicted. When I thought I was beginning to predict what was going to happen I had control over it, but now I have nothing. What's worse, no one else seems to have control either. I want the Taoiseach to come on and announce some shiny new policy, or a scientist to pull up a graph that shows where we are on the timeline of the Earth. None of these things happen, and I don't know who to turn to for answers.

I pick up my phone and start gathering information again. I watch the same four arguments develop on a hundred Twitter accounts, each one linking a new study with a clickbait headline that backs up their point. The crack has caused a spike in domestic violence, one account warns, but not as much as England just playing a football match, another one reminds us. I follow the thread down as far as it goes, observing every possible emotion, until I decide to feel nothing about it at all. On the news, they show pictures of the crack from different major cities, landmarks clearly visible. The graphics they use to illustrate what is happening are clunky; the intern who made them is probably unpaid. One of them has a drop shadow, and I cringe.

Next, they cut to several interviews with leading scientists, but all they can agree is that it's hovering somewhere in Earth's atmosphere. As of yet they haven't been able to detect anything radiating out from it. The usual talking points are bounced around: it's definitely caused by human activity; it definitely isn't, and so on. Someone's saying that it's just the usual life cycle of the Earth. I click into the hashtag for the programming and watch as people parody the words of the guests in real time. The coverage slips from scientists to pundits so quickly I almost don't catch the transition, but I'm not sure there have been any facts on the table to begin with.

There are protests in town over the crack. A reporter standing outside the Dáil asks someone why they've come out today, and they say, 'I'm tired of all these hoaxes, people are just scaremongering, we have bigger issues to deal with,' and it's clear that no one really knows what that means. I can't believe this has made national news. I recognise my purple-shirted friends, who make up about half of the crowd. There is, at least, a man standing on the periphery of the group holding a 'The end is nigh' sign.

Dad says, 'Sure, what are they complaining about? They've nothing to complain about.' And I agree with him. These are not the same people who took to the streets for marriage equality, to repeal the Eighth, or to end direct provision.

My parents get up and leave, satisfied by the information they've consumed. I sit for an uncountable amount of time, opening and closing the same four apps, trapped. Every time I make a move to begin a project or apply for a job, a wave of exhaustion overcomes me. I can't concentrate on anything for more than a few seconds. It's been like this for a long time.

It seems that everyone else has it figured out. Dan's moving to London. Everyone's moving to London. I can't even get a job interview. *I'll never amount to anything.*

I refuse to acknowledge my thoughts and open my email, only to refresh the feed and close the app again. In frustration, I close all the tabs I have open, hoping that doing so will erase all the information they're holding.

I have messages that are unopened, but I don't feel like chatting to anyone. I'm not convinced that people chat any more; they just watch the clock tick down until they can go to sleep again.

Defeated, I scroll through my internet history and start reopening tabs. I keep the diploma in digital marketing open and move the tab so it's first in line. It's the type of thing Mum would suggest I do.

I get a series of messages from Finn. The first one opens with an ellipsis, so I know it's serious. I watch them build up on my home screen, waiting.

. . .

Hey.
I may be a horrible person.

Then:

I need you to tell me I'm not a horrible person.

I think of Grace for a second, and what she'd say, and then cast her from my mind like a magician waving away a trick. I unlock my phone.

Cassie called me.
Her dad got worse.

I wait for the bit of the story he doesn't want to tell me, the reason he's contacted me in the first place.

She won't be coming up to Dublin for a while.
So,
Look I just couldn't see a way out of this.
It was really playing with my anxiety.

He spends a while typing, and I wait for the paragraph I know is coming. There's always a paragraph.

And I know you gave me advice, and I'm so grateful for it, but I just couldn't deal with it, it's too much of an emotional burden. And I know I shouldn't say it like that, it's not emotional labour when it's someone you care about. But Soph, she wanted me to go down and be with her, and I knew it wouldn't be right, and I was so anxious after the call, so I had to break up with her. I didn't think it would be healthy for either of us just to pretend. I took the time to think about it, I really did, but I just let her know there . . .

It's frustrating, giving Finn advice. So many times he's come to me, begging me for help, listening earnestly, and then gone and done the exact opposite of what I said. Sometimes, it's like he doesn't want to change.

i have to ask but i nearly don't want to know
did you break up with her over text?
when her dad's sick?

A minute passes.

Yes.

I press down on his message to select the angry reaction and close my phone.
Then:

please if you're angry with me too i'll know i'm a lost
cause

For a moment I consider not replying, but something about the message feels different, like he's actually being authentic with me. I cave.

you need to stop and think about how you treat people
you're a selfish asshole, do you know that?

trust me, i know
i hate myself more than you hate me

He knows I'm only harsh when I'm not seriously annoyed with him. Things have only been bad between us a few times over the years, and those times have always been marked by silence. In the end, one of us has always broken. He moves the conversation on, and I know he's got what he wants from me.
 I go to the kitchen to get myself a snack, but I'm not

really hungry. I just have an emptiness inside me. I open and close the fridge a few times and then take out some leftover pasta to microwave. I make myself eat it. A full stomach will calm me.

I turn on Netflix and pick one of their originals. Each one I watch is worse than the last, but they make me feel better about my own life. When I finish my pasta I check my phone. The girls from school are discussing something and sending notification banners flicking across the top of my screen, but I can only see the first few words of each one. I'm careful to not open any apps that would give away I'm online. I don't want one of them to drag me into the conversation. I see Grace join the conversation; she'll tell me if it was important later.

Then a message from Rory comes through, like a lightning bolt to my chest:

Hey, feel free to say no but I enjoyed chatting to you at the party. Coffee soon? Before the world is sucked into the void?

My tongue is dry in my mouth. It sits there, useless and taking up space. I can hear my heartbeat in my chest. The frankness of his message catches me off guard; people don't state things plainly any more. I can't help but compare Rory to Finn and how uneasy Finn makes me feel sometimes. I still can't remember what Rory and I talked about, but it must have made an impression on him. It's terrifying to not know who I am to him.

I open up the message I have from Grace. It's a photo

she'd sent a few hours earlier. I react to it and pretend I've only just seen it. I'm not sure she ever believes me when I say that.

I send her the screenshot and ask for her thoughts. Grace has much more experience with this than I do, and even if she's not always the most sensitive, her advice is valuable. It sometimes makes me jealous how boys seem to gravitate towards her and not me. She sends me back a series of heart emojis.

do you think this is a date?
like, a date date?

Honestly Soph, you're so oblivious.

I send her a shrug emoji and wait for more. Grace is never one for giving advice without a little bit of gentle slagging first. I wonder if she's right. I can't remember ever being flirted with, so I don't have much of a sample size. But it doesn't feel like I'm oblivious; it feels like I am mining every interaction for information.

I think it's pretty obvious here, and even if it isn't you should definitely go. Fortune favours the brave!

you have a point
it could just be two friends having a normal coffee
there's good plausible deniability in that
nothing ventured, nothing ventured

One of these days you'll have to grow up.

I decide to change the subject and move on before Grace can really get her claws into me. I ask her what she's up to and start reading the internet. At some point I forget to reply and think it would be too rude to try and pick up the conversation. I'll tell her my phone battery ran out later.

Up in my room, I work up the courage to reply to Rory. Courage I shouldn't need, really, given it's a perfectly ordinary thing for regular humans to do, but I work it up anyway. I read and reread my message to make sure it reads okay and has the appropriate emojis and punctuation, and then send it. I think I've achieved a nice balance between it having no concrete meaning and also controlling every possible meaning.

great!
what should we do?

                                        i don't mind

okay
i'll think of something good

                                        i trust you!

His messages come in one after another, each clause inhabiting its own little universe. I notice immediately his shift to lowercase; he'd have had to fight his phone's autocorrect to do it. He's mimicked the way that I message, and I'm afraid now that he's been able to see my carefully hidden motivations. I lock my phone and leave it upside down on my bedside table.

I stare out the window, no coherent thoughts forming at the front of my mind. I have a general awareness of what is happening around me, and ideas gently nudge me into thinking. I can't help but stare at the crack and think it's what we deserve. The whole world is fractured. Everything from the news cycle to climate change to Twitter algorithms serve only to bring the human race to a crashing evolutionary halt. It's like watching the world slip away between my fingers, too subtle to fully grasp. This crack is just one more thing on the list.

I'm too afraid to ask Rory what he thinks about it. I like the image I have of him in my head, where he's perfect. If I ask him any deep questions, the illusion will shatter, and he'll tell me he's in Young Fine Gael. I worry that it'll put me off, or worse, that it won't. I'm not sure if I have any self-respect, or if my morals will hold up in the face of my general need to be desired.

I lean forward and open the window, breathing in the fresh air. It's possible to pretend that nothing's amiss in the world. I try counting back from ten and thinking of times when I've felt at peace, before the crack and before I cared about politics or any of these things. Sometimes, I think the worst thing I've ever done for my mental health is to start caring about politics. When I breathe out, my mind is blank.

The front door opens and closes with a bang, and Hannah's voice rings through the house. When I look down the stairs there are bags in the hall; Hannah's moved her whole life back here, and now it's sitting on top of mine. I count to ten, chasing the blankness, before I hear Mum call me down to say hello to my sister. Every step reverberates through my whole body.

Hannah's sitting at the table talking to Mum. Her hair's longer, and she looks strong. She's wearing a dress, and I fixate on it, unable to comprehend it. It's like she's walked off the pages of a style magazine, as though I'd modelled for it and some sinister artist had photoshopped my flaws away. I feel distorted, grotesque.

She gets up and hugs me when she sees me, and immediately tries to include me in whatever she's saying to Mum. They both appear interested in each other, but I can't follow the conversation. I'm a stranger in my own home, or my home is a stranger to me. I'm suddenly worried that the familiar walls will close in and crush me, or the photographs will start falling off them. Hannah being here changes the feeling of the space and transports me back into the person I was before she left. She sits back down, but I can still smell her perfume.

I've not adequately prepared my body for the physical shock of seeing her. I'm a little girl again, and everything she's ever said or done to me is swirling in my head at once. I'm the fat little girl, the ugly child that I've always been to her. She's so long distorted my self-image that it's all I see. It's beginning to get hard to breathe.

I pretend I'm getting a call and excuse myself. They both nod at me without looking over or noticing. They never notice.

I lie down on the bathroom floor, feeling flushed and hot. I remember the time Hannah slapped a burger out of my hand, saying I was big enough already. I feel the hot rush of shame again. I remember her telling our parents that they really shouldn't allow me to go up for seconds at dinner. I remember everyone always referring to her as the pretty twin, as though that disguised what they meant.

Worst of all, I remember the times when it used to be okay between us. The memories rise up from nowhere, rose-tinted from the haze of childhood and vague from so much time spent repressing them. It gives me a headache so profound it's like my skull is contracting. It's better to demonise her; it makes her presence in my life easier to dismiss.

I feel my sides and I'm disgusted. I can't find a way to sit or lie down in which I'm not totally and completely aware of my body.

My head is splitting, and I can't breathe. Every bit of air I force into my lungs comes out immediately in great wrenching sobs. I vomit into the toilet three times, each time only throwing up coffee and bile. It's all so bitter. The force of my retching causes tears to spring from my eyes, and I know I'm pathetic. No one has ever been more pathetic.

Accepting this calms me a little, enough to stem the tide of tears. I don't feel better; all I feel is exhausted. The weight of so many years has settled back on me. All the baggage I've managed to work through since Hannah left has just been delivered at my door, returned to sender. At least it's familiar; I've worn these feelings before, and they fit me.

When I go to my room, I take off all my clothes and lie in bed. I read the internet until the sun sets outside my window, and I'm in darkness. I find some free online courses in digital marketing and sign up to them; there doesn't seem to be anything else to do. After a while, I become numb to the point where it's difficult to remember I'd even been sad in the first place. I think it's impossible to express emotion, let alone for me to have just done it. There's no longer a difference between being awake or asleep.

5

The dress won't zip up. It's probably a cheap zip and caught on the fabric, or the stitching's been done poorly. I strain against it, contorting my body, and nearly rip the zipper right off. Eventually, I face facts. I sit on my bed, my head in my hands, until no more tears come. I put the dress back into the wardrobe, where it hangs like a ghost, mocking me. There was a time when that dress had fit me, and I'd liked it.

I sit naked on my bed, and when I look in the mirror I see every line and curve of my body. All of my clothes feel ill-fitting and dated, but I don't have the emotional energy to replace them.

I scroll through Grace's tagged photos for inspiration, trying to figure out what regular people wear when they leave the house. I settle on jeans and a jumper, which is boring, but that's half the point. I can't help but think that this kind of outfit looks better on Grace because her clothes are a lot nicer than mine and she's a lot thinner. I try to get my eyeliner right three times, until I give up and wipe it off in one big smear down my face. I take all my make-up off and start again.

I can't eat any food. My stomach is unsettled, and I

keep running to the bathroom to panic pee and put my head between my legs to stop myself from getting dizzy. I can't get a grip on the day. I load increasingly embarrassing wikiHow pages and the Wikipedia pages for 'dating' and even 'courtship'. The bizarre illustrations swim before my eyes, detached from any coherent meaning.

Rory and I are messaging back and forth. I keep my replies short because I don't want to use up all my content before we meet. I double and triple check each message before sending, wary that I might accidentally send him the wrong screenshot. My phone could easily betray me.

On the walk in, I repeat *act like a normal human* over and over in my head, as if saying it will make it happen. I look at my reflection in every shop front I pass. Not to be vain, but to check that I'm still present, that I still occupy a physical form. My face hasn't changed in the time since I've last seen it. I smile at myself to test that my muscles are in working order. I wonder if anyone can tell my insides are all mixed up when they look at me, if I'm slowly unravelling before their eyes. I stare at each person I pass, wondering if any of them are having the same kinds of thoughts that I am.

I stop in a shop to get a bottle of water because I can feel the control I have over myself slipping. I crave the small thrill of consumption, although I feel guilty that I didn't bring my reusable bottle. The plastic is thin and crinkles pleasantly in my hands. I pay with exact change and smile at the cashier as I hand it over, who doesn't react, as though I'm some kind of horrible thought experiment given flesh. *Just a regular human, doing regular things.* I imagine thinking myself into such an intense spiral that I vanish into nothing. No one would notice.

I arrive early and reopen Google Maps to make sure I'm in the right place. I zoom in as close as possible to the position marker, trying to match my location to it exactly. I've looked up the address several times since Rory sent it to me, but one last time won't hurt.

I'm outside a pop-up museum on College Green, trying my best to look casual yet cool. They have an exhibition on the crack, and we're going to see it and then have coffee afterwards. Another coffee might give me a heart attack, but I can't let that spoil the afternoon Rory's planned.

I have so many tabs open on my phone that I'm beginning to feel nauseous. None of the rabbit holes offer any clarity on either my mental space or the crack, it's all just doom-scrolling. I want to sound confident, to be able to rattle off impressive opinions to Rory, but I keep encountering the same thought wall that pervades this whole problem, which is that no one knows enough to sound confident. I decide to read up on what specific clever people think and cite them when I speak to avoid having to take a stance altogether.

I'm so engrossed in my phone that I don't notice when Rory arrives until he nudges my shoulder. I jump and nearly drop my phone. I reflexively hit the lock button so he won't see what I'm reading.

'Hey, sorry I'm a little late,' he says to me. I check the time; he's not late, I'm early. I smile at him and greet him too, surprised at how calm my voice sounds. I wish my jeans had real pockets so I could put my hands inside them. He opens the door to the museum for me.

The whole room's been painted like the sky, running from sunrise to midnight. There are information boards all around, and we stop at the first one to read it. I'm hyper aware of my own breathing as I stand next to Rory. I fixate on how long the average person spends reading these boards, and if I'll look lazy or intelligent if I walk away too quickly. I wonder if he can hear my breathing as well and if it's bothering him.

'So what's your leading theory on the crack?'

I can't remember anything I've prepared to say. It seems impossible to untangle the ambiguities of the crack, and anyone who's attempted it so far has been wrong. I'm not sure how to vocalise my doubt, and the words are thick in my throat.

He laughs, and I feel more at ease.

'Oh yeah, I agree. Everyone who's already out there with definitive conclusions is either stupid or lying.' He opens his eyes wide when he's being incredulous. 'I think we shouldn't worry about it until we know more. Or, at least, remember that there's nuance here.'

We walk from board to board, and it's easier. A lot of the content is stuff I've read online, or things only tangentially related to the crack. One board is a list of birds that are already endangered, which theorises that their breeding habits might be disrupted by the new light. I think it's been repurposed from a previous exhibit, which makes it worse; it's more evidence that the apocalypse was already happening before a crack opened in the sky. I don't say this to Rory, however, because it doesn't seem like date material.

Instead, we point out interesting or funny things to each other, and I chide him for spoiling bits I haven't got to yet.

'Read faster then,' he says, but I want to prolong the

moments where we stand side by side, and I like it when he touches my shoulder to show me something.

I like being here, with him. Rory has a way of talking that's accessible. He never says anything I can't understand, but at the same time it feels like he's never at a loss for words. I like listening to the cadence of his voice more than the words he says; it's comforting. He looks me in the eyes when he speaks to me, really looks at me, and nothing he says is startling or concerning.

The next room houses some recycled pieces from an old space exhibition and some other things explaining basic physics. We stand around a plasma globe and watch the charge jump between our hands. I feel a flush creeping up my neck. Rory doesn't seem put off, he just smiles at me and winks, acknowledging the subtext. I shake my head in what I hope is an exasperated manner, and when we let go, I give him an electric shock.

'Ouch, unfair,' he says, and then asks: 'Does anyone really know how electricity works, anyway? It's basically magic.'

I took physics for my Leaving Cert and did quite well in it, so I do know, but I decide instead to laugh and shake my head. I don't have to have an answer for everything. It's freeing to let statements hang in front of me uncommented upon.

The final room is fully interactive. We're encouraged to 'play', and the information board makes sure to let us know that it's suitable for all ages. It's a completely padded room, full of blue and purple foam shapes. The floor is on different levels, with grooves and ramps of different sizes. It's some loose interpretation of the crack where *we* are the art. I look at Rory as I take off my shoes.

'Do you really want to play?' he asks. He shakes his

head in disbelief but sits down next to me and begins to undo his laces. He's wearing odd socks, and he's not embarrassed when I point it out.

'Who has time to match their socks?' he says, and I try not to look at my own matching pair.

It's awkward at first. We try to build a kind of uniform structure using the foam blocks, but it quickly unravels. I find an enormous purple triangle that I love, and I insist it's an annex to our house. He laughs and adds a roof. Some children come over and ask to build too. One of them calls me Miss; to him I must seem like a real adult. I laugh, and I don't care who's looking. I feel so at ease, as though nothing matters. I don't have to think, I just have to do. Rory tells me that he doesn't think he's ever had such fun in his life, and it makes me smile.

We get a coffee to go, and walk around the city together. He tells me stories about all of his favourite pubs that have since been knocked down and replaced with hotels, and I'm relieved that he doesn't vote Fine Gael.

'What's your favourite part of Dublin?' he asks me as we walk along Nassau Street, dodging groups of Spanish exchange students with yellow backpacks and Americans clutching large paper bags full of souvenirs.

It takes me a moment to answer. Dublin is as familiar to me as my own face. I see all its flaws and scars, and yet I'm at home here. I'll never be able to buy a house here, but when I breathe in the crisp evening air I feel at ease. The line between security and insecurity is a knife edge.

'Why do you care so much? About buying a house, I mean?' he asks me. 'You're not the only one I know who does, I mean it's not that weird, but personally I'm years away from even thinking about having a deposit together.'

That, I think, is the point. The idea that I could one day own my own house is so far-fetched it feels like a flight of fancy, not something I could realistically aspire to. The housing bubble popped when I was too young to understand things like money, or a mortgage. I've never had that sense of stability, of normalcy. I'm tired of reading articles about generational warfare, about how my generation is somehow destroying the housing market, the stock market, the concept of salaries. Everyone I know just wants the stability of knowing they won't end up homeless, and to not have to pay a landlord three quarters of their salary for the luxury.

'I think it's also just a really Irish thing. Ever since the Penal Laws we've wanted that kind of security.'

I find it funny that this feeling, one that's been ingrained in me for so long, could have a legacy that extends back far before I was born. It seems impossible to think that, but at the same time I can't tell Rory that he's wrong.

We take a turn up Kildare Street and Rory tells me he's never been into the museum here. 'Speaking of history,' he says, and leads me up the steps.

We spend a few minutes looking at all the gold artefacts. Rory jokes that the necklaces are coming back into style; there is a time and place for everything. I haven't been here in a long time, not since trips into town stopped feeling like excursions, and the smell of the place reminds me of my teenage self.

'Oh my God, you have to see this.' Rory's found the entrance to the bog bodies, and I follow him. 'Like the Seamus Heaney poem from the Leaving Cert? Have you been here before?'

I'm embarrassed to admit that I've been here so many

times that I can rattle off the information boards from memory. Rory stares at me and then begs me to give him a tour. I start off slow, the words thick in my throat. Rory has the good grace to at least feign that he's impressed. I've always been fascinated by the bog bodies. They make the past feel more present and give me a sense that time is still marching forward.

'I think I'd have done well in Pagan Ireland,' he says, and so I show him the body of a man that had his nipples cut off to make him unworthy for kingship. 'Maybe not then,' he concedes. 'I probably would have liked to eat more than grain and have access to healthcare and other goods and services.'

We walk, and he asks me what my dreams for the future are, and we talk about how life's both standing still and moving much too quickly. He listens, and I'm relieved. My future feels trapped by the decisions I made in my past, when I was too young and immature to realise their importance.

'Yeah, I get you,' Rory says. 'I know it should feel more uncertain because of the crack but, somehow, it doesn't.'

As the afternoon lengthens I feel some pressure building up between us. If I stay out with him any longer, this nice warm bubble will burst into something more complicated. Either it's something or nothing, and if I stay there will be no more plausible deniability. Possible futures begin unfurling in front of me.

He walks me to the bus stop, and we chat while we wait. I keep my arms crossed because I don't know what to do with my hands otherwise.

My bus disappears off the timetable. I watch it count down from four minutes, to three, to two, and then vanish.

I feel the space between us expand and contract. I'm sure he can hear me breathing. Then, my bus appears on the screen again. I make some joke about the public transport system in Dublin, and how even Glasgow has a subway, but cut myself off when I remember it was Hannah who'd told me that fact. I smile to cover the abrupt ending to my sentence. I think, for a moment, that he's going to ask me to go back to his house with him, or lean down and kiss me. I look away from him as my bus arrives, cutting the invisible string that connects us.

I wave at him from my seat, and he heads off in the opposite direction. It feels simple, and childlike, and pure. I call Grace immediately, and she wants to know every detail. We break down everything that was said into its minutia, until there's no ambiguity.

'Okay, not bad, there's definitely some potential there, but the problem is that Rory is an unknown quantity.'

I listen to her, afraid that speaking will reveal too much.

'Lads are so useless is the thing, the only people who can understand them are other lads. Maybe we could get someone we know to ask him about it over a pint?'

Sometimes Grace says words out loud that she hasn't considered. The only guy I know who knows Rory is Finn. I don't mention this to Grace.

'And I know what you're thinking, the only guy you know who knows Rory is Finn, so yeah, you're right, that's not an option. I think your brain would explode. Steph knows him better, but you know how she is. We'll just have to wait and see, and make sure next time you take detailed notes of your every interaction.'

I get a message from Rory, and Grace makes noises until I read it out to her.

hey
it was great seeing you today
i really enjoyed it!
maybe we could do it again sometime?

'Oh that's eager. Are you into eager?' Grace asks me, and I hang up on her so I have time to process the message in front of me. She messages me immediately.

????

sorry
call dropped for some reason

Yeah, right.
Have you replied yet? Send me a screenshot.

i don't know what to say back
i need time to think about it

You need time to think about everything. The heat death of the universe will happen before you're done thinking.

this is the kind of support I need from my best friend
thanks

Then:

i just want this whole thing to settle in my mind
i need to get used to it

What is there to get used to? Do you like being around him or what?

yes

But?

My thumbs hover over the keyboard for a time, unsure. I don't want to tell Grace that as much as I like spending time with Rory, I prefer having him in my pocket, available, and I'm worried that if our relationship changes that will end. Instead, I say:

look you know how i am
he'll realise i'm a weirdo if he spends any more time with me

If it makes you feel any better, that ship has probably already sailed.

I've got as much out of this conversation with Grace as I will before she turns totally negative, so I stop replying and leave her on read. I don't want to have to share everything with her. I open up my chat with Rory and stare at it before replying:

actually, my birthday is coming up
i'm having a small gaff

sounds great!
i'd love to come!

75

He hasn't noticed I've sidestepped his question into more platonic waters, or maybe he just doesn't mind. The bus window reflects my face back at me as I stare up at the crack.

I scroll through the internet for a while, but it only makes me anxious. Everything's about the crack; people are posting images on Instagram and sharing graphs on Twitter. Most of them haven't labelled their axes, but they're all red lines sharply rising and carefully crafted to ensure panic. I read every headline as though it's the start of a meme before I can stop myself. Barbershop quartets are back and singing about the crack.

I'm not sure when the internet ceased to be a place I could escape to, to get lost down rabbit holes and take care of virtual pets, but it does not offer me the same things any more. I have a feeling it's to do with cyber and personal spaces melding, warping each other. The coping mechanisms I've spent a decade building up are crumbling in the modern world. I think that thought would make a good tweet, so I send it out into the world and wait for other people to agree with me.

On Instagram, I scroll through Finn's last few posts. There's one of his family at dinner. Everyone looks happy. His parents are clinking their glasses together. There's something about social media that allows you to take a photo, add two bars of a song and some gifs, and totally change the fabric of reality. I feel a little warmth at knowing Finn so well that I know when he's masking his pain, but that's something I'll never admit and do my best to never indulge.

Dinner is ready by the time I get home, and we eat at the table. Normally, we eat while watching the news, but today they're making a show for Hannah's sake. I'm tired of watching the news anyway; it's just a constant stream of updates that are not updates. I don't need to see a debate between a scientist and the editor of a right-wing Catholic website just because RTÉ thinks that's balance. They've updated the Angelus to show shots of birdwatchers and repair men staring in contemplation, cast in the purple glow of the sky. I can't even remember what the Angelus is supposed to be for.

Hannah spends the entire meal telling us about a trip that she's planning to take over the next few months. She wants to travel around Southeast Asia with her friends, and as she speaks I can already see the social media posts she'll make. Mum's always asking me what Hannah's up to on social media, because Hannah rarely calls, and I don't want to have to look at her perfect angles and filters for a whole summer. I push my lasagne around my plate, telling myself to only eat as much as I want to, knowing that I am powerless to stop myself.

My parents are less than enthusiastic. Dad finds several ways of asking her how she will pay for it, which Hannah avoids answering. Mum worries she might have a fight with her friends or get kidnapped.

Hannah didn't work through her degree, so I don't know how she's going to pay for the trip. She might be selling nudes online. And I've heard if you find the right community of desperate creepy men, you can make a fair bit from selling things like used tissues or your underwear. I can't decide if I'm uncomfortable with the idea that there could be photos out there that look like me. But of course, they wouldn't look like me, not really. Hannah's barely touched her food.

'What about the sky? Will that change things?' Mum asks, and Hannah looks to me as though I'll back her up. I shrug and the conversation moves on. Hannah knows what to say to convince our parents of anything.

'Well, it sounds like a great opportunity,' Mum says.

'I never got to travel at your age!' is Dad's addition.

'Sophie, you could even come out for a bit if you wanted, meet us in Thailand or something? It's supposed to be amazing.'

I haven't been expecting Hannah to address me, so I can't come up with a way to say no fast enough. For a brief moment I imagine myself on the beach with her, drinking out of a coconut and smiling for the camera, and then crying silently in the bathroom.

'If it's money you need, I could loan you some, and you could pay me back later, no interest! Or, well, almost no interest!'

She's definitely selling nudes.

I stuff my last bite of food into my mouth and clean up after myself, leaving them sitting there at the table. Hannah passes me her plate to put in the dishwasher, 'Just while you're up,' and I take it without comment. The whole interaction leaves me exhausted, so I get into bed.

I pull out my phone and flick though Twitter. It does nothing to lift my mood. If I can't think thoughts for myself, at least I can consume those of others and regurgitate them if anyone asks. Surely, somewhere on the world wide web, someone has some answers to everything that's going on. The crack must be changing something, and someone must know what it is.

All I find are people panicking, other people performatively saying that panicking isn't helpful, and yet more people promoting the use of panicking as a healthy coping mechanism. All of these people are saying more or less the same thing, that it's okay to panic and equally okay to try and pretend things are normal, depending on what works for individual people, but they're doing a good job of acting like they're on different sides. There's nothing at the centre, no one telling me what it is I should be panicking about, only that it's okay to do so.

Rory messages me.

hey

So I reply:

hey

We chat for a while about nothing in particular. I tell him my theory about how memes are restructuring popular humour, and he seems interested. He tells me about the book he's been reading, which he says I might like. There's comfort in the banality of the conversation, and at the end of it I find I can smile again.

6

Grace and I decide to have a drink before showing up to Finn's. The night was either organised at the last minute, or I've been invited as an afterthought. Finn messaged me this afternoon telling me about it, saying it was a casual thing, but when I asked Grace what she was going to wear, she said she'd bought an outfit last weekend.

I meet her at the cocktail bar she's picked out. She's already there, and she waves me over. She's wearing all black and, instead of this making her blend into the velvet booth, she's the focal point of the room. She looks like a chic influencer, and in comparison I look like someone trying to offload cheap products on their friends. Perhaps there isn't a difference.

Grace pushes the cocktail menu towards me. It's leather-bound and heavy, and it takes me several minutes to read and find something that doesn't sound disgusting. The chair I'm sitting in is too high for the low table, and the lights are not bright enough for comfort. My knees keep bumping into the edge of the table. Some nondescript jazz is playing a little bit too loudly. I wonder what I might be wearing if I'd been given a week's notice.

'So,' Grace begins, 'have you been talking to Rory since?'

I haven't spoken to Grace about Rory, even though she's been badgering me. I don't want her to read different things into the messages or, worse, confirm my suspicions.

I evade her questions until my drink arrives and provides a distraction. It's too bitter, but I don't want Grace to know I don't like it. I take two big gulps before attempting to answer.

Earlier, Rory messaged me asking me to confirm the location of Finn's flat, and I felt conspiratorial in telling him. It feels like Finn and Rory shouldn't inhabit the same space, or belong to the same world, and yet clearly they are both part of that elusive social current I always witness but am never a part of, where everyone knows everyone else in South Dublin.

'Well, you better get used to the idea, because they'll both be in the same space soon.' I don't find her funny. 'Okay, fine, but you're the neediest bitch out there. Honestly, I'm just desperate for a bit of drama before we all leave and never see each other again.'

Dan's leaving for London tomorrow, and this fact over-shadows the whole evening. It's hard not to feel like something is coming to an end.

'I'm just worried about him,' Grace says. 'I don't think he has much of a support system over there.'

It's a difficult choice a lot of people I know have had to make, choosing between their career and their friends. I haven't entirely ruled out the possibility of following Dan over. I can't see a future for myself in London, but I also can't see one here.

We scroll through the list of people invited tonight and

discuss the ones that we know. There are a lot of names we don't recognise, and Grace nudges my arm and says, 'Maybe you'll find a third boy to fall in love with.'

Grace has been single nearly the entire time I've known her, but it's not something I've ever slagged her about. I think about suggesting she might find love as well, but I stop myself. The last person Grace loved left her after she refused to carry his child. He was too Catholic to support her decision, but not Catholic enough to not fuck her.

'Oh and don't think I don't have a plan if things get too dull. I mean they will, it's Finn's house. I bet it's covered in indie movie posters and there's a copy of *Infinite Jest* on every table.'

As far as I know he only has one copy.

'Yeah, for putting in the back of his Instagrams.'

Admittedly, that's how I know.

'It all feels very gaslight-y to me. I'm not even sure to who? To reality? I'm not sure that boy tells the truth about his life to anyone.'

I think about saying that he does to me, but I don't. I know how she'll look at me. We all lie on the internet; I don't blame Finn for that. Especially when I know the things he's covering up.

'You mean people actually go on the internet and tell lies? What kind of sickos do that?' Grace laughs. 'Seriously though, yeah, the internet has fragmented our reality. Media, social media, who cares, it's all story and narrative.'

At some point along the way, the way we receive information became more important than the information itself; it became the information. I can't count the hours I've spent scrolling on Instagram just waiting for someone to post something, *anything*. I'm inhabited by a desperate fear that I'll miss something, to the point that I'm willing to waste my life waiting.

'I'll drink to that!'

I finish my cocktail, and Grace orders us another. I should take it slow. I'm worried about what will happen after a few drinks. I haven't spoken to Finn since he told me he's single. I maintain contact with him only via his social media presence: a network of tweets and Instagram stories. It's voyeuristic, and I know it. Even as Grace speaks to me now, I can't stop my fingers wandering, and I refresh Finn's profiles quietly, just to see.

She's talking about her Masters; she wants to go into teaching. I'm not sure she has the patience for it, but she won't be convinced otherwise.

'I just think it's a worthwhile thing to do. I couldn't imagine spending the rest of my life working in some office pushing paper around, funnelling money up to the top.'

I'm not sure what kind of job Grace is talking about, but I know I've applied for hundreds of them. Grace can afford to be idealistic in ways that I can't. For me, a Masters would mean another year spent living at home. My mind flits back to the digital marketing diploma, my stomach churning.

'You're not thinking of signing up to one of them, are you? It's pure credentialism. And do you really want to end up running the Twitter account of some company, pretending you're a relatable fast-food restaurant? It's dystopian.'

I can't answer her, because I don't know what I want.

We stop to pick up some wine in the Spar around the corner from Finn's flat. I get one bottle, and Grace picks up two – 'Just in case we aren't having enough fun,' she says, and winks at me. She uses her dad's credit card to pay, and I wonder what that feels like.

I triple check the address to make sure we're going to the right place. It hasn't mysteriously changed. Grace talks to me about her Masters application, but I'm watching us slowly approach the flat on Google Maps, so I barely hear her.

We buzz into the flat. It's up several flights of stairs, and I pretend I'm not winded. The door is ajar, and noise is spilling out. The building is fancy, and I worry we'll get a noise complaint. I recognise the song after a moment: it's a very popular song by a very cancelled artist. We'll definitely get a complaint.

The flat holds a certain amount of mystery for me, the way physical spaces do. I've only ever seen pictures of it on Instagram, or in the background of the selfies Finn sends me at three in the morning. He moved here at the start of this academic year; his parents thought he needed somewhere quiet to work, but this is the first time he's had us over. I know he has blue wallpaper and paisley sheets.

The flat doesn't look like people our age live in it. There are framed artworks and gold accents on the walls. The hall itself has more square-footage than entire apartments I've seen advertised on daft.ie.

I've taken to browsing apartments in the middle of the night, lowering my standards until I find a place that I might be able to afford in a few years. I follow Instagram accounts that post pictures of the ugliest houses in Ireland, all of which are wildly out of my price range.

I don't see anyone I know when we walk through the

door. For a second, I taste both fear and delight at being anonymous. I adjust the waistband of my skirt. Then I see Finn in the corner of the living room, standing with a group of people I also don't recognise. He waves. My mouth dries.

'Hey guys, thanks for coming,' he says as he hugs us both in turn, perhaps me for a just a second longer. Then, 'Guys, meet Grace and Sophie, I know them from college.'

I wonder why Finn introduced Grace before me and what that might signify. Grace excuses herself to get us some cups, and I stand there nodding at each of the guys in turn. They smile at me, but it's clear that I'm not included in the conversation. They're all wearing the same maroon trousers and blue shirts, and I'm only sure they're not clones because some of them have different coloured hair.

'Sophie's unreal, she's one of my best friends, you guys'll love her!' Finn says, and then he walks away, leaving me to wonder about the weight of that statement as well. Finn's words vanish as soon as he says them; I wish this whole exchange had been a message, so I could have more time to contemplate each individual word.

The group goes back to talking about whatever it is they're discussing, which seems to be the school they all attended. Apparently it's a topic with a lot of content. I turn to the guy nearest me and attempt to engage him in conversation.

'I'm Finn's flatmate.' He laughs as he says it. 'My name's Pearse. Welcome.'

I'm embarrassed and I don't know why, so I thank him for having me in his house. He looks younger in real life than he does on Finn's Instagram, which is why I didn't recognise him. He must have a well-paying job to afford to live here, or else very supportive parents. Maybe he lives far away and Finn's parents allowed him to live rent-free here during the last year of college to save him the commute.

'Oh, I'm from Ranelagh,' he says, confirming my rich-parents suspicions, and then he adds, 'in Dublin.'

I know where Ranelagh is without the specification.

He tells me that he knows Finn from school, and that they'd basically grown up together. All of these details I already knew, and if I didn't I could have picked them up from the other lads talking around us. 'So, what did you study?'

I feel defensive about my politics degree, with the way he looks at me, and the fact I haven't been able to use it for anything. I've finished speaking, but he seems to be waiting for something else.

'Oh, cool, that's great,' he says, in a way that doesn't seem like he finds it great at all. He laughs. 'So, you'll be a politician then?'

This isn't the first time I've been asked that, and it isn't why I chose politics. The more I learn about politics, the worse I feel about the people who actually pursue a career in it. I've only ever seriously considered it when I've felt particularly woeful about finding gainful employment.

He doesn't laugh this time but instead looks disgusted. 'You can't actually be a politics graduate and some kind of communist, can you?'

I don't want to answer, but think I'll be relinquishing some kind of power if I don't, so I go as hard line as possible. I know this argument is futile, but I can't stand people who can't imagine a future that's even slightly better than the present. Pearse doesn't strike me as the imaginative type, however, and I regret my words as soon as they come out of my mouth. His face looks as sour as I feel.

'Well, you haven't actually read Marx though, have you?' His voice rises at the end, but it doesn't have the feeling of a question.

I see Grace returning from the kitchen with glasses and try to silently communicate with her. She's talking to someone I don't know, and she doesn't see me. She's pulled into a side room before she can rescue me.

I try to steer the conversation into more favourable waters. Pearse tells me he wants to own his own house by the time he's twenty-six, be married by thirty, and have five kids. He says things like, 'You have to get on the property ladder early,' as though not being able to do so is a sign of irrationality and not structural inequality. I don't doubt he has his dream well planned out, and pity the woman he finds to marry him. He seems like the type of person who laughs at things that are genuinely anxiety-inducing, not at all like the image of him I'd pieced together from Finn's Instagram and how Finn talks about him.

Finn comes back then, and Pearse turns to talk to him. I use the distraction to make my escape. Pearse doesn't say anything as I go, almost as though the conversation hasn't happened. I find Grace sitting with Dan and Steph on the sofa and beg her for a drink.

'Finn's friends not to your liking?' she asks, and I unscrew my wine in response.

'Yeah, sorry, I'd have warned you if I'd seen you first,' says Dan. 'They're frightfully boring and in love with the system.'

'They're fun to wind up at least,' Steph says. She loves arguing with people, regardless of how pointless it is.

'Which ones? They all look the same,' says Grace. 'Where do they buy their clothes? They all look like economists, like they just sit around silently doing Myers-Briggs tests all day.'

'Myers-Briggs tests are just star signs for people who are afraid to commit,' says Steph.

'So all of us, then?' Dan asks.

'Hey, you've committed yourself to a steady job.'

Grace asks Dan how he feels about moving, and he shrugs and says it's better than staying at least. He's only packed as much as Ryanair's cabin baggage policy allows. I can't imagine stepping out of my life like it's a shell I've outgrown, leaving it all behind. He says he only wears the same four T-shirts anyway. Part of me hopes that the crack expands overnight and causes all planes to be grounded.

We sit and play a drinking game for a while, until we're drunk enough to face the rest of the party. I'm halfway through my bottle of wine and things seem funny now. I wave at Pearse across the room, but he doesn't see me. Grace gives him the finger, and we laugh because he does see that. We do Myers-Briggs tests and post our results on Twitter. Lucy replies to my tweet saying she's glad she's babysitting tonight because we're the most boring people in the entire world. It doesn't feel that way, though.

Finn comes and sits down with us, and Grace gets up to go have a smoke. She takes Steph with her. She can only handle so much Finn in one evening, even at his house. As she leaves I feel myself withdraw, as though she is taking something essential from me with her.

'I want to let you know I'm doing a lot better, I think,' Finn says to me, ignoring Dan. He's sitting close to me, and I can smell cigarette smoke. He puts his hand on my leg, casually. There is a moment of silence where I allow myself to be physically present before I try to unpack what he means.

'Cassie,' he says simply, and moves his hand away.

It takes a moment for the syllables to place themselves into context. It's so easy to forget the girls Finn twirls through our lives, especially when he's so close to me.

'It's freeing to be single, really, I've a lot more space to think about everything – who I am, who I want to be – and I want to start by saying that I'm sorry for the times I've been a crap friend, and I want you to know I'm going to be better.'

Dan asks him if he's drunk, and I can't stop myself from laughing.

'So what?' he says. 'Drunk Sophie loves drunk me!'

I stop laughing.

The front door opens, and I hear Rory saying hello to everyone. His voice shocks me. I'm so used to reading his messages in my own voice that I'd forgotten he had one of his own. I try to merge the two Rorys in my head: my Rory and this flesh-and-blood one.

'Just because I can't have love doesn't mean you can't!' Finn says and playfully punches my arm. The sensation stays with me longer than it should.

One of Finn's friends comes over, I can't tell which one, but he takes over Finn's attention. I leave the room, and Dan follows me out. The hall is full of people, and I feel claustrophobic.

I open a door at random, and it leads into the kitchen.

It's bigger than my kitchen at home. The marble counters are covered in single-purpose appliances. The window looks out onto the street, and there's a seat built into the windowsill. I decide to open the extra wine Grace brought. It doesn't taste any different to the wine I bought with my own money.

'So, what was that about?' Dan asks me.

I decide that I might as well tell him the truth. Dan's always been a good listener and not the type of person who's ever shared my secrets. I'll miss our chats at parties the most; I'm not sure who else will listen to me when I get like this.

'I know. I'm expecting a lot of drunk calls about whatever crisis you're having.'

He's right, it feels like I'm always having a crisis. I wonder how he sees me, and how I can talk to him about this without painting it as just another crisis. I play around with different words in my head, and I stumble over them when they come out. I feel like I'm trying to convince myself more than Dan.

'Yeah, he's a confusing one. I think it's because Finn never really thinks about anything he says or does, even though it seems like he does.' He says it without malice. 'He's the type of person who's a good laugh, but getting too close to him always results in getting hurt. You have to have low expectations with Finn.'

We laugh, and Dan agrees with me that that's true of all men. I raise my glass to my lips and Dan asks, 'Are you in love with him?'

I can't answer, which is an answer.

'It's okay if you are; I can see the appeal. I do think deep deep *deep* down he's a caring person, but please don't

90

get yourself hurt by being a cliché and trying to change him.'

I can't even change myself; I'd never dare attempt to change someone as stupidly complex as Finn. Dan's words are no different to what I tell myself every day.

'I'm going to choose to not comment further because I believe you're an adult.'

Rory comes into the kitchen, and I wave at him. He's wearing a crisp white shirt with the sleeves rolled up. I introduce him to Dan, and they trade banter back and forth. He's so comfortable chatting to people that he makes it look easy. Rory starts to sit down on a chair opposite us, and then someone pulls him from the room. He doesn't take a drink with him, and I amuse myself by imagining he'd come in here looking for me. I'm tempted to follow him. It feels as though there are numerous secret parties happening behind the doors of the flat.

Dan looks at me with raised eyebrows, expectantly.

'Are you a heartbreaker now?'

I don't know where to begin, and the story comes out confused and non-linear. Dan laughs at me when I try to describe our ambiguous date.

'I will honestly miss how much of a mess you are, please never change. How could you not know one way or the other if it was a date?'

I'm drunk enough that I don't feel any shame. I don't feel attractive or interesting enough to have someone like Rory interested in me, and I'm still testing what it's like to have someone interested at all. It's safer to keep him at arm's length.

'But Sophie, you've had other boyfriends.'

Those, for reasons I can't articulate, don't matter.

'I know for a fact there have been loads of guys who've been interested in you, and you've shot them all down.'

I don't remember any of the boys he's talking about. It's never felt like anyone's been interested in me, but perhaps I've been closed off to it. I feel the need to be liked, and the utter fear that I could be loved, all thanks to childhood trauma. Dan looks at me sadly, and I play it off as a joke. I grip the edge of the seat until my knuckles turn white.

'You're beautiful and deserve the world, I hope you know that. And Rory seems to really like you.'

I smile at that. Dan would be the perfect man for me, if he didn't find me so repulsive.

'Hey, it's not you, it's all women. Stop thinking you're special.'

I start to cry a little bit then, not because I'm drunk but because I'm going to miss him. Dan's gentle with my feelings in ways that my other friends are not. He tells me I'm a big dork and that makes me cry harder. Eventually, he admits that he's going to miss me too.

I go to the bathroom to fix my eyeliner. When I open the door, I see a girl sitting in the bathtub. Her knees are pressed to her chest and there's a ladder in her tights.

'Whatever, come in,' she says, not looking at me, and I tentatively comply. 'Have you been crying?' she asks.

I can see her reflected in the mirror as I clean up my face.

'I don't know why I'm here, I don't even know, I shouldn't be here, or have come, or whatever. I don't know what I thought would happen.'

She's cradling a bottle of wine between her legs and slurring her words. There's a flush up her collarbone to

92

her neck, and she's crying silently. Her hair is a curtain over her face.

I close the door gently and crouch down next to her. I'm glad I'm the one who's found her, and I'm afraid of what might have happened if someone else had. I don't know the guys here well enough to feel safe. I fish a bobbin out of my bag and use it to tie up her hair. When I do it, I recognise her.

'I just thought, you know, I just thought maybe he invited me because he wanted to get back together. I mean, why else?'

I take the wine bottle out of her grip and place it gently on the bathroom floor.

'It's not like he left things really clear? He just said he needed time. It's been time. And I'm here. Why am I here? The sex wasn't even that good.'

I can't understand why Finn would invite Cassie here. Earlier he'd told me he was feeling better without her. Her words weigh heavy on me, and I no longer believe that Finn's told me the truth about how he ended things.

I make calming noises and help her out of the bath. I walk her down the stairs, and she tells me where she lives so I can call her a taxi. Her hand is slick with vomit, but I hold it anyway. I've been on the receiving end of enough of these routines to push down my revulsion.

'He's not worth it, is he? So why do I still want him?' I can't answer her, and her question lingers after the taxi drives away; it follows me back up the stairs to the flat. One of these days I'll have an answer.

When I go back to Dan, I can't find the words to explain how I'm feeling.

We sit there on the ledge, watching the party go by. I

crack the window open so I can smoke, and Dublin sways before me. It would be so easy to fall down into it. I wonder if my body would punch a hole in a car roof, if the force of the impact would be enough to curl the metal around me.

Dan tells me that while he's excited to move to London, he's also petrified. I'm sure he'll find his feet immediately, so much so that when he comes back to visit he'll try to colonise us. He says he'll never prefer Walkers to Tayto, or learn how to pronounce Worcestershire.

Periodically, people come into the kitchen to grab things from the fridge. Grace comes and joins us for a while, and she tells us that the rest of the party is boring as she drinks from her bottle of wine. Sometimes, I hear Finn's laugh from the other room. I can't stop myself from seeing Cassie's face. I don't want to rejoin the party; it's safe here on the ledge with Dan.

Eventually, I begin to feel tired and decide it is okay to call a taxi and head home. I'm not sure anyone except Dan notices me leave, but that's okay.

7

It's difficult to ignore Finn. He sends me messages across several platforms, which means I can't exist on the internet in peace. I can't control the way I react to his messages, or the excitement they ignite within me. It's been two days since his party, and he'll begin to wonder why I'm not replying.

I try to focus on other things. I play around with paragraphs on my CV until the words cease to have any independent meaning. I'm tired of redrafting my cover letter over and over for jobs I don't want and won't get. I have a master copy that's over ten thousand words long. It's like gambling: if I can just put the words in the right order, maybe I'll win an interview.

I open up the Google Analytics Academy page and start a beginners' course. I watch the videos at double speed, and the information slides off me like syrup.

Intellectually, I've always been aware that Google tracks my information. It's part of the reason I don't mind the fact that virtual assistants are surveillance devices; my phone is one as well. It's another thing to see it spelled out plainly, in bar charts and Venn diagrams. The video hosts are overly chipper, as though their families are being held at gunpoint just off-screen. I feel a strong urge to rescue Rick and Vanessa, and tell them that polo shirts went out of style a decade ago. It's hard to see how this will increase my employability.

I think Finn would enjoy making fun of these people, but I decide it's safer to message Rory instead. When I open my phone, I see I already have a message from him.

sorry i didn't see you much at Pearse's
kept getting dragged into drinking games!

> *don't worry about it*
> *i wanted to say goodbye to Dan anyway*

totally
are you going to miss him?

> *yes but it's not just that*
> *it feels like with everyone leaving*
> *i'm being . . .*
> *left*

some of us are still here with you

> *yep you're stuck with me*

I'm secretly glad we didn't have much of a chance to talk at Finn's. Our messages feel concrete. I can study them at length, go back and check on them and they'll still be there. I have time to decide what to reply. Messaging him is like having a virtual pet, like that part of the internet is open to me again. It's easy to escape into it.

I want to tell him that I've noticed how he's picked up some of my messaging habits, but I don't want to put words to this feeling. I want to maintain a distance so I can see how far this will go. I want to know what he's going to do next.

> *i like talking to you*

thanks, i like talking to you too

> *since we're practising radical honesty*
> *i think i like messaging you more than talking to you in*
> *person*
> *or anyone in person, not just you*

thanks?
i know what you mean though
it's easy to be honest online

I'm not sure what to say to him, what would be a safe thing to say, so I leave him on read and return to my course.

Rick and Vanessa can't hold my attention by themselves, so I make a game out of it. I begin to unspool entire lives for them, from embryos in the Google breeding facility to death and incineration once they're past their prime. Vanessa doesn't look like she has much time left. In my mind, this is a dystopian future, but I know there are tech bros out there who would pay top dollar to be incinerated by Google and have their ashes fused into some kind of new super metal, now available in rose gold. When the video is over, I add the credential to my CV.

Dan sends a message into the group chat that's just three exclamation marks. I don't understand what it's about for a moment, wonder if perhaps there's been some problem with his new flat, and then I go cold. I check my email and see that our results have come in. I close my eyes, savouring the last few seconds I have before I know the outcome of the last four years. When I open the link, I see a 2.1. I'm both relieved and disappointed. I'd spent a considerable amount of the last year calculating percentages and probabilities, and yet.

Everyone else's results flow across the top of my screen. They all seem happy enough. Grace has got a first, and I do my best to be happy for her. Steph has got a 2.2, but she plays it off. Grace messages me privately to ask if I think Steph's okay, and neither of us can decide. I know she has a conditional Masters offer, but I don't know what it's conditional on.

I call Mum to let her know how I've done. My hands shake slightly, but it's better to get it over with.

'Honey, that's great, really great, are you happy? Hannah's here and her results have come in too! Let me put her on.'

I hold my breath and listen as Hannah tells me she's received a first.

'But don't worry, I'm sure they marked you much harder. So it's like we did as well as each other! I know you had a much tougher time of it than I did.'

Hannah hands the phone back to Mum, who says, 'We'll have to celebrate tonight. We're just out shopping now so I'll pick up a cake or something. See you later!'

I feel untethered, as though my feelings are a kite I've let go.

I open the most recent message from Finn and reply, simply:

i met cassie

Yeah, I thought it might smooth things over if I invited her.

she didn't seem to think so?

Silence. Then:

finn, how did you end things?

I don't know, I just did?

i need you to tell me again

Why?

she was crying in the bathroom finn
you never should have invited her

shit

yeah

I'm not sure why I've messaged him, perhaps on the off-chance he could anchor me, even though he's the main source of imbalance in my life. I'd believed him when he told me he wanted to do right by Cassie. Then:

99

i just called her
you're right
i don't think i understood until now
god i'm so sorry
she hates me
but that's okay
i deserve it

                                        you do

i know
i'm so fucking sorry

                        it can't just be sorry this time
                        you have to actually change

i know
i'm going to really try soph

He's never said anything like this before. I remember what
Dan said, that deep down Finn really is a good person.
He just needs someone to remind him of that and to
point him in the right direction. He's chosen me to be
that person. I close my eyes, thinking. Then I go back
and read some of the other messages he's sent me and
reply to them too. It feels like drawing a line under the
whole situation. I can go back to pretending I don't know
Cassie exists.

   Mum and Hannah come home with armfuls of shopping. Mum's bought Hannah a new jacket for her results.
She tells me she wasn't sure what I wanted, so she gives
me a pair of socks and says she'll take me out for

something bigger another day. I don't want anything to commemorate today because it'd only preserve this feeling of weightlessness.

I read on Steph's private Twitter that she *is* disappointed with her results. I think about screenshotting it and sending it to Grace, but that breaks the unspoken rule of private Twitter, especially since she's posted nothing on her main account. Instead, I message Grace and ask if she's seen it. I'm not sure what kind of social politics are at play where Steph feels okay posting that to the forty-odd people who follow her, and not to us in the group chat. I'm not sure if I should engage with the tweet or message her privately. In the end, I like the tweet and continue scrolling.

I sit through another family dinner, seated at the table. We've reverted back to the seats we've sat in since childhood, despite the new table, chairs and decade. Some habits never die.

Hannah's talking about the crack, saying that maybe she's interested in doing a PhD on it. I remind her she has a degree in social science. When we were kids, we'd both wanted to be scientists; science felt like magic back then. At some point this morphed into Hannah wanting to be a scientist, and forcing me to be the experiment.

'Yeah, I think there's an interesting anthropological approach. Who cares about the atoms and science behind it when the effects on the ground, on culture, are much more immediate and palpable? I'm sure you could find something in your field too, if you thought about it enough.'

I want to say that perhaps we'd all care about atoms when ours are fried by space radiation, but I can't see the discussion ending in my favour. Instead, I push my food around on my plate before finishing it. My parents think the PhD is a great idea. Dad says there's money in that kind of cutting-edge stuff.

The promised cake is a baked cheesecake. After two pieces I begin to feel sick, and I only manage one more. I notice Hannah's unfinished piece, despite her saying it's her favourite. She always eats food like this, like there's an option not to. When I'm clearing up the plates Hannah says, in an offhand way, 'You can have the rest of mine if you like, I'm not going to finish it.' My parents don't react. It's like they haven't heard anything at all.

After dinner I lie in bed, my mind cataloguing every bite of food I had, and I feel nothing. I scroll through my phone to give my brain something to fixate on that isn't my body.

The crack, by all accounts, is getting bigger. There's still no clear evidence that it has any physical effects, but it definitely has cultural ones, I have to give that to Hannah. Instead of covering them, however, everyone seems to be overlooking them. There's been a shift in the news coverage and online discourse. People are no longer posting exhaustive threads on how to prepare for the apocalypse; the apocalypse came and went. I'm getting targeted ads for blackout blinds, guaranteed to filter out any purple light. We've collectively reached our abnormal threshold and have reverted back to how things were before the crack. This, we're told, is *normal*.

There's a certain kind of gap in the coverage that journalists slowly approach and then swerve around: there are parts of the world not bathed in the purple glow of the crack, which should be being upheld as proof that nothing's changed for billions of people. Instead, there's nothing about them. This could be evidence of a grand conspiracy, or simply because we're not used to sending reporters to those places unless there's been some kind of disaster, especially if we can't catalogue the damage in dead white people. We aren't used to looking at these places and thinking *normal*, so they don't exist.

The economy's still shocked, there's still a big purple line in the sky, but it's barely making headlines. We've taken all of these signifiers and forced them through the meat grinder of online culture until they've lost all meaning. The crack's not trending on Twitter any more. We are adapting; I'm just not sure to what.

8

The birthday party arrives on the day it is supposed to. It's crept toward me, on all fours, like a horror-movie monster. And I'm still the same, unchanged, preserved in resin. I haven't lost weight for the event, although I'd idly thought I would.

I wear the dress I'd picked out, which now seems more magenta than I remember. I tug at the collar around my neck. I paint over my skin with make-up, covering the redness in a shade named after a building material. I hold the blush in my hand for a second longer than I need to, wondering why I'm now painting the redness back in. At least it's in the right place this time. My hands shake a little bit too much to get a clean eyeliner line.

Grace does my hair while we listen to a playlist from our teenage disco days. The music doesn't help me to feel any more grounded. Those days were heady and intense and swept me up in a current of teenage hormones. Back then, words had different meanings, and communication was jarring and incomprehensible. 'Meet' meant kiss, and we'd learnt to understand each other on context alone. Now, I wish for that kind of high again, or any kind of feeling at all. Grace tells me I look great, and I smile even if I can't believe her.

Hannah's wearing gold, and she shines. I look sunburnt standing beside her. My parents want some photos before the guests arrive, and Grace acts as photographer. Dad puts his arm around me and pulls me in, and I feel hollow. I imagine I'm pale in the camera flash, my eyes empty. Mum pours me a glass of Prosecco and makes Hannah and I 'cheers' for the camera. The world is too tight. My dress is too tight. Grace refills my glass, and I drink it.

Finn's one of the first people to arrive. Grace lets him in. I'm busy filling up cups with wine and small bowls with too many crisps. He hugs me and kisses me on the cheek, pressing a present into my hands. It's small, possibly jewellery, and there is a card taped to the top. The velvet casing brushes against my fingers.

'Don't open it yet,' he says with a smile. 'But read the card later, I want to be there when you read it.'

I thank him and put it away in a cupboard like I'm shutting away a secret. He helps himself to wine and goes to talk to Dad. I can still feel the impression of his lips against my cheek. I pull at the tights I'm wearing, which are sitting uncomfortably against my thighs. I hope I won't have to continue to adjust them all night. There's still time to excuse myself and change them.

I place the bowls of crisps around the house and try to keep myself looking busy. I take a few crisps and pour myself another glass of Prosecco. I don't want it, but I drink it. I hope I hold the glass in an elegant way, and not in a sad one.

Hannah hugs Finn when she sees him. They're not friends; she's just like that. I move to block her view of the cupboard with my body. Her gold dress clings to her waist, and her hair is effortlessly curled. Looking at her is like looking at my reflection in a funhouse mirror: distorted, untouchable. Only it's my body that's pulled out at all angles, like taffy. Hannah is holding a gin glass the size of a bowl in a hand tipped with red claws. My own nails are bitten down to the fingers.

I avoid my phone. I don't want to look at any messages from people who can no longer come, or who've never been planning on coming. I also don't want to see people's stories of getting ready. It would make the party more real, more present somehow, even though I'm currently living it.

The house gradually fills up with guests, and I begin to understand the current of the party. I don't actually have to talk to people for that long before excusing myself to some other hostly duty. I'm able to flit between groups like a mayfly, killing off each conversation when it becomes too much. No one notices. I take frequent trips to the snack table when Hannah isn't looking, and chew my haul slowly.

Hannah's friends are larger than life, taller than life, and brighter than life. It's like looking at the people Instagram base their filters on. They drink strong drinks from large glasses and their lipstick never smudges. Some of them have flown over from Scotland for the event, and they brag about wearing their heels through security. I hear Dad say something about marks on the hardwood floor, which Hannah ignores. She has a way of always doing that.

One of them approaches me as I'm pouring a glass of wine. I hear her heels before I see her. She taps me on the shoulder hard enough to leave a bruise and says, 'Oh, you're the other one,' as though it's a conversation starter. I smile at her blandly until she walks away, the unspoken conversation evaporating around us.

Rory arrives and I wave at him across the room, but don't approach him. He's wearing a shirt that's in desperate need of ironing. I see Grace grab him by the arm and quickly disappear into the next room. I try not to think about what she might be saying to him. The thoughts buzz around my head like mosquitos.

I go to the bathroom and sit on the toilet, my head in my hands. *Breathe*. I take a sip of wine. When I was sixteen I discovered I could drink just enough to make my birthday bearable, but not enough to make it worse. It's a delicate balance, and I'm toeing a dangerous line tonight. I'm out of practice. *Breathe*. I wash my hands under cold water and splash some on my neck. I try on different expressions in the mirror until I feel like they will hold, and rejoin the party.

'There she is! Sophie, come here!' Mum calls to me across the room, and I feel myself being jostled across the space by the crowd. The distance between the bathroom and the kitchen counter seems insurmountable. I see Hannah standing there, talking to Rory. He's smiling, and she has her body angled towards him. Dad tops up my glass, but all I can hear is the ocean in my ears.

Mum makes her customary speech. She's perfected it over the years, splitting it evenly between her daughters. I can't help but feel that Hannah's achievements shine so much brighter than mine, especially in comparison. When the subject moves towards the present, I zone out. Hannah has a job all lined up. I have nothing. The cake's brought out.

Hannah and I lean down to blow the candles out. Some of my friends pop party poppers, some whoop. Before I can make a move, Hannah's already blown all the candles out and snapped back to a standing position. I'm left bending down, off balance.

I pick up a knife and begin cutting pieces of cake and handing them out to the crowd on little paper plates. Mum's chosen a red velvet cake, which I don't really like. It's Hannah's favourite though, and this is one way to keep the peace. I'm tired. The thought of the cake makes me sick.

Grace comes over to me with Rory in hand and we chat for a while. I feel myself mechanically responding; I can't quite connect with the situation. Rory makes a few jokes, but I can't muster a smile. Grace looks vaguely concerned, but I just shrug and pour us some more wine. I can't hear either of them. I clutch the glass so tightly in my hand that it shatters, and I drop it.

Everyone applauds and I bow, then go to get a dustpan. It's only when I raise my hand to open the utility room door that I notice I've managed to gash my palm. I look at the blood for a second, then go upstairs to bandage it. I imagine what it would be like if I'd cut myself deeply, if I bled out and died right here. It would take the limelight off Hannah for a moment, at least. In my mind, I see her talking to Rory, or Finn; taking my place but doing it better. I've bled on my dress, so I wash it with cold water and hope no one notices.

When I go back downstairs, someone else has cleaned up my mess. Through the open back door I see people smoking, and I watch the cigarettes burn like fireflies. Hannah's out there, cigarette in hand, laughing at something someone's said. The bottom of my dress is wet against my leg. I don't recognise who she's talking to for a minute, and then I realise they're my friends from school. Hannah never noticed them when we were all in school together, but she can't stop herself from trying to take more things away from me. They all look different, impossible, and I can't believe that I was once one of them; they seem too perfect.

I imagine I'm taking photographs of the party, preserving each moment. My phone remains firmly on the table where I left it. I don't want future me to see these scenes. Grace sitting on the kitchen counter, eating a piece of cake. Finn lighting a cigarette outside. The look of my hand, bandaged in white gauze. It is all imperfect, and impossible to capture. All I have is now.

My parents excuse themselves and go to bed, and I open another bottle of wine. I'm not sure how much time passes, only that it does. Grace takes my glass out of my hand, but I roll my eyes at her and take it back. It's my birthday, and this is how I get through my birthday. She takes me outside for some air.

When she goes inside to get me a glass of water, I start chatting to Steph. I can't remember her arriving, and I'm not sure what words are leaving my mouth. She gives me a cigarette and hugs me. I watch it burn down in my hand.

'We should talk more, just us two,' she says to me, before going back inside.

The sky above me is a portal to another world, and I want so badly to cross it. Little fingers of purple light are spreading out from the centre of the crack, like chips in old paint. I can't shake the feeling that it's about to open, that something's about to happen that will shatter reality. I wonder if there's another version of myself across the crack, looking back at me, or if I'll always be stuck with the one here.

Hannah comes over to me then, reminding me that there is already a second version of me. My chest tightens. For a moment, I think she's going to hug me, or ask me a question. Instead, she says, 'It's starting to rain and you look a little bit pathetic out here by yourself, just so you know.'

I'm lost in the party. I put my drink down somewhere and can't find it, so I pour myself another. My tights are soaked from the rain so I peel them off and throw them into the laundry room. I want to peel off my skin with them.

One of Hannah's friends comes up to me, laughing. She says, 'Hannah's always said you're the funny one, the smart one too.' I look at her, trying to understand her words and her worldview. She points to my pile of tights.

'I fucking hate those things,' she says. 'Have you seen Hannah? Last I saw she was trying to get with Tom, or was it James?'

I stare at her, uncomprehending, unable to imagine a world in which she might be asking me these questions. She laughs again, I'm not sure at what, and then vanishes into the party. I find a fork somewhere and eat the last piece of cake, then dump the cardboard platter into the bin.

I hear someone suggest heading into town. I've lost the thread of the evening, but I'm intensely relieved when Hannah leaves. My reflection turns back to normal.

Some people stay; I think I ask them to. We sit around and drink; I think I ask for that too. It's all becoming something of a blur. Grace asks me if I'm all right. Eventually she falls asleep in a chair in the next room. I'm sitting on the couch, a blanket over my lap. Someone says something funny, and I laugh, and then they leave.

Then it's just Finn and me. He pours me a glass of water and shoves it into my hand.

'Drink. You'll thank me tomorrow.' I nod. 'Do you want to talk about it? I can tell something's wrong.'

He sits down next to me and puts his arm around me. I smell his cologne. Cradled close to his chest, I feel safe. I want to share my feelings with him, to give them to him, so he can make them safe as well. I wonder if he thinks I'm pathetic too.

He says, 'That depends, do you mean now in this moment, or generally?'

He looks down at me. I think I'm saying his name. The words tumble out of my mouth on a crest of tears and I'm not sure if he understands any of it. How can I tell him that I hear Hannah's snide voice every time I look at my body? Once, she pushed me down the stairs and then told my parents that I'd tripped. I'll never be good enough, and every time anyone looks at Hannah they see how much better I could be.

Finn tightens his grip around me and still more words come. He looks pained.

'Sophie, I didn't . . .'

I can't hear him. It doesn't matter what he says. I hold his hand tightly, as though it's my only tether to the Earth. I'm like a broken hard drive, corrupted and useless, and I'm not sure what I mean. His voice washes over me, a

111

hum behind my emotion. I imagine that this is how he hears me speak when he needs advice.

'But, you're beautiful. You're perfect. You're not broken.'

Suddenly, he's kissing me. I'm surprised and pull back, but he pushes on. I lean into it. My hands are in his hair. I've never wanted anything in the way I want this. His hand is inside the top of my dress, gentle but determined. My whole body's on fire. Moments pass and I've used up all of my allotted heartbeats. He swings me across his body so I'm straddling him, and lies down on the couch. My dress is hiked up. I'm not sure what kind of underwear I'm wearing, and I'm distantly aware this is something I'll be concerned about tomorrow. In this moment, however, I don't care. All there is, is now.

Finn's shirt rides up, exposing his chest, and I roll off him so we are side by side. Our breaths mingle together in the space between us, and I thrust his hand between my legs. He plays with the elastic of my underwear before reaching his hand inside. My entire mind is screaming and I can't breathe. I laugh and kiss his nose.

Then, he pulls away.

'We shouldn't do this now, not like this.' He looks over, and through the double doors we can see Grace snoring in the other room. His hand has gone cold between my legs, and when he pulls away it feels like something physical is being ripped away from me.

I nod, but my mind's racing, I can only think about how right it feels, about how much I've wanted this. I love him. And he must love me too.

'I should go home.' I nod again and try to keep my voice level when he says goodbye to me. He kisses me on the forehead, and as he leaves he says, 'I'm sorry,' and

I don't know what that means. I think about waking Grace and asking her, but decide to take myself to bed instead.

The evening already has a hazy unreal quality to it. It feels like an extended dream. I stack some dirty plates in the sink and neatly arrange the empty bottles in lines on the kitchen table. My hand is throbbing. I'm not ready for today to turn into tomorrow. I look through the kitchen window up into the crack and wonder, again, if anything is looking back at me. It would be worse if there's nothing but emptiness on the other side.

I remember Finn's present and retrieve it. The box contains a small necklace engraved with his favourite line of poetry, and the card is addressed to 'The best person I know'. The box is heavy in my hands. My brain can't unpick the multitudinous meanings behind this gift; it's slow from too much alcohol. I try to google the words, but my phone screen is blurry.

I change my clammy underwear and get sick in the toilet before making it to bed.

9

Morning comes, although I'm awake long before the sun rises, my mind floating somewhere above my body. My thoughts cascade from one thing to the next, afraid to focus on anything. Every time they flit over the party I'm struck by a wave of roiling nausea, and I can't believe I'd been so bold with Finn. I'm so full of shame I can't exist inside my body, so I scroll through my phone. Every other part of the world is either already awake, or hasn't yet gone to sleep, and I'm able to read endless content. Online, you're never alone.

All the reports are the same: the crack is widening. Wide enough for that billionaire's car to fly through it. In the video, it comes out the other side, and I'm disappointed. It isn't so much a crack, as a trick of the light. Insubstantial, for now. Lying here, in bed, it's hard to believe it's even real. It's hard to believe anything else could exist. The car is being treated like a spectacle, like a firework, something to gaze at in wonder. But I can't find anyone telling me why the crack is widening, and what it means. All I know is that it's now wider than the average motorway; someone suggests sending two cars next time. No one is talking about how much oil they'll need to burn.

At some point, Grace opens the door to my room without saying anything and gets into bed beside me. She pokes me until I consent to be the little spoon. She rests her head on my shoulder, and her voice is loud in my ear.

'Your parents are awake. They woke me up and asked me to check on you. I think they want to make us breakfast. I can tell them you're still asleep if you like. God knows my stomach can't handle any food right now.'

I start to cry, and I'm not entirely sure why. Grace makes comforting shushing noises and holds me until I quieten. I wonder how many times we've been in a position like this, with me vulnerable and crying. I know I'd never have got through any of them without her. Through the crying, I get across to her what happened with Finn, and it's my turn to shush her.

'That prick, that dick, that total wagon of cocks, what the fuck!' she rages, sitting up in bed so quickly that the blanket is pulled off me, and I'm cold. 'You were clearly shook, you were clearly drunk, after you'd just told him all of that, and I just . . . What's wrong with him . . .?' She fades away into rage.

Her words curdle inside me. I can't shake the memory of our religion teacher telling us that all premarital sex is a sin that will be counted when we die. I remember someone looking up words like 'sex' and 'vagina' in the dictionary as though they were curses, and feeling disgusted. The last Laundry only closed a year before I was born. The whole evening now feels wrong, like I've done something wrong. Grace thinks Finn could never actually want me so I must have done something wrong.

When Grace gets like this, I can't think. She thinks she's revealing deep secrets to me, but she doesn't live inside my mind and hasn't lived my experiences. Nothing she says makes sense to me; it isn't connected to anything I feel, but I start to feel it all the same.

I can't focus on any one particular feeling because Grace is filling me up with all of hers. I wonder if this fragile thing between me and Finn is about to snap, or get stronger. I'm not ready for either possibility, and I don't want to talk to him about it. I open and close my messaging apps, my thumbs looking for something to do, and I'm terrified when I see Finn is online. I can't think; Grace won't stop talking.

'Yeah, well, I wouldn't worry too much about that. Just see how many words you can get out of him about it. He might fancy himself a poet, but that boy has no idea how to take responsibility for his actions. You're better off with Rory if you ask me.'

I'd forgotten about Rory. I can't remember speaking to him last night. I've been such a fool though, I've probably fucked up whatever we had. I'm not sure why he'd ever want to speak to me again – I don't even want to speak to me. I close the door on those thoughts, cutting them off mid-train. Grace will tell me if I've done anything particularly embarrassing, so I wait for her to bring it up.

I brush some hair away from my face and notice my bandaged hand. The memory of breaking the glass comes flooding back to me. Grace and I laugh about how badly I've wrapped it up.

'Yes, that was certainly a sight to behold. I was the one who cleared up the glass, by the way. If I'd sliced open my hand for you I would be much less sympathetic this morning.' She shows me her pristine hands, as though to prove she'll never make that kind of sacrifice for me.

'I think you managed to give Rory quite the fright. But he had to leave to collect his little brother from some teen disco before you got too drunk.'

Rory hadn't been drinking, which means he didn't have any rose-tinted glasses to see my behaviour through. I press my palms into my eyes. There are things that are only excusable when everyone is as drunk as you are. I wasn't there to witness my actions, and the idea that he was is terrifying.

We sit for a while scrolling through the internet, showing each other memes and videos as we come across them. I drink some water from the bottle beside my bed and try not to gag. The more I think about Finn, the more anxious I become. I can still feel his touch on my body. I can't live like this: under a duvet, fearing the unknown. I'm sweating in the trapped heat.

Lucy and Steph send some photos from last night into the group chat. I look terrible in all the ones Steph sends, and I can't help but feel that she's done it on purpose.

We call Dan to ask him how he's getting on. He asks about my birthday, and I exhale the air in my lungs. Grace takes the phone and tells him I'm having my regular problems.

'Boys?' he asks over speaker.

'Boys,' she confirms.

I let them talk it over and try on each of their feelings for size, wondering if any will fit. Dan's on my side, and it's comforting to hear him vocalise what I'm thinking when Grace attacks Finn. I'm amazed at how easy it is for them to talk about what I'm feeling.

'Maybe this is the push they need,' he says.

'Please, if anyone's pushing here, it's Finn.'

'Ah, I think he's clueless.'

'They're both clueless!'

It's like they've forgotten I'm here.

'At least you know how we talk about you behind your back,' is Grace's reply. It's true: she could hardly be more blunt in private.

Dan's vague about his new life. I can't shake the feeling that if anything good had happened, he'd tell us, to distract us from asking if he's lonely or stressed. We're not distracted, and Grace looks at me with worry in her eyes. I shrug at her. Grace says she'd love to visit and asks for photos of his apartment. We make plans to get him some kind of plant he'll inevitably kill.

'Did you hear Sophie's going to run the Supermac's Twitter account?' Grace says. I try to contradict her, but Dan's already picked up on the joke.

'Oh, are you going to make them relatable? Remember, Gen Z humour is acting like life has no meaning. Maybe pretend they're serving human flesh?'

'You're not serious?' Grace asks.

'The internet is a weird place. At least our generation isn't defined by hating our wives and aeroplane food?'

I want to defend myself, to make some argument about credentialism and cover letters, but I know engaging with the joke will just spur them on. Instead, I listen quietly and wait for them to move on.

In the end, they help me to draft a message to Finn and I shower, mulling it all over in the hot water. I allow myself a few good sobs, the water drowning out the noise. The night washes off me and circles the drain before disappearing for ever.

When I go downstairs, the table is set with breakfast. Grace comes down, talking to Hannah on the stairs. They sit down at the table with me. I don't want to ask them what they've been talking about. I don't feel the need to; they have nothing in common except for me. The conversation continues on around me, with little input needed. I strategically take a sip of orange juice or deflect when asked a question, and no one follows up. It's a skill that I've spent the last few years honing, but I've always been good at it.

Mum asks if we enjoyed the party, and I let Hannah answer.

'It was unreal. A lot of my friends had a 6 a.m. flight out this morning so we stayed out until they got the bus to the airport.'

I excuse myself to go to the bathroom, and lie on the cool tiles. My thoughts are spiralling themselves into a headache. I can't quite grasp them; they filter through my mind like water. Grace messages me to ask if I'm okay, and I send her a thumbs up.

There are splashes of water on the tiles around the sink, and I blow on them so I can watch them race away from me. I hold my phone above my head and scroll through my notifications. They're all from apps; my fitness app is reminding me to log my breakfast calories, and my language app is begging me to get back to learning French. I feel utterly alone.

I read over the message I have saved in my notes, screw up my eyes and send it to Finn. Immediately, I feel as though I'll be sick. I get up and lean over the toilet bowl, breathing slowly. I know I can make myself sick if I really want to; I've done it before. I can contract my throat and cause myself to cough and splutter, and then eventually bring up my breakfast. It would, at least, provide an answer for my fitness app.

My reflection is darkened in the toilet water. The force of my quiet heaving brings tears to my eyes. I wipe the saliva from my chin and sit with my back against the wall. The alcohol in my stomach is twisting inside me like slugs, but it won't come up. I spit into the water and flush it all away.

I don't look at my phone when I leave the bathroom. It's heavy in the tiny pocket of my pyjamas, and burns hot. Back in the kitchen I nod along with the conversation, but my head is wondering if Finn's seen the message yet, if what happened last night was an explosion of feelings or just some horrible mistake. I repeat over and over in my head that it was a mistake, but I can't make myself believe it.

My parents turn on the TV, and Hannah sits down on the couch with them. I perch on the armrest of the chair Grace is sitting in. Hannah leans her head on Mum's shoulder, and together they look like an accidental Renaissance painting.

I pull out my phone so I don't have to look at them any more and see I have a reply from Finn. It sits casually on my homescreen. All the heat leaves my body, and I feel like I'll actually be sick this time.

Hey yeah, we should talk haha.
I'm sorry I left it like that.

I sit staring at his message, the words burning themselves into my mind. The *haha* torments me. I try to rewind each frame of the night in my head, but the memory is diluted by too much remembering already. I read into the messages so much it takes me a moment to read their truest, clearest meaning.

I prepare myself for the grim reality. I walk myself through how the conversation will go, but I can't make myself open the message. Grace asks if I'm okay, and I wordlessly pass my phone without looking at her. Instead, I concentrate on the news story about the same American billionaire, who's now proposed sending a satellite to observe the crack. I can picture the debate that will play out: a scientist will say it's impossible, some white guy will say it'll look cool, and every news station will cover it.

Grace hands me back my phone and shrugs. She sends me a message to avoid having to speak out loud.

Well, well, well.
If it isn't the consequences of your own actions.

I try not to let any panic show on my face and shrug back at her.

Hannah says, 'I can't believe this is news. Why aren't they covering the election results?'

'Why would they cover them?' Grace asks. 'It's not like anything's changed.'

'Yeah, thank God, I was worried about all those protests. Your lot want some kind of fascist state.'

'Wanting to be able to afford to live is not fascism. You can't just call everything you disagree with fascism.'

'Yeah, right. I just think we need stability to have a functioning society.'

Grace throws her hands up in the air. 'Lack of change isn't stability. Lack of change has caused now.'

'So, you're one of the people who think that capitalism caused the crack? I expected more from you.'

'I hate that argument and I hate even more than you're dismissing it entirely. Capitalism in a vacuum hasn't caused anything, but our continuous exploitation of the natural world in order to maximise production has. A crack doesn't appear in the sky for no reason.'

I zone out of the conversation entirely, trapped in my spiral. Perhaps things *do* happen for no reason, and the universe is a chaotic and unpredictable place. Or maybe we're sold the narrative of unpredictability because it disguises how much power certain people really have. I can't focus on the issues in an abstracted sense, not when I keep picturing Finn's face and reliving his hands on my body.

A few times Grace tries to throw the conversation my way, but I pivot; I know it's not worth arguing with Hannah. My parents make shushing noises, but they're less invested in the conversation than I am.

Eventually Grace leaves, giving me an excuse to retreat to my room, alone. I don't bother to turn the lights on. I flick through Instagram and Twitter, but I find I can't ignore the little red notification any longer. When I open it, I see Dan's messaged me as well.

Remember what I said before I left.
You deserve to be happy.
And don't listen to Grace too much.
She's persuasive, but your feelings matter too.

I start to cry again; having hovered so close to tears all day, it's easy. I don't have the emotional energy to respond, but it gives me enough courage to open the message from Finn. After I reply, I lie on my bed, feeling like I'm made of jelly. I want to tell Dan how grateful I am for him, but I don't know how to. I leave him on read.

Finn and I agree to meet in person tomorrow for coffee. Every possible outcome makes me feel cold and sweaty. I lie on my bed, over the covers, and let it all hit me. I want the crack to end the world before tomorrow so I don't have to live through it.

I track the passage of time by the noises coming from the kitchen. I listen to Mum clean away the dishes and watch the news and start to make dinner. When she knocks on my door I pretend I'm asleep.

I watch Rory's Instagram story. He's at the park with his brother. I think about replying to it, but my thumb won't do it. I ignored him for most of last night, too shy and dry-mouthed to talk to him. He saw me slice open my hand with a wine glass. None of this screams romance. It doesn't even scream functional woman. I send out a vague tweet I hope he'll reply to, and continue scrolling.

I don't want to confront the fact that half of the reason I'm so worried about Rory is that if I can't talk to him, it makes having to talk to Finn harder. There's so much more to gamble and lose.

Thinking about Finn is dangerous. I scroll through his Instagram page, searching his pictures for some kind of meaning. Recently, he's been showing up as the top name on the list of who's viewed my story, but I don't know if that's because of his activity or mine. For a brief moment, I let myself think about what the future could hold in the best possible circumstances. I let a fantasy play out in which Finn confesses his love for me. I picture us getting married, and how we'll arrange the tables at the reception. I imagine kissing him again and remember the feeling of him against me. I masturbate to the idea, and when I come I don't feel so alone.

The feeling fades, however, and I feel unbelievably dirty. Eventually that feeling fades too, and then there's nothing left to feel at all. I wash my hands in the sink and try not to look at myself in the mirror.

I watch some YouTube videos and read through the internet to avoid confronting what I've done, or how I feel about it.

I refresh my email, and there's a response to one of the job applications I sent out. I don't remember applying for it, but the fact that it's not a rejection sends a shock of hope through my system. They've invited me for an interview. I silently thank Rick and Vanessa for getting me this far.

Hannah comes into my room without knocking. She hands me a cup of tea and makes a comment about feeling rough herself. I don't want to take the tea, but I don't feel as though I've any other choice.

She sits on the bed and tells me about her night. She got into a club for free, and some English men bought shots for her and her friend. I nod along, holding the tea in my hands and allowing it to burn me.

'I met someone, actually, well, maybe I did, I never know this early on, you know how things are.' I don't. 'I'm actually kind of sad I went out, because he stayed at the party. One of your friends?'

I close my eyes and focus on the tea's heat.

'I was talking to him anyway, and I'm thinking you could put in a good word for me? With Finn?'

I spill tea over my hand but keep hold of the mug, indifferent. It forms a pool on my duvet and begins to cool. I can feel the wet patch on my belly. I can't look at Hannah. She always gets what she wants, in the end, and I know I can't stop her. I've never been able to stop her. I feel ten years old again. I nod and say whatever she wants to hear until she leaves me alone.

I get up and run my burned hand under the tap until I can't feel it any more, and then get back into bed. The tea sits, undrunk, like a sentry on my bedside table, next to the velvet box Finn gave me. I didn't think I had any tears or bile left in me, but I was wrong. I'm wrong about so many things.

10

I sit on the sofa and flick through Netflix. I can't stop thinking about Finn. Every time I look at my phone I open one of his social media profiles. It's a learned habit that I've never regretted so much. I let trailers autoplay, the noise helping to drown out my thoughts. I oscillate between thinking about the day to come, picturing Finn and our meeting, and darker thoughts, of Finn and Hannah, and the things they would do to each other, with me as a spectator. Reading about the crack doesn't distract me; there's no room for more anxiety in my body, so all the new theories slide right off my brain.

Beneath my chat with Finn is my chat with Rory. I click into it for something to do, unsure if I should message him. He hasn't been in touch since the party, and it could either be a coincidence or a sign of some greater failure on my part. I start typing something banal, but erase it halfway through. I put my phone down on the sofa, and for a second it looks like Rory might be typing to me, but when I pick my phone up again no message comes through. I leave it face down this time.

I can't force myself to eat the toast I make. I'm bloated with guilt and fear, but the emptiness within me just keeps growing. I'm torn in two, fractured and fragile. The crack in the sky calls to me in an appealing way, as though it recognises our connection as world-ruiners. It on a global scale, me on a personal one.

I run through a checklist in my head of the possible outcomes of today, things Finn might say, and resign myself, in turn, to each one. My mood fluctuates between all possible spectrums. He loves me, he loves me not, I love him, I love him not. And worst of all: I love him, he loves Hannah.

I watch the news, but it doesn't provide me with any kind of certainty. Nothing's changed, and the fact that the crack hasn't widened any more has led some people to believe it's actually shrinking. I'm impressed by how much content they're milking from this brief moment of stability. On CNN, the hosts stand in front of a green-screen map showing the length of the crack across the Earth, zooming in and out at seemingly random intervals. Someone makes a comment about how this crisis isn't as bad as ones that have come before, and I turn off the TV.

When the time comes for me to leave to meet Finn, I call Grace.

'Look, I don't even want to talk about it,' she says, in a way that I know means she really does want to talk about it. 'What do you want to happen?'

I feel sick saying the words out loud. I can't admit to her what Hannah told me, or how it's managed to complicate things even further.

'Well, what the fuck is wrong with you, Sophie? For God's sake. Do you like him or not?'

It's an interesting question.

'Well, I for one do not like him, which you know. I don't like the way he treats you. As far as I'm concerned, and I'm sorry if you don't agree, the best possible thing you could do would be to go and give him a piece of your mind.'

I make an uncertain noise, and she snorts at me.

'Yeah, I know you won't actually. You're a coward, you know? Well, I know. That's why you need me.'

I allow Grace to talk to me like this because I know she's right, and in truth I'm holding on to her every word for dear life. Listening to her estranges me from myself, from the whole experience that is my life.

Eventually, after more back and forth than we're used to, she says, 'Look, it doesn't matter what happens here. He doesn't deserve you or half the time you've already given him, and besides if you end up dating him I'll disown you, so you better hope he blows you off. This is either the weirdest love story of all time, or we're about to have a lot of time saved. Both of us.'

It comforts me somewhat, and in some ways it sounds like the truth. I imagine myself as Grace, with her confidence coursing through me, filling my empty shell. She's right. Finn's asked a lot of me over the years, and I've willingly given him everything. Now, I'm calling in that debt. He owes me this one afternoon of honesty.

I message Dan and tell him I'm about to meet Finn. Typing it out makes it feels more concrete; I can't back out now. He sends me back a selfie in front of the plant Grace and I sent him. It feels good to be connected to him, even though he's far away.

Uncharacteristically, Finn's already sitting in the coffee shop when I arrive. I check my phone and confirm that

I'm five minutes early. It puts me on edge, not having to wait for him. He waves when he sees me, and I wave back. I queue to order a coffee before sitting down, my heart hammering in my ears. I think about making a run for it, but I don't know where I'd go. I sit down opposite him. My coffee comes too quickly and my lungs are full of stones.

He smiles at me brightly and asks how the clean-up from the party was. This question confuses me and catches me off guard. I stumble over my words as I spit them out, mixing up the consonants in the longer ones. I take a sip of my coffee and hope he doesn't notice.

We dance around idle chitchat for a few minutes, each topic more mundane than the last. He wants to know if I've convinced my parents to adopt a dog yet, if the new pasta place on Dawson Street is any good, how I feel about my upcoming interview. There are no silences or pauses, because as soon as one threatens to appear he asks me a question that startles me with its attentiveness. I can't concentrate on any of it. Nothing, absolutely nothing, is worse than just ignoring what happened. He's had his hand inside my underwear, and now he can't even look me in the eye. Somehow, this conversation is more awkward and embarrassing.

I don't want to bring up Hannah, but a part of me knows I must, that this is how the conversation starts. I also just want to see his reaction.

'Oh, yeah, we got into an argument about Scottish independence.' I can't read his face, but he doesn't elaborate. I think that people have flirted over stranger topics. He orders us a brownie to share, but I can't make myself eat.

Finn tells me he's been getting into cryptocurrencies, 'In case all the banks collapse soon because of the crack,' and I let him talk without comment, slowly growing more and more numb. We would normally argue about this sort of thing, but if Finn notices something is wrong, he doesn't show it.

When my coffee starts to go cold and the afternoon begins to have that air of endings, I look him in the eyes. I've burned through all of my embarrassment, and I know now is the time we have to talk about what happened. If not now, then never. I can tell I've caught him off balance. I don't usually confront him like this; I've never confronted him like this.

He doesn't know what to say, and it spurs me on. Seeing a little crack in his perfect composure is so alien that it changes something within me too. I'm having an out of body experience. I'm no longer constrained by the limitations of my physical form and the shame that exists within it.

I bring up the kiss.

'Oh, yeah.' He mumbles his words, blushing slightly. For the first time in his presence I feel as though I'm on solid ground. This is the moment, and I won't wait any longer. 'I'm not sure, really, you were upset and it, I don't know, seemed like the thing to do.'

I hear the words, but I can't detect an ounce of meaning behind them. He's well practised at using as many words as possible to say nothing. But I am well practised at seeing through him.

I thumb the rim of my coffee cup and set my resolve. He needs to know I don't regret it, any of it. I go off script and decide to no longer do damage control. I've thrown out the dance steps and he falters. All he says in response is, 'Oh.'

When Finn kissed me, he crossed a line and opened up the possibility that I might have some kind of power in our relationship. I look at him so he can't avoid me again. I'm so deep in shame that I've crawled out the other side, and mainly I'm just tired.

A silence stretches out between us, and I know if I'm the one who breaks it, I'll be lost. I take a bite of brownie and wait. Eventually, he breathes, 'No, I don't think I do either,' which is quickly followed up with, 'but I don't want to upset you or anything.'

Nothing would make me more upset than leaving it like this. He says, 'I just don't think I'm in the place for a relationship,' and I agree with him. He'll never be in the place for a relationship, at least not the kind of relationship that he wants. No one understands that better than I do.

He looks at me with concern, which annoys me. I'm not a child; I'm tired of him trying to protect me. The words don't sound like my own, but they're definitely coming from my mouth. I think I surprise both of us. I feel as though I'm playing tennis, and maybe I'm winning. I picture myself breaking the racket over Hannah's head.

I'm not conscious of the exact moment when our dynamic shifts, and yet it's all I'm aware of. It's like waiting for sunrise and suddenly day breaking. For the first time, it feels like I've some control over him, like I've stumped him.

'Is this really okay? Like, are you sure?'

He's looking at me with uncertain admiration, and I'm beginning to see through the looking glass. I can have

what I've always wanted, just by taking it. I feel unbelievably reckless and alive. I feel like Grace.

'Well, okay then.' I'm conscious of the blueness of his
eyes and the patches on the elbows of his coat. They look
different to me now, somehow.

There doesn't seem to be anything else to say. If this
carries on any longer, we'll talk ourselves out of it. I stand
up, and kiss his cheek. I see him touch the spot I kiss as
I leave the café. He says he'll message me later.

I call Grace right away, barely able to get the words
out.

'I'm not sure whether to be impressed or annoyed.' She
pauses for just a moment too long, and that confidence,
that surety that had filled me up, is gone. And Grace
doesn't even realise it.

'Wait, tell me what happened again,' she says, and I tell
her, testing how the words feel to say out loud.

'So, no strings attached? Hang on, am I right in thinking
that you just pulled a Finn on Finn himself? I think I
actually am impressed. And maybe this will let you get
him out of your system, you Finning him.'

I agree with her, and I can't help smiling as I walk to
the bus stop. It feels like everything's slowly clicking into
place. I like the idea that 'Finning' could be an action
and not an intrinsic part of his personality; it gives me a
new frame to view his actions through.

I get a message and tell Grace to hang on while I check
it. It's from Rory.

hey
sorry for leaving your party early
how is your hand?

no worries at all!
much better thanks
i feel like a total idiot haha

'Two men! Two! Honestly, Soph, you've gone from zero to a hundred here. You're a ladies' man, or well, a man's lady? That doesn't sound right. I think I'll just call you a harlot.'

If anyone's a harlot, it's her. She scoffs at me and says, 'Stop slut-shaming me, I thought you were more woke than that.'

I read out Rory's next message to her.

i'm glad to hear it
you looked beautiful in your dress

My stomach fills with butterflies.

'Yeah, he told me that he liked your dress too,' Grace says. I wonder why he'd said it to her on the night and not to me, and Grace doesn't know either. She says that he asked her a lot of questions about me, about what I liked to do and what I hoped for the future. 'You know, weird stuff, kinda cute, but also might be planning your whole future together kind of stuff.'

This changes the meaning of the messages, and I'm not sure how to read them. It's like Rory in my phone and Rory in real life are two different people, who I have two different understandings of. It suits me to keep them separate, because it prevents me from feeling guilty about Finn.

Grace says, 'Well, you're not dating Finn, it's nothing.' She makes her voice sing-songy, which I know is her impression of me.

I don't want to have this conversation with her any more.

'You're a real player, you know, and you should be careful with whose hearts you're breaking!'

I hang up on Grace as she cackles in my ear. It seems no matter the joke, it's always at my expense.

Dan messages me as I wait for the bus, and I know Grace must have told him about what happened. She's probably told all of them, but for the first time I don't mind that they're talking about me.

See that wasn't so bad, was it?
Well done for putting yourself out there.

The message makes me smile. The evening has a new texture to it. I practise what I'm going to say to Hannah when she asks me about Finn. I repeat the words over and over in my head: *he's not in a place for a relationship.*

I make a mental note to never let them meet again, just in case.

11

The interview is horrible. The room's unbearably hot, and I'm sitting across from three adults who look like they'd rather be anywhere else. I'm wearing some shoes I bought in Penneys, and they pinch my toes. The windows across from me might be one-way, but it's equally possible that anyone passing by could look in and see me.

They ask me questions about my achievements, which are zero, and challenges I've overcome, which are also zero. I use the buzzwords I've been told to use, but I can tell they see through me. My mind starts to wander, and I begin to speculate about how much these people are paid, and whether it's enough to own their own homes. I wonder what special talent they have that landed them their jobs, and if they lied on their CVs as much as I'm lying now. My body detaches itself from the idea of this interview and this job. I don't want to work as a consultant anyway, whatever that is.

There's an older man writing severely on a piece of white paper, who asks me, 'And how do you think your generation is uniquely affected by recent events?' He has a tie pin. His wife might have got it for him for Christmas, if he has a wife. Or maybe he bought it on sale as a way to treat himself, because he thought it would help him feel less lonely. I see the word 'passive' written in block letters upside down.

The question settles in my mind. I look at him, and he looks as bored as ever. The question is vague, and I need him to be more specific, so I can sound engaged and intelligent, and not passive.

'The sky, I mean, the crack, whatever they are calling it. Do you think it has caused anything specific that will hurt your generation?'

It takes all of my composure not to laugh at the ridiculousness of the question. No one has any clue about how the crack is affecting my generation. No one has any clue about how anything is affecting my generation, or the future generations that are being sacrificed at the altar of continuous growth. Who knows if there will be any more generations, or if climate change will wipe us all out before then? I don't say any of this.

What he wants to hear is that, as of recent research, no one can pin down any tangible effects of the crack, and it's unlikely any will manifest. However, my generation should prepare to adapt to the next global event. I make sure to use the opportunity to emphasise my transferrable skills and critical thinking. Even as I'm saying the words out loud, they don't feel like they have any meaning. That's the prevailing narrative, but I'm not sure how anyone can truly believe no tangible effects will manifest. What's more likely is that those in power now are kicking the can down the road until they're retired with good pensions and an apocalypse bunker in New Zealand.

The man nods. I'm asked if I have any questions, which I don't. They let me go, and I know that I'll never see any of them again. I can remember nothing of their faces, only the man's tie pin. I pass a line of people sitting in chairs, looking nervous, all of whom I'm sure the company would prefer.

I stop in the bathroom on the way out to change out of my uncomfortable clothes and shoes, and to get some distance from who I'd been when I was in that room. It's like peeling off my skin, and when it's all off, suddenly I can breathe. I splash water on my face and decide to mark these memories as forgettable. I send them straight to the trash folder of my mind.

Mum calls me, no doubt to ask me how the interview went, and I decline it. I spend some time walking around town, window shopping and trying to get lost in my thoughts. The statues on O'Connell Street look down at me, and I wonder how any of them got to where they are now. At least, for now, I'm not covered in bird shit.

On the walk home I pass more houses for sale. The crack's been bad for the market, not that the market was good before. I spend the walk staring at my feet, avoiding playing any of my games. If I can't get a job, I'll never own a house. That kind of stability will be denied to me, and I'll die alone and penniless.

I think about calling Finn, but our new dynamic still feels mysterious and raw. I don't want to open that door just yet, and it seems he doesn't either. My phone pings, and messages from my school friends start to stack up on my lock screen. I scroll through them for a while, trying to remember who these girls are and picture who they might have become.

Hannah's sitting on the sofa watching TV when I walk in the door. I do my best to will my body to be small and unassuming as I walk behind her to the kitchen to get some water. The sound of her voice is an intrusion into my personal space, and it nearly makes me drop my glass. Without looking at me, she says, 'How did the interview go? Seriously, it's not a big deal if it didn't go well. I've been lucky, God, I've been dead nervous in every interview I've ever done, I don't even know how I got my job!'

She always talks like this, like everything that happens to her is just luck, and she's the same as everyone else. I think she thinks it comes across as modesty, rather than an attempt to play off hard work as nothing. She likes to appear effortless. It makes my failure much more glaring by comparison.

It annoys me, so I pretend the interview went well. No doubt she'll have found something else to fixate on by the time I hear back that I definitely haven't been successful. I send Grace a message without looking at my phone, to vent a little bit of my frustration. I don't care if there are typos.

'Well, that's fab' – everything's always fab to Hannah – 'I really hope you get it, it'd be so fun if we were both working gals! Maybe we could save up and rent a place together? It would be great to get out of this house!'

It's like living in a different reality. Hannah's incapable of seeing any situation from outside her own perspective, and she's neatly erased the fact that we've never been friends from her memory. It's easier to just play along and give vague non-commitments.

'I'm thinking of going for a run later, what do you think?'

I don't think much at all.

'No, I mean, do you want to come with me? I started up running this year and it's so great, really, you feel amazing after, and I'm sure you'd be happier if you did. Get that summer bod ready?' She's so casual, so light; she's always been an expert at cutting me down to my lowest point without even trying. I'm not sure she's even aware of it at this point; it's just second nature to her.

I walk away without answering and make an affirmative noise as I reach the stairs.

'Eight o'clock!' she yells after me.

The whole interaction is so draining that I have to lie down for a while after. I know that if I described what happened to anyone they'd think I'm crazy. It was a perfectly normal, human conversation, and yet I can't help but examine the fabric of the interaction to find the specific threads that have cut me. I break down each word, each look Hannah tossed at me, and I hate her for it. I'd sell my soul to be totally unaffected.

The door opens downstairs and my parents come home. I hear the rustling of bags and them greeting Hannah. In my mind, the scene is domestic bliss. I imagine them unpacking the groceries, laughing, with sunlight streaming through the windows. Whenever I imagine my family, I'm always an observer.

I don't want to think any more, so I open Twitter and start scrolling through it. I like the endless scroll; it makes me feel as though the world is still moving.

I find an article that discusses how the crack is influencing popular culture and how memes have gotten even more surreal, and I send it to Rory. It's the kind of thing that he likes. I refresh my feed for a while until he replies.

that reminds me of this

He sends me a comic that summarises my article into a few sentences, and it takes me a few seconds to understand it. I have an awareness that only someone clever could grasp all the levels of it.

does everything remind you of something else?

isn't that how the internet works?

We chat for a while back and forth, and it's nice. He asks me questions about my life, about my hopes and dreams, and it makes me feel interesting.

what did you do today

job interview

how'd it go

yeah
not well

ouch

We talk about the interview, and he jokes about the man's tie pin. I feel myself unwinding, as though by telling him my anxieties, I'm letting them go a little bit. He makes me laugh, and suddenly the whole thing seems like it was funny. I'm glad that I have him for moments like this.

He asks me what my stand-out moment from college
was:

> *do you want a bad one or a good one?*

both

I think for a moment about all the bittersweet moments,
and settle on one. Grace dragged me to a debate one
night in my second year. I didn't want to go; the building
always seemed stuffy and full of people wearing black tie
and glitter as though they cared about neither. It was an
all-women's debate about beauty standards and body
image. It wasn't so much a debate as a forum for articulate women to express how shit it is to be a woman.

> *that's when I realised feminist wasn't a dirty word*
> *that there are all of these shared experiences*
> *and it kinda sucks to be a woman*

yeah I'm sorry it's so rough
i wish i could help you

> *fix society?*

that's why i vote
my mum taught me to be a feminist

> *my mum doesn't know the word*
> *i think she expects me to not work once i have kids*

hey to be fair

she grew up in a time when we weren't socialised to be
feminists
the laundries and all that
i just got lucky

                    you've never been a toxic man?

i've tried not to be!!

                              sure, sure

He tells me that he went to a rugby school and what it was like. I think of the lads I met at Finn's house and of Pearse. I can't imagine it was pleasant.

so the lads in my year kept this list

                              oh god

yeah
and it was all the girls they'd slept with

                    i'm sick and tired of Irish boys
                              of boys in general
                         and their fucking lists

no it's worse

                                   ??

if two guys had sex with the same girl they had to fight
i'm not even joking

142

it was like this weird hazing thing
the whole year would gather around and chant

jesus christ

i think about it a lot
i wish i'd intervened
but i still don't know what i could have done

i'm not sure you could have done anything

I take a screenshot of this conversation and share it into the group chat with Grace, Lucy, Steph and Dan. I want to know if this is a common thing, and if it is I want them to be equally as disgusted with it as I am.

I watch each of them see the message, but it takes a few minutes for anyone to reply. I wonder if they have a group chat without me, and if they're using it to talk about me right now.

Grace: Boys are fucking gross, no offence to Rory.
Dan: Hey!
Grace: You don't count.
Steph: Yeah that sounds like those lads all right.
Steph: I knew a lot of them in first year.
Steph: Thankfully I didn't sleep with any.

Dan starts telling us horror stories from his time in an all-boys school, and Lucy sends a voice message cataloguing all the psychological torture Steph inflicted upon people in school, although I think she's joking. The conversation hums along, and I'm relieved I shared the screenshot with

143

them. We haven't used the group chat lately, everyone else has been so busy, so it's nice to watch their interactions again.

Rory and I trade anecdotes about our lives growing up, and I unfold. It's enough to get me through dinner with my family, and I can even look Hannah in the eye when she reminds me about her run, and I tell her no.

I feel so comfortable talking to Rory, so safe, that I silence the voice in my head that normally tells me I'm uninteresting or incorrect. We're trading bits of each other back and forth and using them to make ourselves whole. I don't feel ashamed admitting it.

The sun is up before we say goodnight, and I fall asleep happy.

12

Hannah invites me for another run. 'Don't you want to keep the boys interested?' She says it casually, from the sofa, but her words hit me like bullets. Mum thinks it sounds like a great idea, and she acts like it's a harmless statement. Dad isn't paying attention to any of us.

There are a million reasons why I don't want to go; I cast my mind for the one that will cause the least debate. I don't own anything that's suitable to run in. Hannah offers to lend me some of her clothes, but I'm sure they won't fit. I can't stomach the idea of wearing her stuff while doing an activity with her, as though I'm trying to be her. I don't need her image impressed upon me any more than it already is.

'Fine, just one more thing you've failed at because you refuse to try,' she says.

It's the push I need. I message Finn when I'm already on his road. This is something I can win. I'm nervous; our conversation from the other day still feels so tentative. He hasn't liked any of my tweets since.

When he opens the door to me, I kiss him immediately. I'm determined. I need him to take over my body, to inhabit it. I want to give it to him. He bites my lip and leads me to his bedroom. I take my clothes off before I can chicken out or complicate things. I want to win.

Sex with Finn isn't what I imagined it to be. In my head, when I've pictured it, he's always generous and attentive; there must be a reason he's got with so many women. He wants me to go on top, but he keeps slipping out of me. Eventually, he rolls me over and pushes my legs over his shoulders, pinning them until they hurt. It's over too soon, but at the same time I'm satisfied that it's happened.

We lie under the covers together, his arm around me. My skirt is in a crumpled pile on the floor, and I notice his laundry basket is overflowing. He asks me if it was good for me and, after a moment, I nod. Then he asks me if I finished, and I see no point in lying. He's flustered and disappointed, and I'm not sure why. I can't stop myself from laughing, and I kiss him so he doesn't feel insecure. Lying here, with him, is better than sex.

He refuses to get up and throw me my skirt, which I can't do for myself because I'm naked, a fact I hadn't been aware of until now.

'Yes, but I've already seen you naked.'

I know he's right, and it's silly, but I can't help feeling insecure. It's one thing to be naked as part of an action, and quite another thing to just be naked. He'd be able to look at me, really look at me, and potentially get no pleasure from it.

'Well, you've nothing to be insecure about.'

He gets up and puts his pants back on and goes to the kitchen to make tea. Through the open door he asks me how my interview went, and I groan in response.

He smiles sympathetically and tells me I'll get the next

one; it's all experience. Sometimes it sounds like Finn's reading from a list of expressions he found online titled 'Normal Human Things to Say in Conversation'. I don't even want the next one; the idea of redrafting my cover letter another time is exhausting. I plan to never get a real job and just become a trophy wife.

'I'll have to get a high-earning career then, huh?'

I reject his joke offer of marriage before he can reject me.

I get out of bed and gather my clothes from the floor. Finn's destined for a high-earning career. He studied law, and his parents have already hooked him up with an internship. No doubt he'll find himself working fourteen-hour days for a company that doesn't give a shit about him soon, doing coke just to get through it. I'm not willing to sell my whole self to capitalism, even if it'll give me food and a roof over my head. The crack or climate change will take me out in the end anyway, it doesn't seem worth it.

Finn laughs. 'You're very cynical, you know that?'

I emerge into the kitchen, fully clothed, and pick up a mug of tea from the counter.

As I sip, I take in the apartment again. I wonder if Finn will ever be as rich as his parents, if they've done enough to set him up for the lifestyle they have.

He's taken aback. Finn doesn't like to talk about money, even though I know he has it. I've seen photos of his childhood home. I think he's ashamed of it. 'I hope so,' is what he says.

I want to confess to him how much I've been thinking about houses lately, but it feels strange doing so while sitting in his apartment. He probably wouldn't understand, or he'd agree in principle but be unable to relate to my visceral need. When he first moved in, he asked me to move in with him, and I've never been sure whether or not it was a joke. Either way, I had too much sense and not enough money to know it would've been a bad idea.

Finn looks at his phone, and I'm not sure he's paying attention.

'So listen,' Finn says, in a voice that makes me think he's practised this over in his head. 'I have a date on Friday, with someone else, and I know you were clear on all this' – he gestures – 'but I want to check again that this is okay. I can always cancel, you know . . .' He trails off, and I know he doesn't want to cancel. I can't stop myself from laughing that he waited until after the sex to bring up something that could jeopardise his chances of having sex.

I don't want to lie to him. The Finn-shaped hole in my heart I've been carrying around is now full. My need for him is satiated, for the time being. I have an answer for him anyway, and it makes me smile, because I know he won't be expecting it. I'll be seeing Rory that day. It's like a game, each of us trying to show how little we're invested in whatever this is.

I've been single for ever, and I'm not sure that when Finn pictured the idea of us hooking up and him dating, he'd considered that I would be dating too. I like surprising him; it makes me feel powerful.

He just says, 'Well, okay then.'

Pearse comes in then, and he doesn't look pleased to see me. I expected him to be a little bit more subtle, but I suppose he's never had to be subtle about anything in his life.

'Hi, Sophie, didn't know you were over.' He says it in a way that makes me feel unwelcome. I decide to ignore his tone. Finn asks him what he's doing for the summer. I'm grateful because the more Pearse talks about himself, the less he focuses on me.

'Oh, finding myself mostly. No, actually, I'm trying to read through all the modernists and maybe work my way through postmodernism and beyond. I think it'll really give me some perspective. Especially with everything that's going on.'

I don't know the difference between modernism and postmodernism, but I'm not sure Pearse does either. I think he's talking about the crack.

'Oh, you're calling it the crack too, are you? Interesting. I know some people are, but it always seemed inelegant to me, you know? A bit literal, if you ask me.'

Finn doesn't seem to notice our discussion, or any of the subtext. It always amazes me the things men are blind to, as if they've been conditioned to ignore social cues. I wonder if Rory would notice and intervene on my behalf, if he were here.

'Have you heard about these protestors on the streets of Michigan with guns?' Pearse asks me. I have, but I don't know where this is going, so I tentatively nod. 'They're out chanting "my body, my choice" because they want guns to protect themselves from anything that might come from the sky. Your kind of people, huh?'

I repress rolling my eyes so hard they nearly detach themselves from my sockets. I don't want to have an argument with him about the co-option of left-wing rhetoric by right-wing groups to win some kind of manu-factured culture war, but I can't see a way of avoiding it either. I can't properly explain how words can be the same but the meanings they carry can be different. I settle on repeating his words back to him in a funny voice, which feels good enough.

He talks at me for a while, and I make the minimum number of human noises required until he goes back into his room. I'm left with the distinct impression that Pearse has used up the daily quota of words he allows himself to speak to a woman.

I ask Finn what he thinks about what Pearse said, and he says, 'Oh yeah, he just gets like that sometimes.' That could mean anything, so he elaborates by saying that Pearse can sometimes come across as aggressive when he's interested in something. It's the type of thing men say as though it's a neutral statement and not total apathy to toxic masculinity.

It doesn't feel like Pearse is interested when he's talking to me. It's more like he's trying to not only convince me that I'm wrong, but also that I'm a complete idiot. The fact that Finn didn't notice makes me worry he's the type of person who wouldn't call out his friends if they said something he disagreed with.

'Of course I am,' he says, 'what do you take me for?' He kisses me and it's enough to stop me thinking about misogyny. My mind flits unwillingly to Hannah, and I picture her here, in my place. It makes me kiss Finn back more fiercely, as though to prove to her, as she exists in my head, that I'm still winning.

After, Finn asks me to look over a cover letter he's drafted for a job application. He doesn't need my help, but I fix the spelling errors anyway, and he makes more tea. It's peaceful, and I can see our lives developing

150

together. Finn opens the window to smoke, and the height seems less dizzying this time.

When I make a move to go home, Finn leans in to kiss me goodbye, but I duck out before he can. Teasing him makes me happy. It feels like our relationship does when it's at its best; like we're equals, toying with each other. If I just let him kiss me goodbye I'll become boring to him, and I know Finn hates nothing more than things that bore him.

I'm light on my feet as I walk to the bus, and I smile at everyone on it. It's only when I get off that I notice my skirt's on backwards. I swing it back around quickly, hoping no one's noticed. My skin feels greasy.

Grace messages me, and I want to ignore it. I'm not in the mood to deal with her right now. She'll tell me I'm reckless and silly and in over my head. I want to enjoy this, just for a moment, but I know I've ignored too many of her messages to get away with it. She only has so much patience.

Avoiding me?

don't be so dramatic

I haven't heard from you in ages!
When's the last time we hung out?

i've been busy!

Too many boys?
All right tell me all about it.

Grace loves gossip. She loves it so much that I know she'll forgive me for ignoring her if I give it to her. It's the currency we trade in.

> *just left finn's*
> *i had another run in with pearse*

Maybe you can seduce him as well? Make him like you?

> *ha ha*
> *get a new joke*

Get a new best friend.

Her joke falls short. Our relationship is changing: I can no longer be the spinster, and it seems all too real that I could have a string of lovers. She doesn't know me at all.

13

I feel out of place at the restaurant, waiting for Rory. He's just started working at one of those trading companies, and he's invited me out to celebrate. I've read up on crypto-currencies, in case they come up, and try to remember everything Finn told me about them. People are walking by, and I wonder what they think about me. I take out my phone just for something to do, and message Grace.

this place is fancy

How fancy?

like fancy fancy

Lucky you. Remember, just because he's buying you dinner doesn't mean he's entitled to anything else – that's feminism!

stop i know

As she messages me I refresh my social media, waiting for Finn to post something. I'd told him I wasn't jealous, and while it wasn't a lie, I know I'd feel better if I knew who he was with. I want to know if she's prettier than me, and then wonder if I'm even pretty at all. He's left my last message on read, as though he's skirting around the fact that we're both out with other people tonight. If we're both pretending it's not happening, then it's basically not happening.

Rory arrives and kisses my cheek, and I put my phone away. I rub at the spot he kissed, and hope I haven't smudged my make-up.

The waiter leads us to our table and takes our coats. Rory pulls my chair out for me, and I feel awkward in the split second between squatting and sitting.

I'm thinking of ordering the chicken, but Rory says, 'I'm paying!' and insists on steak and wine and dessert. I lose track of the calories I'm counting in my head. The wine is red and dry; I don't have a taste for it, but I enjoy it all the same.

I can't find the flow of the evening. I don't think it's actually possible to be good at flirting, but I know I'm bad at it. Rory keeps steering the conversation onto topics that I dead-end.

'So, what are your plans for after college?' he asks me, and I answer with a vague shrug which is intended as a joke but I'm sure comes across as awkward. There's a beat of silence, and then I search for a different conversation topic before settling on his new job.

I eat my food slowly, using each bite as an excuse to not say anything. I want nothing more than to take out my phone and message him my thoughts. If I could only see our words manifested, the pauses mapped out with punctuation and emojis, I could understand them.

'So, I did an internship at this company last year, and I'm finding this position a real step up. Last year, though, there were some serious problems with sexism so I'm hoping it'll be better. Once, when one of the interns asked what her next task was going to be, one of the male interns said, "To make me a sandwich."'

I can imagine the specific type of man. It's nice to sit here and drink wine with a boy who understands the nuances of just how shitty men can be. It puts me at ease, knowing that I don't have to fear those things when I'm around him.

'Well, the pay is just about worth it,' he says, and I laugh. 'Someone has to fund these extravagant dinners.'

I remember having a similar conversation with Finn, and how I felt like I had to reject his offer. For some reason it's easier to imagine my life with Rory. I picture myself as a happy kept housewife, staying at home while he goes out to bring home the bacon. I'd have an unshakable sense of security, in both my husband and his income. I picture the kind of house I could live in. This future seems so much more tangible than what I could imagine with Finn.

I take the final bite of my chocolate cake, savouring it. My wine glass is empty, and Rory refills it. I watch a drop of red slide down the side and soak into the white tablecloth. The bottle is empty, and he orders another. I protest, but he says, 'I'm paying,' again, without missing a beat.

I like eating in this restaurant with Rory, and I like being with Finn in the apartment his parents paid for. I almost convince myself that there's a way to be a kept woman that's actually feminist. I'll never be able to support myself anyway. My thought train thunders down the tracks. I wonder if I'm pathetic, and if Rory thinks I'm pathetic.

'What?' he says. 'Why would you ask me that? Of course not.'

Suddenly, I feel very guilty about thinking about Finn, about being with Finn at all. I start to panic, afraid that I could lose one or both of them. Part of me wants to tell Rory about Finn, to put all my cards on the table. I'm not even sure that he wants to be exclusive, or what he thinks about monogamy as a concept. He's so measured and reasonable about other issues, this might not even be a big deal.

'Oh, I don't know,' he says. 'I haven't thought about it that much. I guess intellectually I understand that it doesn't have to be a norm, but at the same time I'm not sure I could ever be non-monogamous. Could you?'

I decide it would be a bad idea to tell him about Finn. That conversation can be a problem for a future version of Sophie. I drink my wine, and in my head I play around with the letters of the word 'cheating' until they bear no meaning at all.

'Honestly, I think it's one of those things that is woke and interesting when women talk about it, and really creepy when men bring it up. Like, all the lads I know don't argue about the politics and power imbalances inherent to relationships, they just cheat on their girl-friends.'

He likes it when I laugh every time he describes the horrible behaviour of men, I think because it helps secure his position as one of the good guys. I want to make him feel that way, to thank him for not being awful.

'Really, these kinds of discussions only play out well

theoretically, I've never seen that kind of thing work in practice. It's stuff people talk about in college, it's not real life.'

Rory is correct, college was something other than real life. I'm not quite sure what to say to him, because I'm not sure which well-rehearsed arguments I have that still make sense. There's a moment of silence.

Then, 'Speaking of, can I ask, what are we?'

The question makes me pause for a moment, and I wonder how I've walked myself into it. I feel as though I've been led here on a trail of breadcrumbs, but of course I've participated in laying them. Simultaneously Gretel and the witch.

I don't want things between us to change, and I know I have to say whatever I can to ensure they don't. It's a fine balance. He looks disappointed, and I rush to retract my words. His hand is on the table across from me, but I'm afraid to take it. Being tactile is always easy with Finn; I don't know why I feel a barrier now with Rory.

He says, 'That's cool, I'm just checking.' He reaches across the table and takes my hand, and I let him. I exhale as he does it, and when I make eye contact with him he's smiling, so I smile too. The waiter clears away our plates, and with them the conversation.

I'm drunk after the meal. I've lost count of how many glasses of wine I've had. Rory keeps saying, 'It's a cele-bration!' and refilling my glass. I don't want to know how much money Rory spends, and I'm shocked when I intentionally look at the bill after he goes to the bathroom. I'm secretly pleased that he's willing to spend so much money just to spend time with me.

Rory asks me if I want to get a cocktail, and I'm afraid

of where the evening might go, for reasons I can't explain. I'm aware, in some dimly lit corner of my brain, that things are accelerating. Anxiety is building in my chest, and the world's losing texture. I want to hit the panic eject button.

'Oh, yeah, sure, I'm tired too,' he says.

He walks me to my bus stop, and we hold hands the whole way. I think mine are clammy, and I can't forget that they exist. I feel every fibre of his being where we connect. He talks to me about how long he wants to work at his job, and what kind of house he's hoping to afford. He often indulges me in chats about houses, and I wonder if that's what he's doing now.

I squeeze his hand to anchor myself to the present. I make a joke about stopping for McDonald's and he says, 'But you wouldn't actually though, would you? Did I not feed you enough?'

I can't explain to him that eating is not about being hungry or full, so I laugh instead.

The city is buzzing, and people spill out of pubs onto the street. I want to be part of that yellow glow. I try not to look at them, but that means I'm looking at Rory. He smiles at me, and I'm struck by an impression of how tall he is. The crack is bright in the sky behind him, and when I close my eyes everything is purple.

When we get to the bus stop he turns to me and steps inside my bubble of personal space. It pops. I hold my breath, and he kisses me. Unconsciously, I take a step back, and then he's pressing me into the wall. I've nowhere else to go, and I kiss him back. I picture what we might look like from the outside.

The wall digs into my back, and I laugh involuntarily.

He asks me why I'm laughing, and I'm not sure. It's a little bit sore.

He says, 'Shit, sorry, I'm sorry, I got a bit carried away there.' I laugh again, nervously.

My bus arrives, and I have an excuse to leave. He kisses me lightly one last time, and I wave to him as my bus drives away. I can still see him standing there when the bus turns a corner.

I can't name whatever it is that I'm feeling. I try to call Dan, but he doesn't pick up. I want to talk to him about boys, and about childhood trauma. I pick the evening apart and decide that it was pleasant, and categorise it in my mind as such. Now that I'm alone I can think about everything I've put into my body. I don't like thinking about it.

It's not late when I get home, but I go straight to bed. Rory sends me a goodnight message, and it makes me panic. Finn hasn't messaged me at all, and that makes me panic more. The sky's not the only thing that's cracked.

14

It's coming on three o'clock in the morning, but I'm stuck in a trance. I've ruined my sleep schedule; I haven't seen anyone for days, so there's no reason to inhabit the usual hours. I refresh website after website looking for vacancies from the relative safety of the sofa. There's something permanent about going to bed, a finality in accepting a day has passed, especially when there's nothing to wake up for.

I've exhausted every hashtag I can think of on Twitter. I find an advertisement for a job in a catering company in Cavan, and briefly consider moving to Cavan. My politics degree feels useless; any extra skills I've picked up here or there feel ordinary. Rick and Vanessa can only get me so far. A life change at this early juncture might not be the worst thing.

I'm contemplating applying for a job in Dublin Zoo that's just been posted when I get a message from Rory. He's seen that I'm online and is jokingly telling me I should go to bed. I send him a gif of someone rolling their eyes. This is our rhythm. We text at odd hours, and I never feel too exhausted to reply. He's been busy so we've haven't met up since our date, but that works better for us. I feel closer to him in cyberspace than I do in real life. I feel closer to myself in cyberspace as well.

Rory links me an article about climate change and we chat back and forth about how hopeless and apathetic we both are, which I think is flirting. Every week there's a new disaster. Wildfires are raging up and down the west coast of the USA, apparently caused by a failure in the power grid that was predicted fifty years ago, but which no one did anything about. It's eclipsed the crack in news coverage. My brain is oversaturated with tragedy and isn't coping well with all the new information. For once I'm relieved the news cycle is so short.

did you see the new host of that netflix show is a climate denier?

yes
i wonder who'll be the next person to be cancelled
i keep reminding myself that celebrities aren't my friends
but i'm still disappointed

i hate the word cancelled

you sound like a man about to be cancelled

i know how that sounds
i do
i just think that you can never really cancel someone

true, cancel culture is a lie
horrible men still get awards and money

the circle of life

don't worry
i'm not planning on cancelling you any time soon

thank god

I fall asleep on the couch with my phone still in my hand. The sunrise wakes me up, and I drag my painful body upstairs to bed, but sleep doesn't come. I lie awake with my eyes closed for countless hours before deciding to give up and have a shower. I sit, like a zombie, refreshing the internet until I run out of content I'm willing to consume, including several things I normally never would. I feel a mix of satisfaction and dread.

At some point, Finn messages me and asks me to come over and have brunch with him. I change my outfit three times before settling on something I like, and make sure I'm wearing impractical underwear. I can't find my favourite pair of boots. Hannah asks me where I'm going, and I close the front door before I have to answer.

Finn's in sweatpants and a T-shirt when I arrive. I can't decide if I feel disappointed in how little effort he's put in, or satisfied he doesn't feel like he needs to impress me.

We make French toast, with Finn dipping the bread and me frying. He keeps bumping my elbow whenever he makes a bad joke like, 'You know they just call this toast in France.'

I feel like I always know what to say with Finn, like our conversations have rules and we speak in strict turns.

I don't even have to think about it. It's been a while since we've been alone like this, and I've missed it. No one can match me in this game as well as Finn.

Finn's reading his phone. Then he looks at me and says, 'I had to mute Lucy on Twitter, by the way.'

This surprises me.

He says, 'I don't know if this is unwoke, but it's all the sex stuff. She's just a bit forward? Like, I'm as sex positive as the next guy, but at the same time I don't want to see that.'

I understand where Finn's coming from: I never know if I should scroll past her picture or click onto it, and which one is the more enlightened decision. She says she finds it empowering, but it doesn't seem that all of her followers agree. She's talked about starting an OnlyFans, but when I read their comments I find it hard to separate it from the human trafficking, exploitation and fetishisation of the broader porn industry. Admittedly, it's harder to support when I imagine Hannah doing it.

'Yes, completely, but also, mainly, I don't want to see my friends naked.'

I'm glad he only wants to see some of his friends naked.

He laughs and says, 'Only some.'

I wonder if he likes seeing me naked, if he likes my body. The words leave my mouth without permission: I know the answer could break me. I'm dreading Finn asking me for nudes. I've tried to take them, in the past, but my body can't make the jump from three dimensional to pixels without broadcasting every flaw I have. The comments on Lucy's posts swim before my eyes. *Great rack, a bit too chubby though.* I could try to find whatever corner of the web Hannah's using to sell her nudes and allow her body to replace mine. The thought makes me sick in more ways than one.

He says, 'Of course, you know I think you're beautiful,' because that's the polite thing to do in this situation, but it makes me happy anyway.

'You're not going to start posting thirst traps like Lucy though, are you?'

It's amusing to pretend that I might, but he sees through me immediately. Lucy and I are very different people. I'm not sure we're really friends; I know I'm not the reason she still hangs around. She's much closer to Grace.

'And she can be kind of controlling, right? Grace?'

I drag a piece of French toast through syrup. It feels disloyal to answer at all.

'Sometimes it's like she expects you to have the same opinions as she does, or to not have any at all.'

I'm surprised to hear him say that; I'd always thought of Grace as the centre of our social circle. I'd never thought that anyone else could see the same things I do. The problem with Grace is that her reality is the only reality that matters to her.

'Yeah,' he says, 'that mustn't be nice.'

I stop myself from asking if he feels that way about his friendships, or if he's noticed he's uncritical of his male friends. I don't think he'd admit it if he did, and he certainly wouldn't say anything that'd jeopardise his friendship with Pearse. Instead I eat the French toast and smile at him across the table. He has powdered sugar on his cheek, and I wipe it off.

After, he makes us tea and asks me, 'Do you ever think

about Catholic guilt? I've been thinking about it a lot lately, is it just an Irish thing? Like, I don't understand how Lucy does what she does.'

I've never once thought Finn would be in any way inhibited by feelings of guilt around sex, but he talks with sincerity. I've never unpacked my own feelings about it before, but it explains my general discomfort at the idea of sexualising myself, like it's something I'm waiting for permission for. I sometimes get intrusive thoughts I can trace back to the priest who'd come into our class every week of primary school.

'Once, in school, we had a retreat and the priest told us that if you even think about sinning, because God can see into your mind, that's as bad as sinning, which means we won't get raptured when the time comes. That's a scary thing to hear when you're going through puberty.'

When I was in school we had a religious group come into class and tell us that the more people you have sex with, the fewer people you can love. They made ten girls and one boy stand up, wrapped tape around their arms in turn, ripped it off, and by the time the boy was taped to the last girl, it no longer stuck. Turns out, you should not imply that one boy is fucking half the girls in class if you want cohesion in a group of sixteen year olds.

'I mean, what if you just bought higher quality tape? But no, really, that's mad.'

Sometimes when I have sex I still feel like I'm doing something wrong, which makes the sex we have after much more satisfying. It feels honest, and present. I feel complete when I'm with him, as though he can read my mind and my body.

Afterwards, when we're still in bed, I wonder if he's

sleeping with anyone else. This time always feels the most honest of all, as though neither of us have anything to hide. I'm cuddled into his side, with his arm around me, so I don't have to look him in the eyes when I ask him.

'Jealous?' he asks me, and I don't think I am. 'You?'

I throw a pillow at him, and the silence stretches between us. I realise he hasn't really answered the question himself, but before I can open my mouth he says, 'What about that Rory guy? Have you already broken his heart?'

I'm not sure why I feel comfortable talking about this with Finn when I always evade the subject with Rory, when thus far I've evaded everything with Rory.

'Wow, I didn't realise you were such a prude, throw the guy a bone.'

He accuses me of having too much Catholic guilt, and then he laughs and leans over to kiss me. Maybe we really will be left behind when the rapture comes, if it's imminent.

'Well I hope so,' he says, and then: 'Maybe the crack is the rapture. Who knows? The existential dread of it seems to have passed. No one is talking about it any more and no one's died from it yet, at least. And I don't think Catholics are supposed to believe in the rapture. We don't even have purgatory?'

Purgatory is growing up in Catholic Ireland; or, rather, purgatory is living in Ireland right now, with everyone in their twenties stuck at home with their parents, unable to really start their lives.

'But at least we have good jokes and good looks.'

I reach over and ruffle his hair. Unfortunately, he has a big Irish head on him, which is a pity. He sticks his tongue out at me.

'Oh? You must like that kind of thing.'

The flow of the conversation calms me. It's always been easy to talk to Finn.

We sit together by the window in the kitchen. He opens it so he can smoke. I look out across the city, and I feel no urge to drop down into it. He offers me a cigarette and I decline; I don't feel like I need them any more. Being close to Finn gives me the same feeling.

'Yeah, I'd noticed you'd stopped, but I thought I should offer anyway, being a gentleman. You're an open book to me, Sophie.'

When I leave, he says he'll send me an article later, but I know he won't. Social media isn't our place, not really, and I know he'll forget to message.

I'm in a good mood when I return home. Having dinner with the family is just about bearable, until I bring up the subject of my missing boots. Hannah denies taking them until I get up and bring them back from her room.

'Honey, just share, what's the big deal?' Mum chides me. Hannah sits there in silence.

It's not a big deal, not really, but it would have been nice if she'd asked first. Hannah's been taking my things without asking ever since we were kids, so I know how this conversation is going to go. I feel tears begin to well in the space between my eyes, almost pre-emptively. I breathe in three times to make sure my voice stays steady and retreat to somewhere far above this whole conversation.

'I'm sure she meant to ask,' Dad says, 'and she's sorry.' He says it in a way that seems like an ending to the conversation, although Hannah doesn't say any of the words herself.

'You borrow my stuff all the time,' she says, which I do not.

'Well, there you go,' says Mum, and I get up and clear the table without a word. They sit there chatting as I rinse the dishes, the sound of white noise in my ears.

Later that night, I find the boots in my room again, back where I'd left them, with the zips cut out from the sides. I know there's no point in telling my parents. I get under the covers, fully clothed.

I refresh social media, but Finn doesn't message me. I can see from his Instagram that he's out having drinks. I like one of Rory's tweets instead, and he messages me. This rhythm works for me.

15

Grace wants to come over to hang out, and I decide to let her. It gives me something to do for the day and an excuse for not leaving the house. I haven't seen her in over a week, and I don't know if it's her fault or mine. She has periods where she spends time with her other friends. She maintains friendships so I don't have to, and I don't mind being left on the shelf for weeks on end. It's a symbiotic relationship.

When she comes over, she's excited. She's carrying her laptop in an enormous purple handbag, which she pulls out immediately and sets up on my kitchen table. I put on the kettle habitually. She's cut her hair, and I wonder what else has changed about her since I've seen her last.

'Have you been avoiding me again?'

I haven't. I just haven't been actively seeking her company, and she hasn't sought mine either. I thought this was just how our friendship worked.

'You're such a recluse, honestly.' I don't react. 'Have you been following these super storms in America? Honestly, we should stop calling them super storms and start acknowledging that normal storms have got worse because of climate change and they're no longer exceptional. They think something about the crack is making them worse, but I don't see how.'

She knows I've been following the storms, so the conversation is easy. But I can't shake the unease I feel when she speaks, and how easily she dismisses the influence of the crack. It's like we've all bought into a collective fiction, where we see it and know something is happening, but because we can't explain it, it must not be happening. There's no solution, so we reason there must not be a problem either.

'You and Lucy should talk about this. She was saying the same thing to me the other day at the pub.' I file this information away to use as a conversational topic with Lucy later and try not to focus on the fact that they had, presumably, all been in the pub without me.

'So, anyway,' she says, and waxes into an extended monologue. She tells me her parents are going to let her have the house in Kerry for the weekend, and she wants to make up a list of who we'll invite down with us. 'No one boring, of course, and no one messy.' She begins to list off people, and I don't react when she says Finn and Rory's names. I'm surprised, however, when she mentions Pearse.

'I know, I know,' she says. 'But look, we need more boys, and Steph is kind of into him? It makes me want to vom but arguing is like a fetish for her or something.'

She leaves it at that, and I don't say anything when I hand her her cup of tea. She's lost in a spreadsheet. I wait, the unasked question hanging between us. I don't know how her mind works, if her thoughts are all independent, or buzzing around looking for connections. I'm not sure if she will look at me, or if it will click at all.

'Now, I know what you're thinking, well, two things.' She holds her hand up to me. 'The first is how are we going to budget meal planning with so many dietary requirements, but I've a plan for that, don't you worry.' I raise my eyebrows at her, waiting. 'Yes, yes, the second and more pressing problem is your two boyfriends.'

I look at my phone to avoid having to look at her. Neither of them are my boyfriends, and neither of them have dietary requirements. One of my targeted ads on Facebook is for online counselling, but the picture is of a cartoon woman, and I think it's just a depression meme at first.

'Don't make me roll my eyes back at you. This is the trouble you cause going after two boys in the same extended friend group. I've run the metaphorical numbers, and I'm afraid we can't get away with not inviting both of them, one of them will find out, and then I'll be the one in trouble. Especially because Steph's already invited Pearse, and he's the link between the two of them.'

I put my head on the table. The idea of Rory and Finn spending time with each other is unfathomable, now that I have to care about both of them. I hear their potential conversations in my head. I open and close apps on my phone just to feel like I'm doing something.

'Don't worry. Look, you and Finn aren't *dating*' – she says the word as though it means much more than it does – 'and you and Rory haven't really done anything yet. So I'm going to enact a sacred girl-code rule and say this is a trip you're spending with your best friend, no boys or kissing or sex allowed.' Grace is good at resolving things into simplicities, and I decide it's not worth it to argue. I adopt a veneer of total apathy.

Grace engages me in serious planning for the next few hours. We have to work out where everyone will sleep, what everyone will eat, and how to ensure it will be a drama-free weekend. Grace is sure that if we invite just enough people to allow for minor group splintering it'll be okay and no one will get on anyone's nerves. 'That's just basic social engineering,' she says.

I decide there's no point in being anxious about it right now; there will be plenty of time to be anxious at the weekend. I let her plan, and think about social friction and cohesion. We're all just marbles let loose on a table, convinced that random interactions are connections.

I sit for a while after she leaves, thinking. I know that I'll have to confront this situation at some point, but it's so easy to sink into apathy. It no longer feels like a choice. We haven't hung out as a group since Dan left, and I'm not sure how the dynamic will work. The group chat has been silent since my last message.

I message Finn and, after I've redrafted the message ten times, I tell him about the weekend and that Rory will be there. I try to play it off and tease him about not making anyone jealous. He sees it right away, but takes a while to reply.

Eventually:

Sounds fun!

It doesn't make me feel better.

I open Instagram and look at who has viewed my story. Rory and Finn have been alternating for the top spot. The algorithms they use to decide these things are complicated and change frequently, and I know they are mostly

172

decided by my activity – one of my online courses confirmed as much. I can't help but read into it, however. Just because I know that they're designed to keep me coming back, hooked on the possibility that those little circles could mean something, doesn't mean it doesn't work.

At dinner I tell my parents about Kerry. It takes some convincing for them to be okay with the idea.

'Will there be an adult there?' Mum asks. I'm twenty-two years old and she still treats me like a child.

'I don't know, that drive seems a little bit too long,' Dad says. 'Who's even going, the girls from school? They always seemed responsible. Niamh, right?'

Dad's knowledge of my social comings and goings is always about five years out of date. I nod weakly at him until his fears are eased.

It takes even more convincing to persuade Hannah that she shouldn't insist on coming too. I'm not sure why she keeps trying to spend time with me. The only reason I can come up with is that she's looking for more ways to torment me.

'You know, I'm free this weekend as well,' she says, and I do my best to pretend I can't hear her. 'I really liked seeing your friends the other weekend, it would be nice to get to know them some more.' I focus on eating.

'I met Finn at our party,' she says, and I pretend he isn't invited.

'He follows me on Instagram.' I'm surprised when she says that; it's not something I've noticed. I compulsively take out my phone, and then put it away. I don't want to let her rob me of my cyberspace, not when she already makes my physical space so uninhabitable.

'I'm just saying it would be nice to get to know him, and the others.'

I know I'll have to let her come to her own conclusions about the trip, because the more I try to persuade her to do something the harder she'll fight against me, and my parents will tell me to just let her come. I eat two helpings of dinner and have three biscuits. Afterwards, I still have a hollow pit inside me.

Eventually, Hannah huffs away to her room and emerges an hour later announcing that she also has a trip planned; she's going to go back to Glasgow to visit her friends. She says it with an air of winning, as though she's beat me at this thing, and I let her believe that she has.

Grace creates a group chat to share all the details of the trip with everyone. I don't open it immediately, but I get a message from Rory asking me if I'm going. I know the internet won't be safe for me until I address it, so I open it.

i am!

i'm looking forward to spending some time with you

My hopes that he won't come are dashed.

same
but just so you know
grace has been having a hard time lately
and i think she'll need me

oh sorry to hear that
of course yeah

i'd no idea

                              yeah sorry

do you want to talk about it?

                    it's not really something i can say

The lie surprises me. The words appear, fully formed, as though they're more a product of my phone than my brain. They could have been written by an AI bot that's studied me long enough to predict what I'm going to say. I would happily relinquish control to it; it's easier than continuing to come up with creative ways to avoid this conversation with him.

Grace calls me to tell me that everyone is coming and that we'll have to do more planning in the next few days. I'm not sure there's space in my head for any more forethought, but I agree to help her. She talks to me about the things she wants us to do when we're there until it gets late enough that I can feign tiredness.

I lie awake for hours, looking up into the crack and thinking.

16

Grace drives us down to the house in her tiny blue car. We decided to go down early, just the two of us, because Grace wanted to make sure the house was in order before the others arrive tomorrow. I don't have anything keeping me in Dublin.

The drive is seemingly never-ending, and our supply of road-trip snacks depletes long before we even leave the Pale. The only CDs Grace has in her car are ones she bought when she was a teenager, back when CDs were things people bought, and we blare them as we speed down the motorway. All of the songs are about some kind of heady romance that only exists when you're a hormonal teen, and I long to feel that intensely about anything again. We stop for McDonald's along the way, and it makes me feel a little bit better.

Grace is in full holiday-planner mode and I'm barely paying attention. The sun is just peeking out from behind the clouds for what feels like the first time all summer. There was some anxiety about whether or not the crack would affect the atmosphere and therefore the summer, but it hasn't. Anyone would think it's just an illusion.

I'm beginning to regard it with the same detachment

with which I view myself: as an immutable fact that impresses itself so heavily onto the world as to cease to matter entirely. I find it hard to place within the scale of the Kerry mountains and vistas. It's like it's intruding upon an oil painting, where the painter has made up for what they lack in skill with imagination.

Grace pokes me, and it sends a shock through my system. I jolt up in my seat. Jesus Christ. I apologise for being a million miles away.

'I said, we're stopping here to go to the big supermarket. I still need to pick up some stuff.'

I nod at her, and she slows down to turn into the carpark. When we get out of the car, Grace goes to find a trolley, and I take out my phone. I have a message from Rory.

looking forward to seeing you tomorrow
i've bought some extra snacks

what kind?

you'll see! x

It takes me a moment to digest the *x*. I show it to Grace, but she isn't paying attention to me. I look back at my phone. I'm not sure our relationship has progressed to the point where sending kisses is appropriate, but reassure myself that he's probably the type of guy who sends kisses to his mum. It doesn't have to be read romantically.

Finn hasn't sent me anything, but I haven't been expecting him to. I think briefly of picking up some snacks as well, but dismiss it as simultaneously a gesture too casual and too loaded with meaning.

The Aldi's laid out in the exact manner all Aldis are. I'm not sure why I think four hours in the car will change the homogeneity of global capitalism, but for some reason it feels like it should. There's a sick pleasure in being able to purchase the same vanilla yogurt here as I could anywhere.

We engage in what amounts to a complicated stacking endeavour. We fill the trolley with items, pass them over the conveyor belt and into bags, pack the car, and eventually we leave them resting against the large wooden counter in Grace's holiday house.

It's a beautiful house on its own land, and the driveway is lined with tall standing stones and towering plants. The entire downstairs area is open plan, with wooden columns and too many different coloured sofas filling all the nooks and crannies. It looks as though it's leaped off the pages of an architecture magazine, although perhaps thirty years ago. There's a sense of glamour about the place, shrouded heavily in decay. The corners are full of spiders, keeping watch, and there's a patch of mould growing high up. I wonder whether this house has become something of a financial burden, and how even when you have a house, or multiple in this case, you can still be insecure. I say none of this to Grace, of course, and instead crack open a rusty window to admire the bay.

'I'm glad we got the weather for it,' she says.

Grace sets about unpacking the shopping bags and sends me on a mission to get all the beds ready. There are six rooms in total. Grace is sleeping in the master bedroom. She offers to share it with me, as a handy excuse to avoid the boys, but I feel it would be too claustrophobic. I put cheap satin sheets on the bed and watch as the satin pillows slide off each other. It's like an ice rink: frictionless luxury. I choose Grace's childhood room. It's filled with old books and toys she'd once dearly loved and then finished with.

We make oven pizzas for dinner, exhausted from the journey. I try to check if anyone's messaged our Kerry group chat, but I can't get any of the chats to load.

'Yeah, sorry, the signal's terrible here. But I think unplugging will do you some good,' Grace says to me when I ask her about it. I can't tell if Finn's messaged me or not. She watches me refresh the blank chat and says, 'It comes and goes, don't start freaking out, you'll be fine.'

It's weird to be cut off. I was taught that once something is online, it's there for ever. You could ruin your life with one photo. And yet all of those lines of code are intangible; with no signal or power, they don't exist. One of the courses I've been taking talks about how easy it is to corrupt data and how books and photographs are much more stable. It feels like a lie, but I know it's true.

'Isn't it weird to think that everything is so unstable? Like, we all believe in the magic of technology; it feels so permanent but, just like that, it's gone.'

Something in what she says resonates deep within me. Modern life is a fiction; it feels like nothing ever changes, but when you examine its fabric, its zeros and ones, it's falling apart. We've just collectively decided to believe that it's not.

'Yeah, like the crack. A thousand years ago it would've been an apocalyptic event, a sign of God's wrath. But I think you're right, we're so good at justifying massive changes as normal that we're being told it's just another weather event. They even have the data to prove it.'

Data is only half the story; it's how the data is being interpreted that's shifting the narrative.

I don't have the stomach to finish my pizza. Its stringy cheese and perfectly round slices of pepperoni give rise to images of factories and production lines, so divorced from the animals that produced the food itself. It comes to represent in my mind everything that's wrong with being alive today. Grace also burnt the top of it. When I slide it into the bin – yet another wasted product – I feel a bit more sick.

After breakfast the next day, we finally get a message into the group chat that the others are nearly here. I jump up to shower as casually as possible, and by the time I'm finished, I only have time to lie myself on the sofa before people arrive. I don't quite know what to do with myself, I've forgotten exactly how a regular person acts in moments like this, so I go to the sink and begin washing the mugs Grace and I used for tea. I yell at everyone to come in, but make a big show of having my hands wet so no one tries to hug me. Rory smiles at me from across the room, and Grace shows everyone around.

'And before anyone asks, no, there's no Wi-Fi in the house, and the signal's frequently non-existent, especially if a big cloud passes over. I'm not joking. We'll all just have to talk to each other, like the olden days.'

'I didn't know when I agreed to come I'd actually have to talk to you people,' Pearse says, and Steph throws a sofa cushion at him.

I stop listening and focus on the washing, so I jump when Finn comes up behind me and whispers in my ear, 'Have you missed me?'

I splash water in his face and hand him a tea towel so

he can start drying. We talk about his journey down and the weather, and everything that someone would expect to talk about. It feels like I'm regurgitating formulae in a maths exam. I don't think it's possible for anyone to be more supremely uninteresting than I am in this moment.

Finn doesn't seem to notice. I watch him talk, his lean arms moving as he dries the cups and spoons, and it doesn't matter what we're saying to each other. It's as if I can feel each word move from his lips to mine. Finn's like a spinning top; get him started on a topic he's interested in, and he will just go round and round, propelled by his own momentum.

He asks me what my plans for the weekend are, and it amuses me to spin his question around, to see what he thinks is going through my mind. He raises his eyebrows and says, 'Well, staying far away from me, right?'

I laugh and decide I'll start right now. I walk away from him and move to a big red sofa by the back door that Lucy's sitting on. I remember what Grace said to me, that I should talk to Lucy about the super storms, and we chat for a while about environmental collapse until we are both good and depressed about everything. We tell each other facts we both know the other already knows; there's catharsis in acknowledging just how fucked the planet is. It feels strange interacting with Lucy without the crutch of either Grace or Dan. I can't remember the last time we spoke, just us two, and I'm satisfied that I've come out of the interaction unscathed.

Grace asks Rory to set up the barbecue for later, which keeps him busy for a while. I can see him through the glass of the back door, and it comforts me to know he's so close by. He's there if and when I need him, and in the meantime I can watch him with the comfort of the glass between us.

I haven't able to use my phone all morning; Grace wasn't lying about the clouds. I'm beginning to feel a little bit panicked. My thoughts can't settle on anything without direction. It's been a long time since since I've had to sit and think without prompting. I close myself off in my room for a while and draw the curtains. In the dark, I can hear people talking and laughing in the rest of the house, so I lie in bed and close my eyes and listen.

We drink and watch a movie in the evening, and I sit between Grace and Lucy, a wine bottle nestled into my side. I can't help but look periodically between Rory and Finn and compare them. At times they seem so different, but their contours are soft in the light of the TV, and I can't tell them apart. Their faces meld together in my mind, and I drink.

As soon as the movie's done I start gathering empty bowls and rubbish and move into the kitchen. Everyone's discussing the various artistic merits of the movie, but I'm not in the mood. I consumed it as I always consume things, without thought or comment.

'Did it even pass the Bechdel test?' Steph asks.

'I'm not sure, but you know that's only superficial representation. Like women need to do more than talk for a movie to be feminist? It's a really low bar,' Grace says.

'Really low, and yet so many movies don't pass it.'

'True.'

'I heard that most of *Sex and the City* doesn't pass it?' says Lucy. 'Which is bizarre and yet I believe it.'

'Movies don't have to have women in them to be good,

you can't create a checklist for what good art is,' Pearse says.

'Yes, we all know that you hate women, Pearse,' Steph replies to him, but her legs are draped over his lap.

'That's ridiculous, I don't hate women. It's you that discriminates against men.'

I rinse the bowls in the sink just for something to do. After a moment, I hear someone approach me, and a bowl slips out of my hands. Suds splash back at me and cover my top. It's Rory. He's heavily laden with the rest of the carnage from the movie night.

He asks me where the bin is, and I show him. The bag is full, and he says, 'Want to keep me company while I change this?'

I feel like I'm walking on eggshells around him, as though I'm inhabiting a different and unfamiliar body. This change of scenery, this chance to be alone, expands a balloon in my chest, and I'm unsure what will happen when it pops. We've always had the difficulty of living at home with our parents to put a wedge between us.

We leave the house and the sound of everyone else behind. It's chilly now the sun's set, so I grab a blanket off the couch as I leave.

'The sky is clearer out here, isn't it? I know that's an obvious thing to say, but it's pretty. Sometimes I think we don't look up enough, you know?'

I like the way he phrases things as questions, as though his thoughts don't exist until I confirm them. I nearly tell him that this part of Kerry has protected dark skies, and it's an ideal place for a large telescope due to the lack of seismic activity. I stop myself, however, feeling that that's not the type of information most people are looking for when they bring up the stars. Of course, all that was in the *before* times.

There aren't as many stars any more. The effect of the crack is much more stark out here, its light filling the whole sky. It looks animated, unreal and alien. It's amazing to watch the sky shift and morph in the purple light, without the light pollution of the city. In the city, we've absorbed it into our landscape, just another neon light. Out here, it's easier to see how much has changed.

I open the lid of the bin and he throws the bag in before wiping his hands on his jeans. I shiver and he rubs my shoulders. I like how he notices little things like that.

He stops me before we get back to the house.

'I like spending time with you, just so you know.' He says it in an offhand way, but the implications of the sentence spread out in front of me. I know he wants me to say something in response.

'Do you like spending time with me?'

The question strikes a chord inside me, and I'm not even sure why. I consider it for a moment before replying. I do like spending time with him, but it's not the main thing I like about him.

'So maybe we could spend more time together, then?'

Then: 'You're impossible to get a straight answer out of, you do realise that, don't you?' He says it in a joking way, that makes it seem appropriate that I stick my tongue out and wink at him.

Lately, it seems like nearly every conversation we have is about our relationship, like he's trying to pin me down and make me commit to something. It's getting harder and harder to avoid the topic, and it's starting to make me uncomfortable. I'm not sure how much longer I can conceal the situation from him; guilt is starting to rot inside me.

I move to go inside, but he grabs my hand and spins me around. He calls me a tease, and I find that amusing. I'm standing very close to him now, and I can feel his chest expand and contract with his breath. He shakes his head at me, and I kiss him, lightly. His hand goes to my waist, and I lean back and kiss him on the nose, so he can't accuse me of being serious. I don't want him to think I'm serious, because I don't want him to think any of this is serious. Rory has an intensity about him. He takes me, and us, seriously. It scares me, which perhaps is part of the reason that I like it. I step away from him, and he lets me, then open the door to rejoin the others in the house.

Finn sees me coming back inside with Rory, and he winks at me. He seems genuinely fine with whatever he imagines has gone on, which is disappointing. I consciously don't pay attention to him, and try to pick up what the argument that's going on is about.

'It really does glow!' Lucy's voice is raised. She'd been playing cards with Finn before this argument broke out. The remnants of the game are scattered across the table.

'Maybe in the Caribbean, but not here,' says Steph, who is gesturing with a glass of wine from the sofa.

'I'll prove it,' Lucy gets up.

'You're not serious,' Pearse says.

'Learn to take women seriously, maybe,' she replies. 'Come on, the beach isn't far.'

Rory's standing close behind me, so close that I can feel his body heat. He hasn't moved since we walked in the door, and now it feels unnatural. I grab Lucy by the arm, and together we walk out the door. I don't look behind me to see who's following.

The road is dark, so Lucy takes out her phone. In the light, hundreds of slugs are illuminated on the driveway. 'Fucking gross,' Lucy says, and I hope she turns off the light. I want to disappear into the night.

'God, I hope there's actually some plankton out tonight,' Lucy confides in me. 'I can't stand Pearse, and Steph can be rough when she's proved right.'

I don't know what to say to her; I've never considered her relationship with Steph like that. They always seem so comfortable with each other; communication flows so freely between them that I've felt shut out many times.

'No, no, it is normally. Sometimes she's just a bit much, like tonight. I'm sure you know how it is too.'

Behind us, I hear the others following. Pearse sounds drunk; he's yelling about something, and Steph is calling him an idiot. Lucy looks back at them, her face illuminated from below by the phone in her hand.

'I miss Dan, I wish he didn't have to leave,' she says, and I agree with her. 'I didn't realise until recently, but I think he gave our group a lot of stability; he was always putting out fires.' I think Dan would like that image of himself.

We arrive at the beach, and it's pitch black. I trip over the bank of a stream that's flowing from a nearby field, and my shoes are soaked. It's hard to tell where the sea ends and the sky begins.

'Wait, do that again,' Lucy says. My hands are crusted in sand, and when I look at her she says, 'Fine, just kick your heels in the sand.'

We're close to the sea and the sand here is wet and

dense. I drag my heels across it and when I do, a trail lights up with sparks of glittering light. I do it again, and again, half-convinced that what I'm seeing isn't real and instead I'm having some kind of hallucination. I can't believe that the world, our world, still has little moments of magic in it.

Lucy laughs and yells, 'Fuck you, Pearse!' even though he's too far behind us to hear.

We try to draw pictures in the sand, which disappear after a moment. They're temporary, but they're the most beautiful things I've ever seen. The image of them burns in my vision for a second after they're gone. I'm giddy; it feels like we're uncovering a secret.

'All right, all right, what's going on?' Steph calls. I see the constellation of their phone lights appear at the entrance to the beach. I gaze out across the water and count their footsteps as they approach.

Just behind me, I hear what sounds like Pearse inhaling a large breath. Lucy doesn't turn around and instead wades out into the sea until it's covering her knees. 'Look at the water.'

She splashes at us and the plankton light up again. They look like stars, the sea becoming an unblemished night sky, unmarred by the crack. It's like looking back through time at how the world used to be. It connects now to then, and makes it seem like time might actually be passing. I feel present in a way I haven't for a long time.

'They come in on warm tides.'

'I wouldn't call this warm,' says Rory as he retreats from the waves. He touches my shoulder, as though to pull me back with him, but I shrug him off. I don't look at anyone, but I can sense the solidity of their bodies at my periphery.

I hike my dress up and wade out as far as I can. The cold crystallises my grip on the evening. From the shore, Finn splashes water in my direction, but I ignore him. It's just me, and the sky, and the sea. The water is freezing, but I don't mind.

Lucy laughs, and I'm suddenly thrilled for her. I move closer to her, to observe her joy in this moment, and think perhaps I'm part of it.

'I'm so glad to be here, now,' she says.

I want to take a photo to remember this moment, but my pockets are empty. I abandoned my phone on the sand with my shoes. Grace brings it out to us, swearing at the cold. When she's an arm's length away, she splashes a great wave of water at me.

Before I can get her back, she says, 'Careful, you wouldn't want to accidentally brick your precious phone.'

I weigh my options, caring less about my phone than I ever have, when Lucy jumps onto my back from behind and dunks my head under.

Grace is out of the water before I fully surface, spitting and spluttering from the cold. I grab Lucy by the ankle and drag her down with me. By the time we make it to shore we're both waterlogged and gasping. Out of the tranquillity of the ocean, my clothes are heavy and lifeless, and I begin to shiver.

Steph collects some wood from the beach and builds a bonfire, lighting the world up in brilliant orange. I edge as close to the fire as I dare, and it nearly replaces the warmth of human touch. The others chat around me, but I'm engrossed in the flames.

I can feel my childhood slipping away from me like the sand on the beach. Ageing is a process of longshore drift, moving from one experience to the next, leaving anything that's too heavy behind. These people will all leave me behind, eventually. Dan's already gone.

Across from me, Grace laughs at something Steph says, and her whole face lights up. It's amazing to watch Grace interact with the world. She's totally unashamed of who she is, so confident that life won't reject her that she's almost completely unguarded.

Grace is my best friend, largely through convenience and proximity, but I'm struck by the thought that I'm not her best friend. She could easily replace me with any one of these people. This isn't something that's surprising or upsetting, it just is; it's a fact about my existence.

I stare at my face in the front camera of my phone, as though it might have changed in the time since I last saw it. I try to imagine how I look to the others. My phone lights up with messages from the school girls, which breaks my eye contact. Our fire dies out and we walk back to the house, the crack providing enough purple light to see by now that our eyes have adjusted.

I've never been so aware of the present, and the fact that moments like these come and go, and are lost for ever. It's likely, in ten years' time, I won't know any of these people any more. Some of them may even be dead. I might be dead.

Finn talks at me on the way back up to the house, but I find I can't pay attention to him. His voice is soothing to me, however, and with Finn I never have to say too much. Walking beside him feels like being in a bubble, as though the outside world doesn't exist, and there's only me and him. I try to match my footsteps to his.

'Earth to Sophie?' he says, and I apologise and touch

his elbow. His solidity sends a shock through my body. I hear Rory laugh behind me and release Finn. The walk back feels much shorter.

At the house, Grace tells everyone where they're sleeping and passes out towels. I hardly register it. Rory's sitting beside me, and I'm aware of his hand brushing the side of my leg. I feel formless. I laugh at whatever he says to me, and that pleases him.

'Well, I'm exhausted from that midnight adventure,' Grace says. 'You guys can stay up, but please, please, do not wake me up.'

I make eye contact with Grace, and she gestures for me to follow her into the bedroom. I feel as though I'm leaving a trail behind me when I exit the room, like a slug. As soon as the door closes, the tension eases out of my body.

'So, which one do you love more?'

I pretend not to understand what she means, but she isn't having it, and I relent. I pull the curtains closed so I have something to do with my hands.

'You can't keep ping-ponging between the two of them, it's not healthy. You need to choose soon, before someone gets hurt.'

I find her statement preposterous. I'm not hurting either of them, it's not like it's serious; none of this is serious.

'I'm not talking about the idiot boys, who cares about them? I'm talking about *you* getting hurt. And say it's not serious all you want, but you've never done anything like this before, so it must be serious for you.'

Grace has a way of delivering cold truths at the worst possible time. The tension I had released comes back and hits me with the force of a freight train. Grace does things like this all the time; she's allowed to have whatever relationships she wants to, and I'm never allowed to be anything less than perfect.

I wash the salt from my hair, go to my own room, and then lie in the bed unmoving for hours before I actually drift off to sleep. I can't load any of the podcasts I listen to, so I am alone with my thoughts, which are unusually quiet.

17

The light is pale when I wake, and my body is painful from sleeping tensed up. The curtains are thin and don't keep out much of the early morning light. I check my phone, and it's barely after six. It's been a long time since I've approached the sunrise from this side of the morning.

I open my phone and read through Twitter for a while. It takes forever to load, and all of the pictures are just greyed-out squares. I have to guess at the memes everyone is referencing.

The Americans are still awake, and reading about their political and social climate is not how I want to start my day. Some prominent journalist is in a flame war with a celebrity over whether or not the crack is a government hoax. I can see what's driving the conspiracy theorists; the bigger the event, the more people want to believe there is some reason behind it. Somehow, the decline of late capitalism is never the obvious answer for them.

I avoid looking at myself in the mirror as I dress, unsure how I'll feel if I do. I sit for a while, scrolling through my phone. I have to concentrate on text-based websites, because nothing else will load. The sun is just cresting the horizon, and I watch the world unfold in front of me. It's amazing how many things can happen in the world while you sleep, and how few of them are memorable or important a few hours later. Still, I drink them all in.

I see on Dan's private Twitter that he's awake, so I decide to call him. He answers on the sixth or seventh ring. The connection is bad, as though he's far away.

'Soph, it's basically the middle of the night.'

He sounds sleepy, and something else. I haven't heard his voice recently enough to tell what it is. He says he's fine until I mention Twitter. I'm not sure I should, if it's okay to speak openly about someone's private tweets, but I'm worried about him.

'Yeah, okay, I know, why do I even post that stuff anyway? I'm just being a melodramatic bitch, screaming into the void. On paper it's all good, flat's good, job's good, weather's good. I guess I'm just lonely.'

Loneliness isn't the worst thing in the world; sometimes, it's okay to be lonely. When I was younger, loneliness was sometimes better than the alternative.

'I know,' he says. 'I do. It's just hard.'

He tells me stories about his co-workers and his new flatmate until I can hear his voice lighten up, and then he tells me to fuck off so he can go back to sleep, which lets me know he really is feeling better.

He says that the crack doesn't look different in London, but the British government is acting like it does. 'It's all this Blitz spirit, everyone acting like they personally lived off rations and dug the bunkers.'

I can picture the type in my head. A few years back, some Tory in salmon-pink trousers had thrown an unexplained severed pigeon head at protestors on O'Connell

Bridge, which is now how I imagine anyone who votes Conservative.

'Yeah, exactly, you've no idea. If I have to see one more statue of Oliver Cromwell I actually don't know what I'll do. It seems to be settling down, at least, the crack stuff. I think that's comforting, if also concerning.'

The crack's settled in people's imaginations, as though the photograph of it has finally developed in their heads. It's now something that just exists, rather than threatens the very nature of existence itself. It's like our reality hasn't changed, but rather expanded to contain this new development as well.

'You always have a good way of summing these things up. I think it's all the internet you read and, honestly, I'm concerned. Anyway, tell me about the weekend so far, I want all the gossip.'

I tell him about plankton, and how magical the unexplained parts of the world now feel. It's almost like there are a hundred bubbling possibilities beneath the uncertainty, and I can't find the words to articulate how both present and absent I feel. There's a pressure building in my chest, as though I can't breathe, but at the same time my lungs are clear.

'Huh, sounds like you just need the ride.'

This time it's me who tells him to fuck off, but we're both in a better mood because of it. I get out of bed.

No one else is awake yet, but the kitchen is a yawning space in front of me, so I decide to start making breakfast. Scrolling through my phone, I see that Lucy is online, so I message her. It takes several minutes to go through; it probably would have been more efficient to knock on her door.

awake?

yes
but at what cost

i have bacon

thank god

After a moment or two, I hear a door creak open. Lucy emerges with her duvet wrapped around her. She looks exhausted.

'Let me tell you' – she sits down at the counter and I pass her some coffee – 'one of those boys snores loud enough to wake the dead. Patriarchy in action.'

We laugh, and trade stories back and forth about men. She tells me about a friend she had in her second year who had a stalker, some guy from the debating building who would follow her to the bus stop. For some reason this is funny to us, possibly because if it's not funny, it's too horrible.

She shows me some messages she's received on dating apps and social media sites and says, 'The thing is, the more obsessed a man is with his penis, the less good he is at sex.'

I can't help but feel a bit sad that I'm never on the receiving end of any of these horrible messages and wonder if that means I'm ugly. It feels like something all women experience, except for me. I'm shocked at myself; I think my values are unshakable, but these feelings rise, seemingly, out of nowhere. In truth, I've deleted every dating app I've ever downloaded. The anxiety of staring at my own

195

face and life story repackaged to be as appealing as possible has always driven me away.

'The trouble is,' says Lucy, 'that the bar for men is so low, too low nearly, and yet . . .' she trails off.

And yet.

People wake up in dribs and drabs, and we spend the morning reading various media in the house. Steph's reading the *New Yorker*, which she says she likes because it makes her feel smart without challenging her beliefs in any way. I refresh Twitter, staring patiently at the loading screen until the words start to appear, and think it's the same thing.

'But surely having your beliefs challenged is the only way to be sure that you actually believe them?' Rory's voice sets me on edge.

'Spoken like a straight white man, my friend,' replies Steph. Rory exhales air as a precursor to whatever he's going to say, but Steph cuts him off and says, 'I don't need pain to feel pleasure, I don't need bad days to make the good days, yada yada yada. I can believe things without having to debate literal fascists over them. Stop being an edgelord and playing devil's advocate.'

Rory looks at me in an imploring way, but I can't save him from her.

'Don't worry, she's always like this,' Pearse says to Rory, as though we can't hear him.

When Grace rouses herself into a conscious state, she announces we'll be walking down to the beach. She throws a towel at my head, and I know I can't argue with her. I'd brought some togs down with me, at Grace's instruction, but I haven't mentally prepared myself for actually wearing them.

196

Pearse says, 'But we've already been to the beach.'

'There's nothing else to do down here, idiot.' Steph says 'idiot' the way some people say 'honey'.

Someone goes to wake Finn, who still hasn't shown his face. The others busy themselves getting ready for the day, and I stand for a moment amidst them, not thinking about Finn.

The sun is just about bright enough to justify it, the Irish summer as ever holding out on us. The walk down to the beach is lovely. The hedgerows are full of wild-flowers and brambles, and the road is lined with people enjoying their holidays. Steph and Pearse are arguing loudly, and Finn is kicking a football. I ask Grace if she thinks I could afford a house down here, since it's prob-ably much cheaper than Dublin.

'Yeah, but then you'd have a house down here,' she says, as though it would be a bad thing, and she doesn't already have a house down here. I imagine what my life would be like if I allowed it to play out in this place.

The beach is empty when we arrive, no one else deeming it nearly nice enough to test the waters. Swimming in the Atlantic is an endurance activity I've learnt to avoid willingly partaking in. I sit down on a beach towel, and Rory sits down next to me.

'Not going in?' he asks me, and then, 'That's okay, I'll keep you company.'

'Of course she's coming in, she's no choice,' Grace says, and she eyes Rory suspiciously. 'No boys, remember?' she whispers, just to me. It seems easiest to go along with her. Rory shrugs, takes off his shirt, and heads down to the water.

Taking off my clothes makes me nervous. I approach

the water, letting it wash over my feet. It's ice cold, somehow colder than it was last night.

Finn says, 'Nice togs, Soph,' and I blush.

It seems unlikely no one can see how my body morphs around the swimsuit. When I look down at myself, it's all I can see. I don't have the cover of night or the joy of the plankton to hide behind today. I wade out until the water touches my waist and dunk my head under.

'Jesus, that was fast,' Rory says.

I think about saying that's not the only thing I'm fast at, just to see how Finn might react, but he's talking to Grace and no longer paying attention to me.

I float in the water long enough to get used to the burning chill, to feel comfortable in it, and then I get out. My whole body is numb with cold, and I can't feel it.

I watch the others from the safety of my beach towel, and for the first time don't wonder what they might be talking about. I let the feeling of the air wash over me.

After a while, they come out, shivering from the cold.

'Worth it,' says Grace, who has a flask of tea.

'Almost worth it,' says Lucy, who doesn't.

I close my eyes, nothing but white static playing in my mind. The boys and Lucy kick the football around, and I hear it evidently end up in the waves and someone go out to get it. Grace and Steph make fun of the players, their chatter a running commentary. I eat the sandwich I'm given slowly, imagining each bite making its way to my stomach. My body is cold, but I barely inhabit it. Eventually, we leave the beach. Back at the house, Grace keeps us to a strict shower schedule so the hot water doesn't run out. Somehow, I'm last and left with a luke-warm drip. I contort my body under the showerhead, goosebumps prickling my arms.

By the time I've dried off and changed, Finn has started making dinner. He's a spectacle, putting on a show just for me. He asks me to peel the potatoes for him, so I sit at the counter and watch him as I do it.

Rory doesn't approach me, but I keep catching him looking at me. He doesn't look away from me when I catch him, and that feels indecent somehow. As I sit at the counter peeling the potatoes, my phone screen lights up with a message from him. I look around, and he's deep in conversation with Pearse. I turn the phone upside down so I can pretend I haven't seen it and to prevent Finn from seeing it. The whole scene feels like a play, like everyone has lines and stage movements practised and I'm sitting in the centre of it all: an immersive audience experience.

The girls are sitting at the table, a bottle of wine open between them, and they don't offer me a glass. The normal thing to do would be to pour myself one, to assert some sense of dominance over the scene, but I don't think that's the role my character's supposed to play. Instead, I pick up another potato. It's half rotten on the inside, and I show it to Finn.

'Throw it out,' he says and returns his attention to the pot he's stirring.

It sparks a moment of panic inside of me, to see the blackened potato, like somehow the blight's back. I can't bring myself to throw it out.

'I don't think we'll starve for lack of one potato, and even if the blight is back, our supply chains are good enough, and we don't have the Brits taking all our food this time. There wasn't a famine in Ireland, it was manufactured.'

I think what I'm feeling is intergenerational trauma. Finn shakes his head at me and asks me if I'm done with the rest of the potatoes yet.

I chop them into small pieces, all the while wondering about the word 'trauma'. I keep turning it over and over in my mind, thinking about the pieces of our lives we hand down to the next generation, and the pieces of our lives we give away to others. I poke at my own trauma, wondering if it can even be called trauma, if it's too insignificant.

All of these feelings, I put into the potatoes, until Finn takes them away from me and puts them in the oven, and I can't help but feel like I'm handing over some of these thoughts to him as well, as though that's what's at the heart of our relationship. He takes away and absorbs the bits of myself I don't like, and I feel lighter for it. I'm aware that my affection for him is growing, and he hasn't done anything at all to spark it. I consider confiding in him for a moment, but figure he would get too much satisfaction from it.

I sit down next to Grace, and she passes me a glass of wine. She's arguing with the others about the ethics of the deep web, but what they really mean is the dark web. The deep web is the parts of the internet that search engines can't readily access, while the dark web is where you can buy drugs and hire hitmen.

Steph says, 'Oh, of course you'd know that,' and I put my hands up in defence. I recently listened to a podcast on the topic. I frame it as though I'm the one who's at

fault for spending my free time consuming endless information, and not them who've just had an extensive argument
about something none of them really know anything
about. This, I feel, is my role in the play. I finish off my
glass of wine.

Rory sets the table around us and then sits down next
to me. He grabs my hand under the table, and I playfully
hit it away, hoping that Finn, who is bringing the food
out, doesn't notice. I don't want to spoil what had, admittedly, been an entirely self-indulgent moment.

The food is delicious. I keep my eyes on my plate to
avoid making prolonged eye contact with anyone and
inviting them to ask me a question about what I'm thinking
or feeling.

There's a lot of wine flowing; nearly everyone's brought
a bottle or two to thank Grace for hosting. I'm on the
red, and the ashy taste is beginning to spread warmth
throughout my body. The more I drink, the more I feel
as though I'm estranged from the evening, like I'm
watching a soap opera with the TV screen separating me
from everyone else, preventing me from making an impression on them.

I'm trapped by the concept of the present, by the idea
that time is moving forward and I'm witnessing it. I take
several sips of wine to quell this rising feeling, but it
doesn't help. Rory brushes his leg against mine under the
table, and I make direct eye contact with Finn. He winks
at me. I feel hot, as though I'm under a spotlight.

Grace says, 'Does anyone remember Megan?'

Megan's a girl that we spent all of freshers' week with,
before she vanished off into the drama society the following
semester, never to be seen again. She'd insisted on going

out every night and chasing the taste of the evening with several Beroccas mixed into a naggin. I know people sometimes buy drugs from her, but that's the extent of my knowledge of her comings and goings. She's another person who once burned brightly in my life who I've completely lost touch with. I can't remember who I was when she was important to me. There have been so many versions of myself since that time. Too many versions.

I feel shut out of the conversation and light-headed. The wine is beginning to taste like water, and my mouth is dry. My hand shakes as I pour another glass.

'I still see her sometimes!' Lucy says. 'She's on my train home. I have her on Facebook as well. I think she recently got kicked off the voluntourism thing she was on?'

'How do you even get kicked off one of those?'

'I don't know, but hey, at least she managed to get something resembling a job!' Lucy tips her glass to mine and says, 'To unemployment, eh?'

I excuse myself to go to the bathroom.

The tiles are cool against my hand, and I stumble my way towards the sink. I'm more drunk than I'd thought. My head is rushing, and without conscious thought I find I'm lying on the bathroom floor. It's so cool here. I fixate on the little pattern of blue along the wall, and try my best to count the tiles. I keep losing count after seven.

I decide I'll feel better if I vomit, and so I do. Chunks of potato come up, along with a significant amount of red wine, and my head feels clearer. It looks like blood in the toilet bowl, and I try to connect it to some kind of potato-based Famine metaphor, but nothing makes it seem any less pathetic. I flush the toilet.

I get up and look at myself in the mirror. The force

of my vomiting has brought tears to my eyes, and I wipe at them, trying my best to keep my make-up intact. I wash my mouth out with water and a little bit of tooth-paste on my finger and decide I'm fit to return to the others. I'd be surprised if anyone notices anything is amiss.

When I open the door, Rory's there. 'Hey,' he says quietly, 'are you okay? You seemed a little bit off.' I smile at him, at his warmth, and I hug him. I need the cradle of his safety. I need the rhythm of our connection; I want to scroll through the screenshots of our conversations that I've saved.

He bends his head down to kiss me, and I kiss him back. It's warm and soft and nice, and it makes me feel warm and soft and nice. He pushes me against the wall, and I'm drowning in the kiss. I can't breathe. Something is digging painfully into my back, but Rory doesn't release me. It's all swirling away from me, and I'm a tiny presence in my head. He has his hand against my neck, choking me, and suddenly his other hand is inside my top.

'I've been waiting for us to be alone together,' he says in my ear, his body pinning me to the wall so tightly I can feel every part of him. Some primal part of my brain wakes up, and I connect his pleasure to my pain, and I am afraid. Very, very afraid.

I can't think. My vision lights up with a thousand stars. He's not giving me enough air to breathe. He's crossing lines I never thought he'd cross. I push back against him and try to move away, but he's everywhere. I don't want this; I've never wanted this. He is consuming me.

I fumble with the handle of the master bedroom and get it open. He seems surprised at that and bites my lip. It's painful, and I can taste blood. He releases my throat, and then it all stops. I take one shuddering breath and push against his chest with both hands. He goes stumbling back a step.

There are tears in my eyes, and I can't breathe.

'I thought this was what you wanted? I thought this was okay?' He looks genuinely confused.

Something resembling my voice says that he's not allowed into the master bedroom, it's Grace's parents room, and I slam the door between us. It's only when I hear his footsteps moving away that I start to cry properly.

It feels like my sanctuary has been ripped away from me. My body is not my own; my brain isn't connected to it any more. A moment ago I'd been full of tense energy, but now I'm deflated.

I lie on the bed under the covers with the lights off. I left my phone at the dinner table, and I miss it now. I still want to read through the screenshots of my conversations with Rory and pretend I still inhabit those times. I watch the light of the crack twist and turn in the night sky, and I remember the plankton. I hear a few people joking outside and imagine smoke curling up and away from their perfect figures.

I feel empty, like a car that's run out of petrol. In my mind, Rory was the safe option, the nice option, the shy guy who respected me. That image has come to a shuddering halt. He's taken away any control I had over our relationship. He's made me realise that I'm powerless in a way that I didn't know it was possible to feel.

The door cracks open and I jump, but it's only Grace. 'Sophie? Are you in here?' I make non-committal noises and open up the covers for her. She slides in next to me. 'Are you okay? You never came back after you left to go to the bathroom, and we thought maybe you'd just gone for a nap or something.'

She flicks on the bedside light, and I imagine she sees me there like a corpse, with glassy eyes. 'Hey,' she says. She brushes a strand of hair out of my face. 'What happened?'

I swallow painfully; I can feel my throat beginning to bruise. My voice cracks as I try to speak, to tell her that Rory had done something, maybe nothing, maybe *something*. I'm unintelligible, speaking through a fog. I can still feel Rory's hands on me. Something that I'd once wanted, once idly fantasied about, suddenly makes me feel like I'm dead.

'What happened to your lip? And your neck?' Her voice goes from concern to anger. She jumps out of bed and turns on the overhead light. She takes me in, and I feel the need to cover up, like I'm indecent. In straightening out my T-shirt, I notice that the seam has split on one side. 'Did Finn do this?' It's not a whisper, it's more like a scream that is forced out between tight lips.

I shake my head.

'Rory?' she says back at me. She nods slowly, so slowly it scares me. I can't hear any words coming out of my mouth.

'I do not want that bastard in my house,' is all she says.

I've never seen Grace look so angry. Looking at her is exhausting, so I roll over in the bed and pull the covers up to my neck. I feel Grace tuck me in tightly, and her presence leave the bed. She turns off the light and closes the door.

I feel like a child, like Grace is my mother. I reflect upon all the times she's sheltered me. I've often felt overshadowed and powerless, some addendum to her personality. I'm grateful for that now, because it means that I don't have to have a personality of my own. I don't need to be myself when Grace takes charge.

What happens next comes to me in snippets. I hear something shatter, and then silence. I hear Grace yelling, and ripples of sounds trying to calm her down. Rory's voice saying lots of, 'I just thought,' and, 'I thought she,' which I think is funny, because I now see he's never done any thinking in his life. More shattering. A door slamming. The sound of a car engine.

Grace comes back into the room. She hands me a mug of tea in a hand with a crisp white bandage on it, and I wonder what that means.

I'm asleep before I finish my tea.

18

I wake up sometime before the sun rises. Grace isn't asleep beside me, and I dimly wonder where she is. I've usurped her claim to the master bedroom, and I hope she won't be mad at me because of it. I search for my phone in the folds of the duvet and under the pillows, but I don't have it.

It takes me a moment to remember what happened last night. I slept dreamlessly, and it feels as though I'm emerging from a fog. When I open the curtains in the bedroom I see that a dense fog has indeed rolled in from across the sea, as though the entire landscape has been swallowed by a cloud. I can't be sure that it hasn't, and I want so dearly for it to have been.

My stomach is growling so I get out of bed, only to realise I'm still wearing my ripped shirt. I shrug on a cardigan Grace left on the floor and walk down to the kitchen. It's eerily quiet, and the grey morning light makes everything look cold. I shiver. My phone is on the table, and when I click it on, my lock screen is full of messages. I don't have the energy to read them; scrolling through them is hard enough. When I unlock my phone, the internet connection isn't strong enough to download them.

I sit and stare at the notification bubbles, and I want to scream.

I walk around the room waiting for my toast and try to piece together what might have happened last night. I prevent myself from thinking about my part in the situation, and try to examine the events in abstract, as though they happened to someone who, despite looking and talking like me, is not in fact me.

The dustpan and brush are leaning against the wall, observing the scene. There's a brownish stain on the skirting that someone's dabbed at. When I open the bin, I see the remains of a broken glass. Dread pervades my body. I remember Grace's bandaged hand and piece the rest of it together.

I eat my toast and watch the sun begin to rise, burning away some of the night's fog. The rosy glow is competing with the light of the crack, turning the sky a shade of fuchsia. It isn't scary at this hour. The crack keeps changing, but it hasn't killed us yet, and that thought is comforting. Although, if it did kill us, that would be okay too.

It hurts to chew and swallow, but I do it anyway. I play with the crumbs on my plate, swirling them in different patterns, trying my best to think about nothing at all. I contemplate challenging myself to eat the entire loaf of bread, just to see if I can, but for once I think that eating won't be the solution to the yawning emptiness inside me.

I don't know how I was so wrong about Rory. We'd talked about men on our dates. He'd laughed when I told him about the woke misogynist, the proud feminist man who uses the language of social justice to manipulate women into sleeping with him. He'd told me he hated how unaware some of his friends were, how he'd taught them about consent. And yet I'd never once wondered how he could be so close with Pearse. I flick through the old messages I have saved now, trying to understand.

After I'd sent him an article about another woman who'd been killed by her partner in what the media called 'sex games gone wrong', he'd said:

that's actually disgusting
i hate how many men think that's what normal sex is

He had all these woke things to say about sex work, respecting women's bodies and the harmful normalising effects of the porn industry. I'd listened to him uncritically, never once thinking he could be lying, When I run out of anguish to feel, there is anger, and when I run out of anger, there is nothing.

I run everything I remember him saying to me through my head, combing each sentence to find the thread where the lies began. It's my fault; I should never have made the mistake of trusting him in the first place. I should never have let myself want to be wanted. I want to tweet this feeling, but I stop myself.

When I go to shower, I see my bruises for the first time. The cluster of fingermarks on my neck are indistinguishable from hickeys. I scrub at them with soap, but I know I can't wash them away. My bottom lip is bruised; it looks like I've been in a fight.

I think about what the others would say, if they saw, and what they know. I don't know how to tell them; what words are available to me to talk about this. I don't want to think about what Rory said to them, but I already know what he's going to say. It's so easy for men to say that they made a mistake; it's so much harder when you're a woman and forced to be the mistake. I try to come up with a list of off-the-cuff remarks I can employ when they ask me about it, but I find it impossible to imagine a future beyond this agonising present.

The scene beyond the window is serene. I watch clouds move across the hills on the other side of the bay, the light and shadow playing with perspective. The crack is huge in the sky, and I feel so small. I walk to the window and press my head against the cold glass. It's only then that I notice Finn asleep on the couch, which is facing away from the kitchen.

He looks cold, curled up in a ball. His grandfather's coat is crumpled beneath his head. Seeing him here, while I feel like this, is like something from a dream, or a nightmare. I take one of the blankets from an armchair and lay it across him. His eyes open, and I sit down with my back against him.

'Hey,' he whispers, and I echo him. 'I spoke to Grace, she told me . . . she told us about that bastard.' He shakes his head, and I don't move. I can't move. I swallow. I wonder what Grace told him, and I'm grateful she did so I don't have to test out the words myself.

'Do you want to talk about it?'

I do, but I don't have the words to do it. My tongue won't form them. Finn takes my hand in his, and I watch him do it. My fingers feel heavy and numb. His hand is warm. He traces circles across my knuckles with his thumb.

'I'll kill him, if you want me to. I'll end him. I thought you had something nice going for once.' The severity of his tone shocks me. I'm distantly aware that these words should mean something to me, but they don't. I'm swimming through a current of meaning and being swept away.

I squeeze his hand in mine, and this, at least, is nice.

'It is,' he says, 'but you know what I mean. Something real.'

Of course. His touch feels real, the feeling of his chest expanding and contracting as he breathes feels real, but it's not. I can't quite comprehend what's going on. I've forgotten my lines.

I don't want Rory any more, at all. But part of me still wants what he represents, and that disgusts me. I want what Finn won't give me, and it's ruining me. My thoughts have shattered; they exist only in fragments, and I cut myself whenever I try to grasp one.

I don't think he thinks I'm real.

'No, I'm pretty sure you're real.' He brings my hand to his lips and kisses it.

I'm real, and he's real, but we can't be real together.

I move away from him, scooting to the very edge of the sofa. I want to look at him one last time like this, to feel as though it could be natural to look at him and have him see me.

He looks bemused; his hair is ruffled.

He tells me that Lucy suggested they all check into the local B&B for the night because Grace didn't want anyone to stay. He tells me the mood shifted considerably when Rory left sporting a black eye. He looks at me sideways when he says that, and I don't think it was Grace who punched Rory. I trace bruises on his knuckles. He stayed when everyone else left.

'Yeah, I just thought, I don't know, I wanted to be

here if you needed me. I stayed on the couch in case you reappeared, and I must have fallen asleep.'

I need him, like this, right now. The problem is I can't need him any more. I don't want to stop being with him, but I can't be with him. I just need the world to slow down. I'm a little bit surprised when the words come out of my actual mouth. It might have been better to wait, to hold off on saying anything until I could type it out in a message, perhaps with Grace's help. But that no longer feels authentic, and I want Finn to see me as I authentically am.

He asks, 'So friends at least? You know you're my best friend.'

I smile, which is as much as I can muster. All the lines feel so blurred right now. I'm not sure about anything.

He nods and tells me he understands so many times it punctuates my sentences for me. And to his credit, he does look like he understands. The thread that weaves us together loosens, and I feel like crying once again. *Space,* he calls it.

He says he's going to get a lift back to Dublin with Pearse, that he'd rather be back early, but he can stay later if Grace needs his help to clean up. 'I think Pearse is a bit spooked by the whole thing, if I'm being honest, and he wants to leave.' He shows me some messages Pearse sent him. It's pretty clear things won't be progressing any further between him and Steph, but I find it hard to muster myself into caring.

I want so badly to tell Finn to stay, to take it all back, to rewind the clock to twenty-four hours ago, or several weeks ago, to a point where I could be honest with him that he's what I want. All of him.

He heads off, and I hand him some food for the journey; we have so many leftovers.

'You're always thinking about food, aren't you?' He says it with a smile, but it doesn't make me feel any better.

I clean the kitchen and take out the bins, erasing the evening's physical presence. I want to take out my phone and scroll through Twitter to dull the noise in my head, but I'm afraid of what I'll discover when I open it. I don't want to see anyone sub-tweeting me, or worse, messaging me directly. I think about reaching out to Dan, but I know it would break his heart more than it's broken mine. I turn the phone off and put it into my bag without looking at it.

In the end, I wait for Grace to wake up, and then we drive home. The CDs in the car no longer hold the same meanings, so we sit in silence for a while, neither of us sure what to say. I look at Grace's bandaged hand, much neater than how I'd bandaged my hand during my birthday party. It turns out there are some things she's willing to sacrifice for me, after all.

Somewhere around Moneygall, Grace turns to me and says, 'Do you want to talk about it?'

It's not so much about wanting, but needing, and yet I'm unable to. As she pulls off the motorway, I point at the billboard in Obama Plaza in the hopes of distracting her, but she's wise to so many of my tactics.

'We should talk about it, about what happened, I think it would be good for you to talk about it.'

I don't know where to begin, what to even call it. I wonder, idly, if it would have been better if what he'd done to me had been worse. If I could give it a fright-ening name that would make people feel like they had to whisper around me. It would stop me from wondering if it had just been normal. Maybe it had been normal.

'No, stop. Stop spiralling. I don't want you to rationalise all this in your head as okay, as normal, okay? Because women do that all the time. And it's fine to cry, or be angry, or feel nothing at all. But regardless, this shouldn't have happened to you.'

I let her words echo through me, hoping they will resonate in some hollow place.

'Are you hurt?'

It's a curious question. I've detached myself from the physicality of the situation. I'm numb to it; my body no longer aches. Already, I feel as though it hadn't *really* been that bad. I know women who've had it worse.

My mind wanders to what might have happened if I hadn't been able to shut the bedroom door, if we'd been alone, if I didn't have Grace. Maybe I'd been too quick to startle, to push him away. Maybe it's my fault.

'This isn't your fault,' she says, but she can't know that. She wasn't there. I was barely there.

'No, I absolutely can know it. If it was normal, you wouldn't feel this way.' But she doesn't know how I feel.

'I'm so sorry this happened to you, and I'm sorry none of us stopped it. We should've seen through Rory. Last night, Steph was telling us some stories from when they were in first year together, and he got away with treating some girls like absolute shit just because he's charming. We should have seen through him. It's not only you he fooled.'

Grace has tears in her eyes. I've never seen her like this before.

'This isn't normal. Or it shouldn't be fucking normal,

even though it is. Every woman knows another woman who has been assaulted, or raped, or harassed at work. Every single woman. But I bet if you ask a man if he knows a rapist, or a harasser, he'll say he doesn't. Finn didn't tell us about Rory. Pearse didn't tell us. And we're supposed to believe they didn't know? I'm so sick of it.'

I know that what she's saying is true, but I still find it hard to accept. Pearse didn't know about me and Rory, and I'd always led Finn to believe I was in control; I'd thought I was. Everything Grace lists are causes I fight for, slogans I chant, and things I march to end. They're not things that happen to me.

'They're things that happen to all of us.'

My understanding of Rory, and the world, has been overturned in a single night. I think about the conversation Grace and I had so many weeks ago, about uncertainty and insecurity. Rory had let me believe, for a moment, in the concept of certainty.

'And I will kill him for taking that away from you,' Grace says to me.

We drive the rest of the way home in a heavy silence.

19

I've signed up to that diploma in digital marketing. All of the lectures are pre-recorded, so I've been burning through them when I run out of other content to consume. The professor doesn't have the same charm as Rick or Vanessa, but I am less worried for her safety. She doesn't look like she's going to be incinerated any time soon.

I have a lot of unread messages from Rory. Every time I open my phone I see the red notification bubble. Several times, I've opened my phone to message him out of habit before I've been able to stop myself.

I've been learning more about the algorithms that control me; I'm taking a module in them. Rather than solidifying my grip on reality, the more I learn about them, the more I feel like I have no free will. I know now that they feed me whatever they think will keep my attention, keep me clicking. It's not an accident that I want to message Rory. I've been trained by my phone to do so.

I'm desperate to talk to someone, but my messaging apps now feel tainted. I don't know who's on my side. I can't even face Grace's matter-of-factness. She gives too many names to things that I don't want to confront. Her unread messages stack up in my inbox, amongst other unhappy company.

I'm listening to a lecture at double speed and refreshing my feed when it happens. There's a sound like paper being ripped in two, and an explosion of light fills my room. Dogs start barking, and I still can't see.

I blink, my eyes watering, and my vision comes back. My whole room is violet. I rush to the window, and where the crack had been there's now only purple. It's as bright as noon, but when I check my phone it's still the middle of the night. I can't see the moon any more, but I know it's supposed to be full.

Someone screams, and I want to join them. Tears start falling from my eyes. Deep down, through all the doom-scrolling, this is what I've feared. This is what I've been waiting for, even though no one had predicted it. Something is happening, I knew something had to happen. There's almost a relief in being right, in having my anxiety justified. It's like all of my unease flows out of me and puddles somewhere around my feet; without it, I'm empty.

I reach for my phone. No one I know is awake; no one has any cause to be. I try to call Grace, but she doesn't answer. My room feels smaller. The walls are closing in on me. I can't breathe. I can't think.

People are tweeting strings of nonsense, or single words all in caps. Each tweet beats through me like a drum. I need someone to tell me what's going on. The crack was never insubstantial, it's all been building up to this moment. I just need to know how bad it's going to be so I can start to prepare for it. I'm almost giddy, high on a sense of purpose. I watch it start to trend, first five thousand tweets, then twenty thousand, then over a million. I scroll, barely aware of the words I'm reading.

And just like that, the light fades. My room is dark again, and it's hard to remember how it had looked bathed in purple light. I begin to think I imagined it, but the tweets are still there.

Out the window, the crack is back. It quivers and coils in the sky, the same as it was the day before: back to normal. I'm deflated, elated, not sure what to think. Online there's already talk of a false alarm from those monitoring the crack. It was just a freak event. I get back into bed and close my eyes. I can't tell if I fall asleep, or just lie still for a few hours.

The next day is a blur. I spend hours in bed, scrolling. No one can explain what happened last night. The best theory I see is that the crack was discharging built-up static electricity. Someone describes it as similar to a prolonged lightning strike. No one I know was awake when it happened, so none of my friends are talking about it, and I'm afraid to reach out to them.

The usual arguments unfold on Twitter: people say I told you so; people post detailed threads about why there's nothing to be afraid of; people make memes involving dogs and skeletons and lightning flashes. It's so expected, so ordinary, so boring.

When I check my notifications, Rory has liked a meme I retweeted. Suddenly, I'm no longer panicking about just the crack any more. I touch my neck. My bruises have only just faded.

I eat dinner with my parents, and they don't notice anything is wrong. They're not interested in talking about the crack; as far as they're concerned, everything is normal.

'They said it was nothing on the radio,' says Mum, as though that's that.

Dad asks me how my friends are to prove that he's not worried about the sky any more, and not out of real interest. It's my turn to deflect.

I am glad that Hannah's come back from Glasgow with enough conversational content to fill any gap that might have let them know I'm in the process of slowly becoming another piece of furniture.

'We went to this pasta place we used to go to all the time, it was unreal,' and, 'I missed the campus!' and, 'Why don't we have a Greggs in Ireland yet?' It's all word soup. I barely need to be present. I eat a lot. I eat until I'm so disgusted with myself, the only thing I can do is eat more.

The ground under me is uncertain. It feels as though I'm on drugs, unable to concretely trust my reality. I stay up late watching conspiracy theories and news coverage about the crack, as though I can consume myself into a fixed position. But the crack is unknowable; it defies all the structures of reality we have. It's an object so large and so utterly universe-changing that the only thing to do is to memeify it in the hopes of conquering it. I've moved a chair beside my window so I can more easily look at it.

I stop looking at the social internet and instead dive into more anonymous forums. I know that most of the theories I'm reading are made up by people with nothing better to do, writing from a very specific part of the world, but I need something to quench my thirst for information. I forget about my online diploma. It doesn't seem important any more; money doesn't seem important any more.

The crack is caused by climate change; the crack is

caused by nuclear power; the crack is caused by fracking; the crack is caused by China; the crack is caused by the subterranean lizard people; the crack is a hoax designed to take away the world's second amendment rights, even in countries without two amendments; the crack; the crack; the crack.

Days pass, and nothing changes. I comfort myself, at least a little, by thinking that if reality is so elastic that it can expand to include a crack in the sky, I can warm myself to my new reality as well.

I feel now, more than ever, that there's no past or future, and the present stretches on for ever.

My phone starts to ring. It's Grace.

'Hello? Sophie? Are you alive?' She sounds annoyed, 'I've been trying to reach you for ages.'

She doesn't want to hear about any of the posts I've been reading, even when I tell her about the really wild ones.

'Yeah, I've seen the videos, they said it was just static electricity, right? And it's back to normal now.'

She doesn't understand what it was like to witness the flash; for a brief moment I thought I was dying. I thought everyone was dying. It doesn't feel like things have gone back to normal. The crack is still there. It's still growing. I want to scream and cry and yell that this is not at all normal.

I listen to Grace update me on our mutual friends' lives until the actual reason she called me comes up. It starts to rain.

'I'm worried about you, anyway. I know everything with Rory was bad, but I don't want you to think that it defines you. I haven't seen you in ages. I miss you.'

I don't know how to tell her that Rory hadn't just been one guy, he'd been much more; he'd made me feel wanted, for a little while.

'I know it feels like this unique thing, it always does, and I don't want to diminish what you're feeling, because it's important and real, but I can assure you that thousands of women have gone through the same exact thing. I'm sure there's a support group somewhere. Google it.'

I have googled it; I've googled everything. That's how I found the parts of the internet I've been inhabiting for the past few days. I want her to move on from this topic of conversation. She asks me to meet her for drinks later, and I agree, thinking that I'll come up with some excuse closer to the time.

'Great, I'll see you later then. And don't think you can come up with some kind of excuse, I'll be able to tell! What kind of other plans could you have?'

She knows me too well.

I know they've all been talking about me, and I don't want to see any of them. Dan messaged me the other day:

Hey
What happened in Kerry?
Are you okay?

The red notification bubble still sits on my home screen. I don't know who told him, and I don't want to find out. I've seen the vague subtweets, and perhaps he has too. I've watched the story morph and grow, people I barely know twisting it until it fits nicely into their belief system. Someone I recognised as one of Steph's friends had tweeted, *if I'm friends with anyone problematic, message me and that will change.* I'd clicked into her profile and read through screenshots she'd posted. In them, she confronts Rory about his behaviour, but I have been reduced to 'that girl' who's 'obviously a bitch'. Every day I think about liking one or two of them, just to point out that I still exist, that I can see them. But I don't want to make drama by pointing out they're about me. That would rip them out of cyberspace and bring them into the real world.

'I can't stand subtweeting,' Grace says, 'but it's honestly just not worth the drama. Who cares about what those people think?'

I do. Everything on the internet has taken on new meanings now I know that it could be about me. Even things that could not possibly be about me feel weighed down with secret significance.

'Yeah, look, people gossip, and people have no backbones, and everyone knows everyone and thinks their opinion is valid, but that doesn't change who you are. Just because they take the path of least resistance doesn't mean you have to.'

Over the last few days I've seen people posting Instagram stories with Rory and tagging him in tweets. I can't help but feel that if there's any fallout from this at all, it's entirely directed at me. It's easier that way, for them. For some reason people feel that doing nothing is not a choice, that they can't be blamed for the fallout.

There's a lull in Grace's monologue, and I see my opening to end the conversation. She messages me after.

Look I'm really trying to be here for you, but you have to let me.

The buzzing in my head is almost painful, impossible to drown out. I try to listen to music or a podcast, but it doesn't help. Everything fills me with anxiety, and I have a lump in my throat. I can't even look up at the sky without being reminded that existence is transient, and we're all going to die. The crack is inescapable, and my world is being consumed by it. I'm just waiting for it to finally be over.

I run a bath, light a scented candle and open a bottle of wine. The hot water nearly feels like comfort. Mum knocks on the door and asks me if I'm okay, and I ignore her. Every time I read something online that threatens my grasp on reality, I take a swig straight from the bottle and put my phone face down on the floor. The crack really does look beautiful in the sunset.

Hannah knocks on the door and yells, 'Can you get out of there? I need to get something before I go out,' and I ignore her.

Half a bottle in and I begin to melt. I'm one with the water, and the wine no longer tastes acidic on my tongue. Grace calls me wondering where I am, and I find myself agreeing to meet her at the pub in an hour. I exist in a liminal space between sober and drunk, aware and unaware. I am perfect.

Like a robot, I dry my naked body, dress myself and put on make-up. Some adventurous part of me decides that eyeliner is like warpaint, so I slap it on. I am dreaming.

I finish the wine and arrive at the pub. I think there's a taxi in between. Grace is here, and so is everyone else. There are people I haven't seen since Grace's party, who I recognise only from their little circular profile pictures. They all blur together, unimportant. I wave at them and buy myself a drink. I can't see Rory, and I breathe a sigh of relief. I can't remember if this is a single or a double.

When I sit down at the table, I arrange myself into a sitting position that feels powerful in my mind. I find myself laughing a little bit too loudly, but I enjoy it. Everyone's attention on me is intense; I drink it up. It feels so much like I'm performing, and I'm performing well. My body somehow knows what to do, what they want me to do.

Every interaction is false, as though we carry between all of us a glass secret, and if anyone mentions it, it'll smash. Eventually, after a few drinks that make me feel confident, I edge the conversation towards who else will be joining us.

'Finn should be here soon, though I think he's meeting other people.'

I don't let this bother me. Finn's always had other friends.

'Actually,' someone says, it doesn't matter who, 'I think Rory will be here soon. Is that okay?'

It's a question that everyone knows the answer to, but it's more convenient to pretend that they don't.

I shrug in a careless way and excuse myself to get another drink. A small voice in the back of my mind whispers that I should slow down, but a louder one is screaming that I should do whatever I can to get through this evening. If I can get through this evening, I can get through any evening. I order a double. Grace meets me at the bar and asks me if I'm okay.

She says, 'I'm sorry, I didn't know he was coming when I invited you. We can leave if you want?' I can see the concern in her eyes, which makes me resolute. Of course

I'm fine. My throat feels tight. I wonder if they always go to the pub without me, and if this is why I'm never invited.

I hear Rory arrive. My whole body stiffens and stills, like rigor mortis setting in. I move my arms as though in slow motion, gesticulating randomly and trying to keep my train of thought. I can be indifferent. I carry my drink carefully back to the table, sipping when I can to avoid having to make eye contact or conversation. Everyone tenses around me, and it almost feels like power.

I notice Rory sitting opposite me, trying to catch my eye, but I pretend I can't see him. I look around mechanically. If he wants to talk to me, it's because he thinks there's something between us he can salvage, and if he thinks that then he doesn't understand the weight of what he's done. I feel phantom hands. I swallow around a lump in my throat and hate being a woman.

Lucy's sitting next to me. She leans close and whispers, 'I can tell him to leave, if you want.'

But I don't want her to; I don't want him to know that he's rattled me. I grip my glass tighter and laugh, in a careless way, the whole time imagining I am floating.

'Every guy I've ever slept with has tried to choke me. Did you know that?' I didn't. 'Porn's addled their brains so much that men actually think choking is normal, and not something they need enthusiastic consent for.' If she keeps talking I will cry, so I lean away from her and laugh again.

Something's about to shatter, and I don't want it to be me, not this time. Someone buys a round for the table, and I cheer with the others, determined not to let it affect me, to rise above it. I want to explode outwards, like the crack did; I want to do the shattering.

Rory looks at me, and I smile back at him, which catches him off guard. *Good.* I want another drink. In my mind I'm glamorous, seductive, irresistible, unobtainable.

The night meanders on, and we're dancing. Lights are flashing. I feel amazing. The beat moves fluidly through me, through my arms and out of my feet. Grace is here, and we are laughing. I've never laughed so much at anything. I spill a drink down my top and I'm soaked, drying myself in the bathroom. Someone yells that they love me, and I've never felt so whole in my entire life.

Vomit. On the pavement. Outside the nightclub. My hair is tied behind my head. McDonald's.

Home. Bed. Sleep.

20

My mouth tastes like cotton and bile. Opening my eyes is like cracking open a can, my whole vision fizzing. My brain doesn't record the time between being in bed and being on my knees in front of the toilet. I retch and only bile comes out, like big globs of sulphur. I'm crying. The whole world hangs around me, heavy and dark.

I can't remember coming home. Did I get a taxi? A sense of shame pervades my whole body, and I don't know why. My phone is clutched in my hand, cold. I'm sweating. I unlock the screen and see I have several missed calls from Grace, and a string of messages from her from throughout the night.

Where r u
?????

Im bathroom

Have you left??

Then, this morning:

Have you died yet?

not yet
but nearly

I retch again and wash my mouth out with water from the sink. It's warm and tastes thick.

I remember getting myself another drink so I wouldn't feel. I remember seeing Finn with someone, but I can't remember who. I resolve myself into not caring. The whole night is a blur. Looking at my phone, I see I tried to call Dan five times, but he didn't answer. I climb back in bed and decide it will be future Sophie's problem to deal with.

When I wake up, sometime later, I call Grace. I'm fragile and have to be treated gently.

'Yes, no wonder. You were absolutely trashed last night. I don't think I've ever seen a woman so eager for a vodka coke. And I don't think I've ever seen you vomit so much. I'm not sure we can go back there ever again, with the way the bouncers were looking at you.'

I laugh it off, which feels like my only option.

'And, yeah, you also sort of confronted Rory. I mean, not really, but also yes definitely.'

Everything in my body stops moving at that. I utter an affirmation which makes it clear that I don't remember any of it.

'I mean it was bad, but also you were dead right, but also it wasn't your hottest look. He was just leaving and then suddenly something came over you, and you called him entitled and a misogynist and also said you hoped no woman would ever touch him again. I think you also started going on about Taylor Swift for some reason?'

Snippets are coming back to me, like flashes of light in the dark. The reckless feeling inside of me had gushed out. I remember approaching him, gin glass in hand. I remember feeling like a queen, but looking at the memory again, I was just drunk.

'Yes, indeed you were. But you were also kind of iconic. You told him that he had no right to make women feel special just so he could make them feel vulnerable, that bit sticks out in my mind. You should put it on a shirt or something. You also said that you never wanted to see him again, and I mean fair enough.'

I decide that I don't care. At least Rory knows to leave me alone now.

Grace laughs and says, 'You certainly have a way with men. And I wouldn't worry about it too much if I were you. My memory is a little bit fuzzy as well, but the phrase "too pathetic to even be a soft boy" is burned into my memory.'

I feel discomfort at not remembering what she's describing. It's like being told stories about a child I'm responsible for.

She then reminds me that Finn had been out as well, not with us but with a group of school friends. She tells me she thinks he went home with some girl, and I don't react, although it feels like she's testing me. I refresh my social media to see if he's posted any clues anywhere; he hasn't.

We chat until suddenly I have to puke again, and when I do I feel much better. I hear the door open and Hannah saying she's brought some doughnuts from town, and I ignore her. One more nap and I'll be able to fully react to the day, at around three or so.

When I wake up again, I have a message from Rory. I don't want to read it, but it occupies my mind with a certain kind of buzzing. Eventually, after some googling, I install a Chrome extension that lets me read it without him knowing.

Each sentence is a stone that drops in my stomach.

Before anything else, I'm genuinely sorry that I made you feel uncomfortable like that. It was never my intention to do so, but you're right that it is totally my fault for making you feel that way, and I don't expect you to ever forgive me. I clearly misjudged our whole relationship, and I'm so so sorry for that. I'm generally sorry for having misjudged a lot of things. It's really hard having feelings for someone who doesn't like you back, but that's just life, and it's not an excuse for my behaviour.

It reads as though it's been drafted and redrafted over and over again until it sounds nothing like him. I wonder if he got some of his friends to help write it, and what he told them about me to make him sound like the good guy. His return to capitalisation feels like a betrayal somehow, like a wall that has been erected between us.

Then:

But I have to say that the way you acted was out of line, you embarrassed me in front of my friends and were totally irrational. I wanted us to talk about this maturely, but I'm not sure I'm going to be able to do that any more. I think we need some space.

I don't know how someone's view of the world can be so incorrect.

I lie in bed for a while, thinking and not thinking. Unthinking. It feels like hours pass, but time's ticking by slower and slower. I don't want to dignify it with a response.

I spend some time reading reddit for inspiration, mustering up righteous anger on a subreddit about relationships and personal problems. This is the corner of the internet that bitter people come to when they lose all hope. I open up so many tabs that I can't see which one I'm clicking into.

I send a screenshot of Rory's message to Grace. She tries to call me, but I decline it and message her that I don't want to talk. She sends me a voice message.

'I can't get over him, I mean really, really, his tone's so condescending. Did you catch the part where he says he's sorry for *making you feel* uncomfortable, as though it's the act of you feeling that's the problem? Honestly, it's so textbook misogynist I don't even want to talk about it. And maturely? He wanted to talk about this maturely? That ship sailed the moment he fucking shoved you into a wall. Also how fucking cliché is it to call a woman irrational? I'm screaming.' I play it several times, until the words start to make sense to me.

After some consideration, I turn my read receipts on again and open the message. I ponder the efficacy of the humble thumbs up, or a gif of someone giving the finger, and then decide to just leave it blank.

I open up Twitter and see that Rory's tweeted something vague about someone who's overreacted to him just trying to show affection. He follows up with the

231

shock revelation that they also cheated on him. Reading it causes a shiver to go through my whole body. I can't believe he has the audacity to put something like that out into the world. I don't know who told him about Finn – it was probably Pearse – but I don't care if his feelings are hurt. We were never exclusive, we'd never had that conversation.

Rory knows what happened, he says he's sorry for it, and yet that hasn't stopped him from trying to publicly claim the narrative. It takes all my willpower to not reply to his tweet and give him the satisfaction.

Instead, I scroll methodically through all the replies, trying to see if any of our mutual friends have anything to say about it. People add to the thread, and it's like I can see the group chats whirring. The same people react to and retweet each other as soon as they post; they've probably run a few drafts of each tweet by their focus group, countless people poring over screenshots of Rory's tweets.

Steph messages me:

Hey Sophie just checking in, I hope you're okay.
I know you're upset but it might be best to just let it
go. The whole thing is really awkward for everyone.
And the thing with Finn wasn't fair to Rory, he's really
upset . . .

I leave her on read as well, and ignore the follow-up messages she sends me. Multiple people are typing to me, the hive of social media buzzing. I close the app, but messages start scrolling across the top of my screen.

hi sophie . . .

Soph, look . . .

Okay, I just want you to know . . .

I'm drowning.

Rory's post is gaining traction amongst people I don't know, and plenty of people are calling me a bitch or saying I'm behaving like a classic manipulative woman. My body is hot, and I want to be sick. No matter how many times I refresh the app, there isn't enough content generated to hide their replies.

I call Grace in tears, unable to say exactly what's happening, so I send her screenshots. They're concrete facts that I don't have to explain, and I hope she'll read them in the same way I do. An errant ellipsis or question mark can totally change the tone of a message, and I might be reading too much into it.

She's fuming. I listen as she drafts message after message, totally detached from how they relate to me. She's articulating things that I'm not sure I'm feeling, but they sound righteous and pure.

'Okay, I'm going to come across as very calm,' she says, but she's not calm. 'You can't argue with calm. I'm going to ask him why he thinks this is an acceptable way to treat a person. Maybe just that? But I actually want to fucking ruin him, so maybe I should go harder? Call him a fucking prick who pretends to care about consent and feminism but actually doesn't? Okay, hang on, I'm just going to send it.'

I picture the message in my mind's eye and hold it there. I hear the sent noise, and then wait.

'Fucking prick! He says he doesn't know what I'm talking about, and, hold on, he's telling me that he thinks I'm being rude? Me? Fuck off.'

I'm exhausted. I don't want to deal with this any more, and that's enough to unfollow him. It feels like a particular betrayal, as though Twitter was our space and it's now corrupted.

'Go for it, Soph, it's for the best,' Grace says in my ear.

I hope he notices, that he's refreshing my profile wondering what I'm thinking, as I'm doing with his. The post is only gaining more traction. It's being ratioed, presumably because no one wants to like it, but the comments aren't in my favour. I wish I could remove him from my life with the same ease. Our relationship has only really existed online, has never really worked in person, so unfollowing him feels like tearing our connection in two.

I need to reclaim cyberspace. I need people to believe me.

'Are you sure you're ready for this drama? I mean, I support you fully, but just so you know, there will be drama.'

I want to argue with her that it's not me who's the source of the drama, but I know that's not what she meant. I want to be reckless. I begin to methodically like tweets that I know are about me, and with each one I feel more powerful. I decide to tweet this feeling, and I don't care if people like it. Grace tells me that I might as well get it all out. I am relieved afterwards, like I've finally set the record straight.

I get my first DM after I hang up the phone. It's from someone I don't know, but who's following Rory.

Why did you lead Rory on?
Are you just a fucking slut?

My world is collapsing, like I'm in a paper bag that someone is sucking all the air out of. I don't want to reply, but I can't stop myself.

how can i be a slut and also lead someone on?
surely sluts are easy

They're not usually ugly either.

My response isn't as strong as it sounded in my head. I suppose that this guy, who is holding a dead fish in his profile picture, doesn't spend a lot of time weighing the significance of words and whether or not it is possible to reclaim slurs. It doesn't matter if what he says is true or makes sense; that was never the point of his message. I block him, but he's not the only one who messages me.

Can't take a joke can you?

You're the reason men hate women.

I can't stop refreshing things, just to check on them, to see how many people think I'm awful. None of the comments make much sense, and it seems like some trolls or bots have picked up on the hate and are fuelling it. I know that these things happen in the abstract, but I've never thought they could happen to me.

I've always used social media as a way of distracting myself from my immediate present, but now it serves only to remind me of my recent past. My escape route to reality has closed up. I get several notifications that there have been attempts to sign in on my account. I get three Facebook requests before I turn everything on private.

Eventually, when I can't cry or laugh hysterically any more, I message Rory.

you are a horrible person
i regret ever trusting you
and i hope no one ever does again

I block him on all platforms before he can reply, so I get the last word. It feels like cutting off my own arm. I can barely see my phone through my tears, and I bite down on my duvet to stop the sobs that threaten to overcome me.

I make a thread of all the things that have been messaged to me, and tag the boys responsible. I ask if anyone knows who their mothers are and if they can pass it on, then I delete all the apps and turn off my phone. It's the only way to make it stop. I can't understand how I've become the bad guy in this situation, and how Rory has so easily dominated the narrative. Even I'm beginning to feel guilty about how I treated him, which makes me cry harder.

None of my friends have taken my side, which I don't understand; they've known me longer, or at least I thought they had. Maybe they've all been hanging out with Rory without me. Apparently, it's easier to allow me to suffer than to call him out. He's lost nothing from this, and I've lost everything.

I remember, at the back of my mind, talking to Lucy about men online and wondering if the fact that I hadn't attracted hate and unsolicited sexual images meant I was ugly. Now, I know how stupid that desire had been.

I delete the screenshots from my phone, and it nearly feels like I'm deleting the memory. I wait until I'm in the shower before I let myself cry properly, so that no one will hear me. I cry like a wounded animal, and the water runs cold before I leave.

21

I haven't seen anyone for a week. I keep my phone off and in the bottom drawer of my bedside table. It's peaceful, and dull, but I need dull. I don't miss social media, although my fingers are bored and looking for something to do. I pour myself into my online diploma and finish watching all of the lectures in the span of two days. The information sits on the surface of my mind, and I take the exam in a dream state. I don't care if I pass.

Afterwards, there is nothing. I start the job search again, completing the circle. I'm back to where I started, one more line on my CV. No matter what I do, life will always be like this. There's no escape.

I spend a lot of time looking at the crack. A sixteen-year-old in Kyoto has made an app for people to measure the light of the crack in their area, and every hour it produces new graphics showing activity hotspots around the world. I've set up notifications for it. There's a comfort in watching the graphs morph and change, in seeing the raw data, and knowing that even if no one in power is paying attention, teenagers are.

A new theory has been going around the internet: that the biggest effects of the crack are manifesting in the places furthest from it. I scan forums in languages I don't understand, using Google Translate to decipher reports about climate destabilisation in the southern hemisphere. The jargon doesn't mean anything to me. It seems appropriate that the apocalypse we've all been predicting is happening, just not here.

Mum calls up to me and tells me that Grace has texted her and wants to know what's wrong. I don't want to have to explain everything to her, so I make up a lie about dropping my phone in the toilet and being too embarrassed to say anything.

'Ah sure, what are you like? You'll have to get a job soon enough. I'm not paying for a replacement.'

I'm already looking for a job, I've been doing nothing else, but she leaves and I'm not sure she hears me.

I turn on my phone, flinching as it lights up. I don't have the torrent of notifications I've been expecting. Then I remember deleting all my social media apps. I hadn't factored in silence as a consequence of my actions.

I do have several missed calls, however, and some text messages from Grace. She's left me voicemails.

The first one starts with, 'Who even uses voicemails any more, you bitch,' but I can hear worry in her voice. She doesn't tell me what people are saying about me, and that makes it worse. A part of my brain wants to reinstall Twitter to find out, but I take control of that impulse immediately. My fingers hover over the keyboard for a long time before I finally text her:

thanks for all the voicemails

You're alive!!

are any of us alive?

She starts and stops typing several times; I watch the bubble appear and disappear until I begin to feel afraid of whatever she might tell me. I don't want to find out, at least not right now.

coffee?

She stops typing for a moment, then:

Coffee? That's all you have to say to me? Are you okay?

of course

I don't believe you.

you never believe me

Yeah well what am I supposed to think. You've been ignoring me for days.

I don't want to continuously have this debate with her, so I use the same lie about dropping my phone in the toilet. It's better to lie.

and after that it was just easier to not engage

Hmm.
Fair enough.

I often find that when I mix in a grain of truth, a small morsel of vulnerability, Grace doesn't ask for more.

> *i'm actually upset*
> *but i think that's reasonable*

Yeah, definitely very reasonable.

I pass whatever test she's laid out. She's forgiven me for not contacting her with my every emotion.

I get dressed and go downstairs. Mum's sitting on the couch and says, 'Good afternoon, lazy bones.' I do my best to smile at her.

'Are you going out? Speaking of, have you noticed Hannah's been out a lot lately?' I haven't. 'Do you think she has a boyfriend?'

I stop smiling. Even when she doesn't know what's going on in my life, Hannah still finds ways to be better than me. There's no winning.

I walk into town, and I'm conscious of how much time I'd normally waste looking at my phone. I feel freed from that burden, although I'm now noticing with fresh eyes how grimy Dublin is, and how big the seagulls are.

Unplugging from social media has ripped out the roots of the complicated parts of my life. There are things I'd never say out loud, but I'd be expected to put on Twitter. Now, those thoughts are mine alone, and I feel giddy at reclaiming that secret part of myself.

The café Grace suggests is a place off Camden Street that I've never heard of before. It has several different roasts. I hold the coffee in my mouth and think about the caffeine slowly entering my system as Grace chats at me. I picture it spreading warmth throughout my body. I'd been worried it would be weird with Grace, but she's the same as ever. I swallow.

I'm sitting facing the window, and from here I can read the posters on the shopfronts across the way. One of them is advertising telescopes for viewing the crack, and I'm struck by the innovation within the crisis. The crack, at least, is something that's visible through the light pollution of the city. It's just a regular, unexplainable feature of the landscape. It's part of society in the way that other unexplainable things are – not unexplainable in the way aliens or ghosts are, but more like the stock market and oil prices. And like those things, the wealth and novelty they provide us are paid for by people far away who we don't have to care about.

'How are you feeling?' Grace asks me. 'I know probably not great, but it's polite to ask.'

I don't want to talk about this; I haven't practised telling anyone about my feelings yet. There was no one I wanted to tell, and so the words are unfamiliar to me.

'I think our friends are trying, but they're just not sure what to say to you. You know how they are.'

I do. Or maybe I don't. Grace has always been the one to tell me how they are.

'Don't be silly,' she says, and then, 'So there's something I have to tell you. I got a little wine-drunk watching Netflix the other night, and I may have messaged Finn.'

I nod at her, and wait, my thumb circling the handle of my mug.

'I may have told him that the way he treats you isn't fair, and he owes you a lot more than an apology. I mean, when I saw him going home with that girl it made me so angry, and I just couldn't not say something. I've been watching this happen to you, and I just couldn't. I don't like the way he treats you, or, frankly, the way he talks about you.'

Grace's impulses are a force of nature, something she can never control or monitor. I think, for a moment, that Grace is actually a very destructive person. And she's not self-destructive; she explodes outwards and hits us all with her shrapnel.

I take a sip of coffee and let the situation wash over me. My emotions are still fragile, and I can't be sure exactly what I'm feeling. I wonder what Finn's been saying about me. Grace is complicating the reality that I've just got under control. My sense of calm and secrecy is waning, and I'm gripped again by panic that people are talking about me, or reading my thoughts. I feel out of control. She refuses to show me the messages she sent him, and so I can't get a grip on anything.

I picture myself very far away from this whole situation, as though it involves neither me nor anyone I know. I keep my voice steady and concentrate on adopting a facade of calm and resoluteness.

'Yeah, no, I know, I'm just trying to help. But I do think it could be good for you, for both of you, if you did have a big chat.'

I don't respond. Outside the window, two pigeons are fighting over half a sandwich.

'Okay, but please do consider it. And what was I supposed to do? You were ignoring me for over a week.'

I've been ignoring everyone, not just her. I don't feel bad that I didn't engage with Grace, and I'm a little bit annoyed that she expected me to. She doesn't look impressed.

My phone goes off, and it's a text from Finn. He's asking if we can meet up and have a chat. Outside, one of the pigeons is victorious.

I pass the phone over to Grace, who takes it wordlessly. When she's finished reading the message, she says, 'Look, maybe it's for the best,' as though it's of no consequence. I can't believe her. I have so few relationships that are uncomplicated, and she has to ruin this one. I need her to set this right; she has to set this right.

She picks at the remains of a muffin she's eating and finally looks at me and says, 'No.'

The coffee cup is shaking in my hands. I look at her, wide-eyed and confused, my head rushing. I'm acutely aware of every detail of everything around me, yet also completely detached from the concepts of space and time. I repeat myself.

'Look, I just think this had to happen at some point and now is as good as any.'

I'm clutching at the tatters of my life, the pieces she's left for me. Thoughts are swimming in my head, and I'm drowning. I need to disconnect myself from her, to cut the threads that allowed her to do this to me. I don't know how she can be so selfish, so manipulative, so conniving.

'Selfish? Really? Me?' She throws her hands up in the air at me. 'Do you have any idea how much I do for you? I'm just concerned. And, sorry, you don't remember this, but the other night I had to comfort you as you puked and cried about why Finn didn't love you, or didn't want you, or whatever.'

I've been there for her when no one else has, I've supported every decision she's made, even when it's cost

244

me all my savings, and I can't believe this is how she's repaying me.

'Don't bring up that time,' she says, but I can't hear her. I can't hear anything.

'You know what your problem is, Sophie? You think everyone hates you because you're awkward, or you know more than them, or whatever. But you're wrong. Everyone hates you because you think we're all beneath you, and you're incapable of thinking about anyone but yourself.'

I stand up to leave, but she tugs at my sleeve. 'No, look, come on, I'm sorry, sit back down.' But the wind is rushing in my ears. I feel hot, like all the blood in my body is moving to all the wrong places, incredibly fast. I can feel my tongue in my mouth. It's engorged and useless. I know that if I get up and leave this table, something between us will snap. I don't care.

I need to leave this place; I need to get some space. The very concept of space feels elastic and uncertain. It stretches and contracts before me, and I can't get a firm hold on it. The little bell above the doorframe dings as I exit.

My phone burns a hole in my pocket the whole walk to the Liffey. It's a wild animal I'm afraid to even acknowledge. When I get to the Ha'penny Bridge, I think about throwing it into the river. It seems like a dreadfully romantic thing to do. I can see it framed in my head as a shot in a movie.

I look at the locks fastened to the white railings of the bridge. I doubt if many of the couples are still together, and try to imagine what they were thinking when they locked their initials in place. Probably, they were searching for the certainty that physical manifestations tend to have.

I stare out over the water as an apathy washes over me, all-consuming, until I become aware that I'm holding up pedestrian traffic, and my hands are white from grasping the railings. I don't know why I came here.

I walk the whole way home, my mind as empty as a broken vase, and only when I'm safely tucked up in bed do I reopen the text message from Finn.

My immediate instinct is to text Grace, but that door is closed now. I think about Lucy, or Dan, but I don't feel connected to them. I haven't ever been close to Lucy, and Dan hasn't been answering my calls. I remember Steph's messages. I don't feel connected to anyone.

My mind is running hot. I'm flushed with a heat so intense it feels like all my body's energy is burning off. Finn wants to call me, and I can't form coherent thoughts in my head. I can't believe Grace has landed me in this situation.

He calls me, and I can't come up with a reason to ignore him. He asks me question after question, gives me excuse after excuse, and I remain unmoved and non-committal. I recapture my feeling of detachment, that need to be anywhere but trapped inside my life. I become a robot, my mind blank and malleable.

'Oh.'

I let his voice take over.

'So you don't think, you know, this is unhealthy or whatever? That we can't be friends?'

An eternity passes, and I'm not here to bear witness to it.

'And you aren't mad at me for . . . any of it?'

The question is funny; how can I be mad when he's never owed me anything?

'We all owe each other things, after all, we live in a society.'

I feel that familiar pull towards him, as though we're on the same wavelength. When Finn and I work, we really work.

'I miss you . . . Maybe we could hang out again? Just hang out, I don't mean . . .'

I swallow.

'And hey, I just want to say . . .' He's gentle. 'I've seen that stuff Rory's mates have been posting, and it's not cool. I'm sorry this is happening to you, and I wish there was something more I could do for you.'

He understands, and it floods me with ice-cold relief. I hadn't realised how much I needed someone to just understand and listen to me, to take what I say I'm feeling as fact, instead of what they think I'm feeling. It feels like authenticity.

It's for that reason that I find myself spilling words out of my mouth, about Grace and how controlling she is, and how she always makes me feel like I'm lesser. She doesn't even mean to do it, and that's the worst thing.

Tears are pricking my eyes, and as the silence on the phone extends between us, I visualise the satellites and radio towers reflecting it back and forth as it grows.

'Yeah,' he says, 'I'd also been wondering about that. Not in a bad way, I mean, but not in a good way either. Sometimes, it feels like she sets the rules, right, and you just follow. And you never follow anyone else. She definitely had some choice things to say to me, anyway. I was worried.'

Everyone else sees me as Grace's shadow person; that's all I really am. My mind flits between memories, every time I've let Grace's personality overcome my own. I've never been anything more than what she's made me. I feel an illusion shatter, like glass.

'No, you've always been more than that. To me, anyway, you have.'

I smile for the first time in a long time.

'I'm happy we're okay,' he says.

After our connection is severed, I pull the covers over my head and cry as my breath fills the little space I'm occupying. I am utterly alone.

22

With each passing day it's like a physical thing is solidifying between me and the outside world. Reaching out to people is impossible. I draft messages in my head, but none of them feel right. The pressure of occupying a physical form threatens to break me; my brain floats somewhere above my body, and I'm merely an observer. Finn hasn't contacted me since we agreed we were okay, and I try not to think about it.

Hannah's started her job at the civil service and every day comes home and asks me how my day's been, as if to point out how much more eventful hers was. She's started seeing someone new, which I know because she pointedly refuses to tell me where she's going, as though she's inviting the question. I don't care enough to ask her.

I've fallen back down the conspiracy rabbit hole. Some people have started ironically calling themselves the Crackpots; some of them deserve that name. Everyone is waiting for it to flash again and theorising about how long the next episode will last. Some are hopeful that we'll be able to harness the crack's energy, but that seems unlikely to me. We'll never get enough investment to make the energy input worth the output; it'll take more than that to convince people to give up our glorious petroculture.

I can tell my parents are worried about me, but none of us have the vocabulary to talk about whatever's happening. Instead, Mum leaves treats outside my door and I eat them hatefully. Sometimes, I can hear them talking about me when they don't know I'm sitting on the stairs.

I've lost my sleep rhythm. Daylight no longer matters to me, and I sleep whenever I feel like I have to, or need to, like a dog does.

I'm asleep when Finn calls me the first time. My phone's on silent, but the light coming from it is enough to wake me up.

I'm confused when I answer. His voice is breathless. He sounds drunk. I take the phone away from my ear and check the time. It's after four in the morning.

'Hey, hello, hi, hi, can you hear me? Soph? Sophie?' I wait for more information. He doesn't say anything, and I listen to his ragged breath and the sounds of chatter around him. I can't tell where he is. He says, 'I need you. I just need you, okay? I need to talk to you.' I don't know what to say to that. He tells me where he is and asks me to meet him at his flat. I've never heard him beg for anything before.

I think about telling him to go home and sleep it off, but I can't. I can't shake the fear that he really doesn't have anyone else to talk to, and I know how down on himself he can get. I'm tormented by the idea that he'll do something stupid. I'm pretty sure I'm the only person who's ever seen him cry.

I jump out of bed, my heart thumping in my chest. I pull on tracksuit bottoms over my bare legs and a hoodie over my nightdress. I wash my mouth out with mouthwash and call a taxi. My mind is incapable of wondering what kind of scene awaits me when I arrive. As I sit in the car, I run through possible things I, or any other human, might say. *Don't worry, it will be okay. Everyone feels like this sometimes. Drink some water.*

It's a warm night, and I'm beginning to sweat from either my layers or my anxiety. I ring the flat bell a few times, but no one answers. I can see the faintest hint of a sunrise, the pastel colours washed out against the purple of the crack. I feel as though the skyline could swallow me.

I ring the bell again and eventually I'm let in. I can't help but worry about what's happening and comfort myself by deciding Finn is just passed out somewhere.

When I arrive at the flat door, it's closed. I bang on it a few times, fed up. When I check my phone, I have some texts from Finn.

Hey.
Sorry about earlier.
Just go home.
Chat later.
Xxx

I'm confused and try to call him. I'm used to him pushing me away. He never asks for help when he really needs it, when it's serious. He likes to just talk around problems, to bring them up like the weather, when he wants someone to listen. I've never been explicitly needed

251

by him before. The thought of him calling me here fills me with nervous delight. I've been waiting to be wanted, to be needed.

I bang on the door again and try to ring him. I can hear his phone go off in the room beyond and then be immediately silenced. Someone laughs.

Pearse opens the door and seems surprised to see me. I begin explaining why I'm here, but he interrupts me and tells me to go home. I'm so tired of him that I just ignore him.

I push past him and follow the sounds of life. I open the door to Finn's room. I can't quite compute what I'm seeing at first; the room is dark. His paisley duvet is crumpled on the ground. It's only when the girl laughs that it all clicks into place. I gasp, and she looks at me, and I see my own face looking back. I don't know how Hannah's here; I can't understand it. I try to pull the door closed, but it catches on their discarded clothing.

I don't see Pearse as I leave. Maybe I do, but I don't register it.

The walk home is long, and the sky lightens over me. I don't understand why Finn called me, and I don't want to understand what I walked in on. I don't know what it means for me.

I stop at McDonald's on the way home. The glare of the light is blinding. They've just started serving breakfast and I order hash browns. I sit in a booth, tracing swirls in some salt, and eat until I cease to be a person any more, until I'm more potato than girl, until I convince myself that being alone isn't so bad. I think about potatoes and trauma.

My mind is white static, and I can't leave it blank for fear my thoughts will betray me. I take out my phone and reinstall all the apps I'd deleted. Tears blur the screen in my hands, but that doesn't stop me from consuming.

23

Finn hasn't messaged me. It's possible he doesn't even remember calling me, or me being in his apartment. It would be better if he forgot. I open and close my messaging apps a few times, in case he's messaged me and it just hasn't come through yet. I feel smaller every time I do it, but I don't stop.

I listen to podcasts and stare at the ceiling above my bed, and the idea of independent thought is impossible. I can't think about last night; I can't think at all. The image of what I saw is too painful to hold, my thoughts parting around it like a rock in a river.

I want to convince myself that it didn't happen, that what I saw wasn't real, and thus take control over my reality. I know if I think myself into spirals I can gaslight myself, but what I want most of all is to have someone to talk to about it. I feel the absence of communication as a physical thing; it impresses itself upon me, choking me.

I want to call Grace, but I also don't want to give her the satisfaction of being right. She always thinks she knows better than I do. I lie in bed, my eyes open but unseeing.

I've read all of the things Rory's friends have said about

me. I think he deleted some of them, because there are gaps in the Twitter threads, or maybe I already blocked the commenters. Reading it all was satisfying, in its own way, because where I had once been full of sadness I am now hollowed out and empty with the realisation that even strangers see I deserve to be sad. The only consolation is that social media drama moves so quickly they've already forgotten about me, like I never even existed.

I draft several messages to Dan, but I don't know what to say. I haven't spoken to him in so long I fear that he'll have forgotten me. I can't be sure Grace hasn't got to him first and turned him against me. They're all Grace's friends, not mine.

I've barely slept; every creak in the house makes me sit up in bed. I'm sick in the toilet a few times. The contents of my stomach come up like wet cat food. I still haven't heard Hannah come home.

The idea of leaving my bed is utterly unappealing. I spend a lot of time researching the crack, without really learning anything. I let the data consume me, each tweet or article saving me a moment from my own thoughts. No one is predicting any more anomalies, but then no one had predicted the first one. I read so much that I can't find anything new. I only notice the time when the screen of my laptop goes orange and lets me know the sun's set. Night, somehow, is comforting.

When I sit up, I notice the little velvet box on my bedside table. I open and close it a few times, then take the necklace out and play with the silver chain. It's never felt like the right time to wear it; I didn't want Hannah to see it. Reading the card again makes me sick to my stomach, and I vomit one last time in the toilet.

I'd let myself read into the necklace; the idea that it could have a hidden agenda kept hope alive inside me. I feel stupid for indulging that desire. By not settling on one concrete meaning I've allowed some part of me to believe that he meant it, that he meant any of it.

I'm not the best person he knows, because he doesn't know me at all. I wipe the bile from my mouth and throw the necklace, box and all, into the bin.

A notification banner pops up on my phone. It's a reminder to respond to a Facebook event. I can't remember the last time I used the Facebook events function, and I didn't think I knew anyone who still did.

The event is some kind of last hurrah before Niamh moves away. I'm sure I'm invited as an afterthought. I scroll through the guest list, and Grace hasn't clicked 'attending'. I check her Instagram and she's put up a story of a family movie night.

If I go, I can be anyone. I don't have to exist in this body; I can fashion myself a new one. Or I can go back to an old one. I want to remember what it's like to be one of those girls, to go back to a time when I didn't know Rory, or Finn, or have anyone else. If I could go back, maybe I could make different choices.

I think about Facebook and the people I'm friends with who I haven't spoken to in years. At one point it was a status symbol to have as many friends as possible, but now my friends list is a reminder of everyone I've lost touch with. Some of them could be dead, and I wouldn't know. I scroll through people's profiles at random, trying to glean a sense of their personalities, and wondering what people would think about me if I died. My page would become a gravesite for someone who'd never really existed.

More than anything, I want to exist. It's with this mindset that I don some red lipstick. Mum doesn't say anything to me as I head out, and I think she must be glad that I'm finally leaving the house.

I meet the girls in a bar with music that's too loud and drinks that are too expensive. Dublin's not a city where people can comfortably exist. The bar is not really my place, but I decide that I can become the type of person whose place it is. My cocktail tastes like cough syrup, and I watch the people around me interact with each other.

The girls sitting around me all gel together, their forms shifting and laughing at cues I miss, but I take a drink every time I feel uncomfortable and the feeling soon passes. I find that when we get talking, these women – who seem so put-together at first – are actually struggling with the same things I am. None of them have moved out of their parents' houses, only one of them is working at a steady job that pays above the minimum wage, and everyone loudly complains about how they'll never own a home. There are words and phrases I can use and they respond with, 'No, yeah, exactly,' and it feels amazing.

'Every job I've ever got has been from nepotism.'

'Even the dental secretary?'

'Especially the dental secretary.'

'I have an interview my cousin set up for me.'

'I'd love an interview, I feel like if I could get that far it would be easy, but I can't even get a rejection email.'

The table in front of us fills with empty glasses, but I'm distanced from them as a concept. My problems feel universal for once. The people in the bar move in shapes around me, silhouetted in the flashing green and red of the lights, surrounded by chatter. I imagine what it would be like to be one of them.

Niamh asks me what I'm doing now, and when we talk about unemployment she clinks my glass and laughs in a way that's infectious. I don't know if any of this is even real.

Another girl, who's blonde and perhaps called Ciara, asks me if I'm seeing anyone, and an image of Finn flashes before my eyes. I was never seeing him, though, and he certainly never saw me.

'That's the same as me, honestly, I just can't pick a good one!' She nods enthusiastically and buys me a drink. These people will believe anything I tell them; I'm the master of their reality.

Thoughts of Finn have entered my mind, infecting it. I'm drunk enough that my defences are lowered, and I can no longer control my involuntary reactions. I open his Instagram and scroll through it. In his tagged photos I see a graveyard of his exes. He never liked me enough to date me. All his previous girlfriends are much prettier than I am, so of course I'd never make the cut. Even if I did make the cut, why would he settle for me when he could have me, but better? Thinner.

On Twitter I scroll through his liked tweets, hungry to get an insight into his life. After a little bit of scrolling I see one of Hannah's tweets, and then another, and another. I saw them together, but this makes it somehow more real.

I'm at the bar ordering a double when Niamh comes over and tells me we're all leaving and going somewhere else. I tell her to wait for just a second, and down the gin in a few big gulps. I leave the empty glass on a table by the door.

We end up at a club on Harcourt Street that I've both been in and never been in before. They're all laid out more or less the same way, and they keep changing hands and names. I remember the floors being stickier. The landscape is disorientating, hovering somewhere between familiar and unfamiliar.

The bartender is cute, and I fall in love with him when he hands me my drink. The smoking area's laid out like a pub, with the addition of climbing plants. One of the girls – I've forgotten her name already, or perhaps I never knew it – leads us through it with military precision. We sit at a table, and she tells me that she thinks everyone here hates her. I don't know otherwise, and we both laugh.

The dance floor is flooded with smoke and neon pink light. I can see myself reflected on the mirrored walls and ceiling, a tiny ant among all these people. Lost.

A circle forms and I'm pushed into it, suddenly adrift from the group of girls. As I dance, my arms above my head, my feet shifting, a guy smacks my ass. It goes through me like a bullet, and my body goes rigid. I turn around and slap him, my hand moving without thinking. As I exit the circle I grab Niamh or Ciara or whoever's hand, and she follows me.

Out in the smoking area, the girl asks me what happened. The evening feels as though it's closing in on me, and I can't help but think of Rory. I lost my drink somewhere along the way, and I need another. The panic will stop if I have another drink.

'Oh no, I'm sorry, want to go back and dance?'

I stare at her, uncomprehending. The idea of dancing now fills me with dread. I want to rage and scream at every man I see, to ask them why they think it's acceptable to do that. I can't explain this though, and tears push at the edge of my vision. I just shake my head. I'm overwhelmed by the fact that another man has managed to steal my feeling of safety away from me. She asks me again, and it becomes clear that she's lost interest in me entirely. I don't know why I thought coming out with these people was a good idea.

The girl is gone, and I'm vaguely aware that I told her she could leave. She vanishes into the normalcy of the evening. I'm in a stall in the bathroom, my head between my legs. My nose is full of snot, and I'm crying. A girl in the stall next to me tells me it'll be okay, and I cling to that.

Out on the street, it's cold. I dimly remember that I haven't brought a jacket with me. I start walking, unsure of where I'm going and unable to comprehend the night around me. I stumble past groups of people smoking outside bars, hiding my face so they don't look at me.

Panic is beginning to rise in my chest. I'm not sure where I am. I don't have any cash to hop in a taxi, and I don't know where the nearest ATM is. The thought of walking home makes me burst into tears again, my teeth chattering. The city is swallowing me whole.

Without conscious thought, I'm on the phone to Grace. I can't understand what she's saying, and she can't understand what I'm saying. I'm sorry I'm sorry I'm sorry over and over again, the memories of why I'm so sorry lost in the alcohol. I manage to send her my location, and twenty minutes later she comes to pick me up in her little blue car.

She doesn't say anything at first, and I fill the silence

with whatever babble is on my mind, fulfilling my urge to minimise what's happened.

After an unknowable amount of time, we arrive at a 24-hour drive-through. My vision is blurry, and I can't read the menu, so Grace orders chicken nuggets for me.

When I begin to sober up, she asks me what happened and clicks her tongue.

'It drives me mad,' she says, 'that you were sexually assaulted in a club, in broad daylight, or broad neon light or whatever, and it's so normal that no one said anything.'

It startles me to hear her put it like that, but she's successfully put a name to what I'm feeling, and that helps to settle the storm inside me.

'And I'm sorry about Rory and everything that's happened since. I know you feel stupid that you let it happen. I feel stupid that *I* let it happen. It's tempting to think it's your fault because you ignored all the red flags, but don't forget that he ignored all of your boundaries. Because you weren't important in the equation to him, only he was.'

Her words settle inside me, give me concrete sounds to attach to what I'm feeling. I've always needed Grace for this.

'I'm happy I was able to come and get you tonight, but you only get so many rambling crying calls to me, okay?'

I nod and doze in the car as she drives me home, and that's that. It's like nothing's happened, and I think about how comforting it is knowing that whatever happens, I'll always have Grace. It's enough to make me cry, and then I'm crying about a lot of different things. Grace makes comforting noises and offers me the last of her chips. She doesn't ask me why I'm crying; she never has to.

It's all too much, with Finn, and Rory, and that guy in the club. I'm tired of crying over stupid boys who aren't worth it.

Grace says, 'I don't want that either, isn't that what I've been saying all along?'

Now, with the benefit of hindsight, I can see that she's right. She's always been right. She asks me about Hannah and I look out over the dashboard. Grace's hands run over the steering wheel, and she tells me she knows about Finn and Hannah; she saw them go home together. I can see the sky beginning to lighten beneath the crack.

'You're stronger than her, strong enough to handle it, no matter what she does to you.'

She drives me home, and I repeat her words in my head as a mantra. Hannah's coat isn't hanging on the hall bannister, but I don't care. She can have Finn, but she will never have Grace.

24

My mouth tastes like vomit, and I have the unbelievable urge to get sick into the toilet. My head is heavy, and I almost don't make it the whole way there. The porcelain is chilly in my grip as I retch so hard I cry.

I lie on the floor and think about how often I'm in this position. There's something so soothing about the caress of the icy tiles beneath my back and pressed to the side of my face. I feel dried out, like an old husk, so I cup my hands and drink some water from the tap. I can feel it swishing in my belly.

When I drag myself back to bed, I check my phone. I have dozens of messages, but none of them are of consequence. I have a few with too many question marks from the girls wondering where I've gone, to which I reply with a shrug emoji.

Grace sends me a message, and as I read it images from the night swim before my eyes. I'm both ashamed and relaxed, because I know I'm a mess but I'm also relieved that things are almost back to normal between us.

I feel like a sliver of a person. I've given away so much to other people, and to drink, that I have no emotional energy left for myself. I've been living a shadow life. I can't remember the last time I saw myself with fresh eyes, instead of reflected in other people's perceptions of me.

I scroll through Twitter, and I'm aware for the first time of what a tremendous waste of time it is. I'm reading the comments of people I don't know or care about and using them to avoid interrogating myself.

A crack's opened up in the sky, the world's nearly ended, and the internet's run it through the same cycle it does with every bit of information. Pulled it apart, disputed it, ground it through memes until it reached a shape suitable enough to slot into our agreed-upon reality. But the problem hasn't gone away.

I'm so tired.

It's after two by the time I drag myself out of bed, warm on the verge of hot.

I call Grace. I'm desperate for our familiarity. She comes over and I open the door. She nods sadly when she sees me, and then forces me to go and shower. She sits on the toilet seat and looks through her phone, and I don't mind. When I look at myself in the mirror I see huge dark circles under my eyes. It is difficult to work the shampoo through my hair; my body doesn't want to obey me.

I wrap myself in a towel and sit down on the floor next to Grace. My hair is wet and hangs around my face. She puts her phone down and looks at me, but I can't meet her gaze.

'Soph,' she says softly, 'I know you don't want to hear this, and I know maybe you're very fragile right now, and all that, but honestly you've been a bit of a cunt lately.'

I don't say anything, I just let her words wash over me.

They're familiar to me, like the tide coming in. This is all so familiar.

'No, come on, this is serious. You never want to hang out with your friends any more, and when you do it's like you're a million miles away, messaging Finn, or Rory, or whatever. You never have time for us, it's like you're not even here. And now maybe this shock's the thing you need to actually come back to us. I know it hurts, but I've been saying all along that Finn's a piece of shit and you deserve more. It's not fair what he did, but you know neither he nor Hannah are worth this. They deserve each other.'

My heart has stopped working, but I'm too tired to argue. I go to my bedroom to get changed, and Grace follows me, still talking. I force my arms through the sleeves of my jumper, and my feet through the legs of my pants, feeling all the while like a puppet whose strings have been cut. I try to pinpoint the exact meaning of Grace's words, and when I do, I slump down on the bed and hug my knees to my chest. Everyone hates me, and I have no one. I have no friends.

'You're so melodramatic, always, honestly. Here's what's going to happen. You're going to give that boy a piece of your mind, and try to talk to him so he doesn't do this to anyone else, and for your own sake as well, and then you're going to take responsibility for your own actions. You're going to get through all of this, and it will be okay. You're going to move on. And I can't even tell you how many conversations I've had with Dan and Steph and Lucy about how worried they are about you. They do care.'

She says it in a soothing way, but it shatters my world.

I wonder if it really could be so simple, if Grace always lives her life so simply, if things can be stated so plainly and still be true.

'Also,' she begins, in a tone that makes it clear that she doesn't really want to begin, 'I have to tell you something, and it's good that you're already crying and mad because you might as well get it all out of your system at once.'

It's as if I've swallowed a bucket of ice, each piece congealing the acid in my stomach.

'So, that argument with Finn I had? That wasn't just me being my general drunken self. I didn't want to tell you this at the time, but I'd heard he was saying some not nice things about you. I won't give you the full details, no one needs that, but I heard that he'd said things about you being pathetic, and things about your body as well. And Hannah.'

Of course Finn thinks I'm pathetic. I'm not sure why it hurts so much to be told something I already know. I feel as though I've been looking at an old-school 3D image, with these two different Finns jarring and incompatible, and Grace has just given me some glasses. It clicks into place. I understand. This feeling, at last, stops the tears.

We order takeaway and watch movies, and in the evening the messages start arriving from Finn. They come at regular intervals, each one insistent yet bland.

Hey can you talk?

Are you there?

Hi, are you free?

I watch them warily. On impulse, I open them, not to reply, but to leave him on read. I want to make him feel the same awkwardness he's always inflicted upon me. This is a mistake, because five minutes later he calls me. Seeing his name on my phone makes my stomach flip over.

Grace sees my face and grabs it off me. 'Hi Finn, Sophie can't get to the phone right now, she's busy, um, making dinner, so can I take a message? Oh, is that all? Cool.' She hangs up the phone. '*Prick.*'

She rolls her eyes. 'He wants you to call him when you can. As if.'

I used to think I never believed in romance, not really, but what I now realise is a starry-eyed view of functional relationships is shattering before my eyes.

Grace sees me fiddling with my phone and takes it from me, so I pick at the skin around my fingers instead. To distract me, she tells me more about her Masters, and we spend some time scrolling through websites looking for something I could do. She says, 'We could move out together, maybe not this year, but next year,' and potential futures I'd never considered suddenly seem possible. Some of them even look appealing.

I wait until Grace leaves, and I feel stronger, and then I call Finn. Hannah's still out, and I can't be sure she's not with him. Some sadistic part of me wishes that she is, so that he can't lie to me any more. He answers on the third ring. The sound of his voice shocks me.

'Hi Soph, Sophie, hi, how are you?' He's breathless and I can't help but imagine what he's just been doing. Surely he can't have just been having sex? That's not what he sounded like when we had sex.

I wait. Finn's always most honest when you don't give him the opportunity not to be. He tries to initiate banter, but I find the words leaden in my mouth. I remember our easy jokes with a kind of nostalgia. I understand now that for all that time, all the times I let him slip past my guard and make me smile, I was actually incredibly fragile. I feel that version of me crack and shatter. Remembering the past only serves to make the present even more unbearable.

Eventually, I cut him off, showing definitively I never really knew him in the first place. I'd thought that we were equals. And if not equals, that we'd existed in that sweet romantic spot where power is exchanged through some kind of game. But for him, it's always been nothing more than a game, and I've lost.

He called me the other night, and I need to know why. The answer could break me, but I still need to know. My voice is remarkably steady, as though it's coming from a speaker in the back of my mouth and not a real human organ.

'Yeah,' he says, 'yeah, I don't know. That's a good question, honestly, I don't know. I was drunk, and I think I realised that you wanted space, and I shouldn't have called, which is why I didn't call again.'

I think once upon a time I might have been charmed by this; I think it would have worked. The idea that he'd needed me, but had reminded himself to respect my boundaries. The words feel hollow now, a shiny surface paving over empty meaning. I nod, even though he can't see me.

I work through his words one by one. He told me he needed me, but I guess it wasn't me specifically. He's willing to settle for someone who's just kind of like me.

'Hang on now, Soph, that's harsh, of course I need you, it's just I remembered I can't need you. You're my best friend, and that means something.'

I think of all the times I've let him get close to me, emotionally and physically, and how little he seems to know me at all. I think of all the times I let him away with things when he talked to me like this. I long to be that connected to him again, but I know it's impossible. All of those carefully constructed bridges have been lovingly burnt.

The words come out of my mouth as though I've been working on the script for as long as I can remember, longer than I can remember feeling this way. He never really cared about me, just the idea of having someone like me; he uses women for validation, and once he earns their trust he tosses them aside in favour of a bigger conquest. He doesn't understand that we are living, breathing animals and not static collectables.

'I just . . . I don't want to end up like my parents . . .'

But that's what's going to happen; that's what he does. He did it to Cassie, and he's done it to me, with my twin, even after I told him everything. He knew what he was doing to me, and he did it anyway.

'But I love you,' he says, which we both know is not true, and that's the reason he says it.

I'm pacing around my room now, energy coursing through me. It feels as though I've been struck by a bolt of truth, and my words hang around me as physical things the moment I utter them.

He doesn't say anything for a long time. I can hear his breath hitch, and I think he's crying. At one point, this would have broken my heart. I still feel the impulse to reach across the space between us, but it's weaker than it's ever been.

Instead, I listen quietly, as though I'm keeping vigil to the fact that he has a heart. Perhaps this is the first time he's ever faced consequences in his life.

After a while, he says, into the silence, 'Can we go back to just being friends?'

When he realises the answer is no, he hangs up.

I sit on my bed, unfeeling. It's better this way.

I refresh social media, looking for someone to talk to, but there's no one. My chat log is full of the names of people I no longer speak to. Grace is right: I've let distance grow between me and everyone I care about. She says they still care about me, but I can't break the barriers I've constructed in my mind. It feels impossible to message anyone, and even more impossible that they might reply.

I scroll up through our group chat, to before Dan moved away and Steph started working, back to when it was all normal. The messages feel as though they're from strangers. I want to go back to that time, to when things felt like they would never change. To when I could believe the words I read. But even now, looking back, I'm not sure that kind of certainty ever existed.

I listen to a podcast about the crack. The camaraderie of the hosts almost feels like friendship. Their banter is at odds with what they're talking about. No progress has been made on the crack; no one knows what it is, and they're saying no one ever will. This is just something we have to get used to. They've started attaching words like *emergency* and *crisis* to the discourse, but in an almost quizzical way. Everyone keeps repeating that it's not going to end the world. I'm not so sure, although I've never been sure the world's not already ending.

Finn's words echo in my ears: *I don't want to end up like my parents.* He spent so long running away from the idea that he's circled back: trapped. I don't want to end up like my parents either; I don't think it's even possible I could. When they were my age, the world was different, and full of possibilities that no longer exist.

I'm tired of apathy, especially apathy towards the future. The hosts of the podcast seem secure in the idea that the present will continue like this for ever. But that present is based on a past I never got to live. The future is yet unmapped, and I can't keep looking back before taking a step forward.

My phone goes off. It's a notification from the app that Japanese teenager made. I'm filled at once with a kind of longing, which in other terms might be called hope. Maybe the podcast hosts are powerless, maybe I'm powerless, but there are people using the tools they have now to imagine a better future. Maybe, somewhere out there, there is a solution. We just need to look in the right places.

I want to move on from now. I want to grasp the future that is available to me and stop fixating on what I've done. I'm not alone, I've never been alone; I just had the wrong idea of what loneliness meant. I want to stop pretending I believe what I've been taught happiness is: I have to find out for myself.

The future starts like this: I look up flats in Dublin, in London, in Tokyo; anywhere I might like to go. I could stay with Dan for a while. There's nothing keeping me here, in this moment, except for me. Maybe I could do a Masters, or teach English abroad, or write a novel. Maybe I could do all three. Things are changing, and I want to change too.

I send a message into the group chat, and I wait.

ACKNOWLEDGEMENTS

This book would not exist without so many wonderful, weird and inspiring people, and this acknowledgements section couldn't possibly do justice to the debt I owe them.

Without Paddy O'Doherty, you would not be holding this book in your hands. It would be gathering meta-phorical digital dust and never have seen the light of day. Her support and guidance started me down this path and gave me the confidence to think I might be able to walk it.

Thank you to my agent, Marianne Gunn O'Connor, who has more faith in me than I do myself.

Thank you to all the team at Canongate, who've quite literally made my dreams come true. In particular to my editor Megan Reid, who understood my vision for this novel and whose carefully considered comments were invaluable. And to Jamie Byng. I never thought I'd be lucky enough to find such a supportive and enthusiastic team.

Thank you to my mother, for everything she's given me. To my father, who never laughed when I talked about fantasy literature. To John for his early encouragement, and to Sally for showing me this was possible. And to Paul, who was always so sure I would end up surprising everyone.

Thank you to every member of my extended family. To Sunny McDonagh for loving books as much as I do. To Josh Oren for giving me my first favourite book, and to his parents Diane and Bill for giving it to him. To Bríd O'Doherty and Denise Milmo-Penny, because even though they never knew about this book, I can't help but feel that they had something to do with it. To my grandmother, Georgia Prasifka, whose love for me I know is unconditional. And to the grandmother I never got to know, Roisín McDonagh, who was also a writer.

Thank you to my dear friends. Dee Courtney, who read it first. Lorna Staines, who was always ready for three a.m. conversations and five-minute-long voice notes. Julia McCarthy, for dreaming big ideas with me over a few glasses of wine. And to Heather Murray, who's been here for it all, who always knew I could do it, and without whom I would be a fundamentally different person. And thank you to the entire Murray family.

Thank you to Clare Hanlon, who's been there for the start of nearly every good idea I've had, and to her family for their hospitality. To Molly Barnicle, and Emma Jackson, and Doireann O'Brien, and Robyn Lawrence, and Chris Paschali, and Suzanne Elliot, and so many others whose support helped me to bring this book into being. Thank you for being there to discuss ideas and listen to me talk through plot points. Thank you for laughing at the jokes I considered putting into the manuscript and then cut for not being funny.

Thank you to Catriona Fyfe, who was there when this

wild journey started, although it feels like much longer. And to Niamh O'Connell, whose early comments on the first chapter were so insightful and brilliant they changed the whole book.

And thank you, reader, for giving this weird little book a chance.